Bewitched on Bourbon Street

Books by Deanna Chase

The Jade Calhoun Novels
Haunted on Bourbon Street
Witches of Bourbon Street
Demons of Bourbon Street
Angels of Bourbon Street
Shadows of Bourbon Street
Incubus of Bourbon Street
Bewitched on Bourbon Street

The Pyper Rayne Novels
Spirits, Stilettos, and a Silver Bustier
Spirits, Rock Stars, and a Midnight Chocolate Bar (Winter 2015)
Spirits, Beignets, and a Bayou Biker Gang (Spring 2016)

The Coven Pointe Novels
Marked by Temptation (a novella)

The Crescent City Fae Novels
Influential Magic
Irresistible Magic
Intoxicating Magic

The Destiny Novels
Defining Destiny
Accepting Fate

Bewitched on Bourbon Street

A Jade Calhoun Novel

Deanna Chase

Bayou Moon Publishing

Bayou Moon Publishing
dkchase12@gmail.com
www.deannachase.com

Printed in the United States of America

Acknowledgments

To all the Bourbon Street readers: Thank you! Your love for this series makes it possible for me to do what I do. And to my team, Lisa, Rhonda, Angie, Janet, and Lynn, thanks for all your hard work and putting up with me. I couldn't do it without you.

Chapter 1

"I never thought I'd be drinking honey-flavored jizz from a plastic penis," Pyper said, inspecting the phallic-shaped straw.

I sputtered, choking on the honeysuckle daiquiri. "Pyper!"

"Jade!" Pyper mimicked my tone and smirked, the bright-blue streak in her dark hair falling forward as her shoulders vibrated with silent laughter.

My best friend, Kat, put her drink down and pushed it into the middle of the table. Her hazel eyes narrowed. "That's it. I'm switching to wine."

"You two are so easy." Pyper smirked and took a long sip.

Kat gave her a side-eye glance and then got up and crossed the crowded room to the open bar. She was elegant in her skinny leggings and flowing silk shirt, her bright-red curls done up into a fancy bun.

It was afternoon on New Year's Day, and we were currently with the rest of my coven at a private residence in the Garden District for a fertility party. My coven member, Rosalee, had asked me to host a blessing for her older sister, who'd been having trouble conceiving. When I'd agreed, I hadn't realized she'd intended to throw a party and invite half the magical community of New Orleans.

"Was it something I said?" Pyper asked me, her big blue eyes round with mock innocence.

I plucked the penis straw out of my untouched drink and flung it at her, reveling in the joy swirling around me. As an empath, I usually tried to block out other people's emotions, as they often just wore me out. But happy ones filled me up and made me stronger. And today I was enjoying the boost. Especially after the rough morning I'd had.

For whatever reason, right after I'd had my morning chai, I'd gotten a searing headache and almost vomited in the sink. A couple ibuprofen had knocked the pain out, but man, for a minute there I'd thought I wasn't going to make it today.

Pyper caught the straw and winked as she slipped it into her drink next to the other one. "Looks like I'm having a ménage this evening."

A bubble of laughter escaped my lips as I shook my head. "You're insane."

"I know."

"Looks like y'all are having a good time." Rosalee appeared from behind me, a smile on her full lips. She'd left her long dark hair loose and wore a flowing skirt, playing up her earth witch side. Sliding into Kat's empty chair, she handed out twig crowns twined with honeysuckle vines. "We'll wear these during the blessing. Honeysuckle is supposed to help with desire."

Pyper raised a skeptical eyebrow and stared at the handmade crown with distaste. She opened her mouth to no doubt say something inappropriate, but I cut her off. "Are they spelled?"

Rosalee shook her head. "No. We made them for the sym-bolism. We didn't want the magic to get out of hand and…" she leaned in and whispered, "you know, affect the guests."

"Good thing, considering we're all sucking on these. Wouldn't want the blessing to turn into something more suited for the Sex Dungeon." Pyper held up both penis straws and then slipped one into her mouth as she made suggestive eyes at Rosalee.

"Oh, goddess," I mumbled and took a gulp of my ginger ale. I wasn't taking any chances with alcohol today. Not after the headache this morning.

Rosalee laughed, her dark curls bouncing around her face. "That would be awkward." She turned to me. "You ready to start in about five minutes?"

I glanced over at Bea, my mentor, who was sitting a few tables away. She was radiant in her royal-purple sheath dress and matching heels. Elegant. Absolutely stunning. I only hoped I managed to look half as good as she did when I was her age… which I guessed was mid- to late sixties, but you'd never know it based on her appearance alone. She met my gaze and smiled, her eyes full of kindness.

"Sure," I told Rosalee and nodded at Bea. "I've never done one before, so Bea is going to help me."

Rosalee clasped her hand over mine and squeezed. "Thank you so much for doing this. It means a lot to Dani. It's all she's been talking about for the past few weeks."

Her gratitude zinged through me as we all turned and looked at her sister, the woman of the hour. She was an older, plumper version of Rosalee with one major difference—Rosalee was a powerful witch, and Dani wasn't. It wasn't unusual for family members to have varying degrees of magic. But in this case, as far as we knew, Dani didn't have any magic at all. And according to Rosalee, she'd resented that fact for a long time. But now that she was married, all she wanted was to start a family.

"It's not a problem. I'm happy to do it." I smiled, warmth filling my belly.

Kat returned and sat on the other side of me, her hand wrapped around a chilled wine glass. She faced me, her expression earnest. "When you have your blessing done, I expect it to be less 'ladies' tea' and more 'let's party,' okay? I mean, the props are fun, but I prefer a night out to really get everyone in the mood. Know what I'm saying?"

"Yeah. Whatever happened to letting a drunken night of debauchery end with hot sex and a bun in the oven?" Pyper added.

The pair of them got lost in their laughter, but for once I didn't find their teasing all that amusing. From what I understood, Dani and her husband had been trying to conceive for the last few years without much luck. And she wanted to start the new year with a little help.

I knew it shouldn't, but it bothered me that my friends were joking about this day without really understanding her struggle. Sitting back, I crossed my arms over my chest and frowned at them.

"Jade? What's wrong?" Pyper asked when her laughter faded away.

I shrugged, fully aware of what my problem was. But now wasn't the time to talk about it. My fingers dug into my biceps as I tightened my grip.

"Hey." Kat gently pulled on one of my arms, forcing me to relax my hold on myself.

I let her and met her apologetic gaze.

"Sorry. I know you've been thinking about trying."

"Trying what?" Pyper asked and popped a chocolate-covered caramel into her mouth.

We both just stared at her.

She stopped mid-chew. The chatter of the others around us filled the silence. Pyper's throat worked as she forcibly swallowed the rest of the chocolate. Her eyes softened, and then she smiled. "Are you and Kane trying for a little witch of your own?"

I cast my eyes down, pretending to inspect the fruit I'd left untouched on the plate.

"Jade?" Pyper asked softly.

I shook my head and dipped a strawberry into the whipped cream.

"But you want to?"

"Yes," I finally said. "We've talked about it, but we haven't decided one way or another. It's probably not the best time to start right now." Kane and I were constantly fighting demons, black magic users, and other power-hungry magical creatures. As much as I wanted to—*we* wanted to—the idea of bringing a child into our crazy life wasn't exactly practical.

"Aw, honey," Kat said with a gentle smile. "You know what they say. It's never a good time to start having babies. You just do, and it works itself out."

"Yep," Pyper chimed in. "If it's what you want, put the witch B.S. aside and go for it." She waggled her eyebrows. "Besides, who wouldn't want to make a baby with Kane?"

"What she said," Kat added. "I'm so jealous. Your babies are going to be gorgeous."

"That's quite enough," I said, chuckling. "You two talking about Kane like that is weird. You're creeping me out."

"Please. I was just referring to his superior good looks. I don't want anything to do with his man parts." Pyper wrinkled her nose and winked. They were best friends and behaved exactly like brother and sister.

"Me neither." Kat said and gave us a sly smile. "I've got my hands full with Lucien."

"That's better." Their advice warmed me, and if I was honest, it was exactly what I wanted to hear. Only I needed to hear it from Kane, and he still had reservations about the timing. I shook my head, clearing the thoughts from my mind. I had a job to do. "Enough about me. Time to get this blessing show on the road." I stood and walked over to Bea. "Ready?"

She nodded and followed me to the small temporary stage Dani had installed. I cupped my hands around my mouth and whispered, *"Amplify."*

A small tingle of magic touched the back of my throat, indicating the spell had worked. "Happy New Year, everyone!" My voice boomed through the room, instantly quieting the guests. I met Dani's gaze and smiled. "If we can get the guest of honor up here, I think it might be time to add a little magic to the baby-making process."

Everyone hooted and hollered as Dani blushed and joined us.

"Yeah, girl. That's all you need. A little magic in the bedroom while Todd does his thing," Mati, a Coven Pointe sex witch, called from across the room.

Dani's blush turned bright red. She looked like she'd rather have the floor open up and swallow her whole than endure the good-natured taunting.

Rosalee, who was sitting at the nearest table, clamped her hand over her mouth, hiding her laugh.

I shook my head, swallowing my amusement. For a girl who'd decided penis straws and sperm-shaped cookies were a good idea for her party, she sure was modest. "I'm certain there's plenty of magic in that department." I winked at Dani and took her hand in mine. "This blessing is more about clearing any muddled energy and creating the right environment for welcoming a new soul into their lives."

Dani took a deep breath and gave me a grateful smile. While the teasing was fun and entertaining, this was serious business to her. That was clear. I squeezed her hand, letting her know I understood.

Bea took a step forward. "Thank you all for joining us today. Each of you was invited because of your personal connection to Dani and Rosalee and because of your unique energy. While Dani would be grateful if you participated in the blessing, it's not required. There's magic involved, and your energy will be used as part of the spell. So if you choose to sit it out, it's understood. Your presence indicating your support on this special day is quite enough."

Most people were nodding their agreement, but I noticed Lailah and Zoe whispering as Zoe shook her head. Lailah was our resident angel and soul guardian. She was dressed in a muted cream skirt and peasant top, void of color except for the red poinsettia hairclip tucked into her honey-gold locks. Zoe, by contrast wore black wool pants and a button-down shirt that made her look ten years older than her twenty-four years. Gone was the fresh vibrant blonde I'd met a few months back, replaced by the somber witch who was struggling to fit in.

A few months ago, Zoe's soul had been stolen by a lesser goddess and used for evil purposes. But thanks to Lailah and the Angel Council, she'd been given a new one. From what I understood, there'd been some challenges adjusting, and Zoe's magic wasn't up to speed. So I wasn't surprised when Lailah stared at me and then shook her head, indicating neither would be participating. Lailah could, but she was really only here to keep an eye on Zoe.

I nodded and faced the crowd. "Those of you willing to participate, please stand."

Sure enough, everyone in the room stood except for Lailah and Zoe.

"Great," I said, smiling. "Now grab your honeysuckle crowns and place them on your heads. When you're ready, join hands."

The two dozen or so guests moved to the middle of the room and formed a circle.

"Perfect. Since this is my first blessing, I'm going to let Bea lead." I stepped back, giving Bea the stage. She was the former New Orleans coven leader, extremely powerful and more than capable of doing the blessing without me. But since I was the current coven leader, it was up to me to bind the magic once the blessing was ready.

"Welcome, friends and loved ones," Bea said with her arms stretched out wide. "We're here today to cast a fertility blessing for one of our own. Dani?" She gestured to our hostess. "Please take your place in the middle of the circle."

Dani smoothed her pure white dress as she slowly made her way into the circle. I followed, placed a white pillar candle in front of each of the participants, and then took my spot on the northern-most point of the circle.

"Jade, raise your candle," Bea said.

I held the unlit pillar out, and when Bea nodded, I whispered, "*Levitate.*"

The candle floated right in front of me. Pleased everything was going according to plan, I joined hands with Kat and Pyper. Across from me, Rosalee repeated the step, followed by the two witches occupying the east and west points.

With the four candles elevated, Bea raised her arms skyward and called, "Aphrodite, goddess of love, beauty, pleasure, and procreation, we ask you for your blessing of fertility. We, the friends of Dani, offer our support and our strength in her journey to motherhood. From earth, wind, fire, and sea, we call forth to thee."

The four candles lit simultaneously with an elegant flare.

Bea met my gaze and gave me a slight nod. I let go of Kat and Pyper's hands and raised mine, palms up. The remaining candles rose, completing the candle circle. I repeated Bea's words, ending with, "We call forth to thee."

Magic glowed in the palms of my hands.

"Everyone except Jade, please place your hands around your candles," Bea said.

The entire room was silent as they did as they were told. Once everyone had a firm grip on their candles, Bea said, "Now, Jade."

The magic sparking in my palms glowed brighter the closer I got to my pillar candle. The two were like magnets, wanting to be connected. Good. This was working exactly how it was supposed to. Confidence swelled in my chest as I cupped the candle with both hands.

The flame on my candle shot high in the air, the strength of it surprising me. It flickered twice, then held steady, pulsing with clean energy. Nice.

"With these candles, we call upon the Goddess Aphrodite to bless Dani with the gift of life," Bea said.

Closing my eyes, I clutched my candle and chanted, "From north to south to east to west, we call upon the earth, wind, fire, and sea to bring a new life to thee."

Magic burst from me through the candle to the flame. Sparks of fire shot around the circle, uniting with the other flames, and a collective gasp sounded from the participants at the exact moment my magic touched them.

"Repeat the phrase 'bring new life to thee,'" Bea ordered.

Together as if one unit, the women chanted, "Bring new life to thee."

The candles blew out, leaving a trail of white smoke. Then a wind kicked up, and the smoke shot toward Dani and wound around her, seeming to seep right into her skin.

"Well done, Jade," Bea said. "I think that—"

The white smoke separated from Dani, concentrated into a ball, and then shot right at me, sucker punching me in the gut.

I stumbled backward, clutching my stomach, barely able to breathe.

"Jade!" someone called, but I couldn't make out who. I was too busy gasping from the dark magic burning my abdomen.

"Oh, God," I forced out. "It's black magic." I barely heard the horrified cries from the other guests. "Bea!" Tears of pain blinded me. "Help!"

A cool stream of magic engulfed me, and I felt nothing except Bea's strong, soothing energy, rejuvenating me from the inside out as she pulled the darkness from me.

My vision cleared, and with a powerful force I rarely called on, I shot my own magic at the black cloud hovering in front of me, blasting it into nothing.

I stood there, my breath coming in short bursts as the collective shock in the room left me completely unable to move. The weight of everyone's emotions was too much to bear, and my knees buckled. I fell to the side, barely missing hitting my head on one of the rented tables.

"Jade!" It was Kat. She kneeled in front of me, worry lines marring her usually smooth complexion. "Call Kane!"

"No." I pushed myself back up. "I'll be fine. I just need everyone to take a step back, please."

Everyone except Kat did as I asked. The relief was instantaneous. My body was lighter and my breathing turned to normal.

Kat placed her hand over mine and squeezed. "Take what you need."

I shook my head, unwilling to use her energy to fortify myself. I had in the past and likely would in the future, but not unless it was absolutely necessary. "Really, it's okay. I only need a minute."

She studied me as if she wasn't sure she believed me, but after I gave her a reassuring smile, she bent her head in agreement and got to her feet.

Bea kneeled down in front of me and handed me one of her energy-boosting herbs.

I took it without resistance.

"What happened?" she asked, worry streaming off her in waves.

"I have no idea. Everything was going fine, then when the magic hit me, a stream of black magic came out of nowhere." I glanced around, searching for a rogue witch. How else could I have been attacked? "Did you see anyone? Someone must've cast a spell at the same time."

"No." Bea frowned, confusion mixing with her worry. "And it didn't come from anyone else. It came from you."

My mouth fell open in shock. "That's impossible. I don't use black magic."

"No. Not on purpose, you don't. But if something's off with your powers, then you could've—"

"Jade's been cursed," Zoe said, her voice carrying over the whispers of the guests.

Bea started, and we both turned to eye the young woman. "Are you sure?"

Zoe nodded. "The black cloud is from the curse, not Jade."

My heart raced, and my hands went clammy. How was that even possible? Wouldn't I remember being cursed? But the pity on her face and the sudden acceptance on Bea's spoke volumes. I glanced between them, my stomach turning over from the magic-induced nausea.

"Do you know what kind of curse?" Bea asked.

"Whoever cursed her..." Zoe swallowed, and a pained expression claimed her delicate features.

"Zoe?" I prompted, my voice full of tension. "What is it?"

She closed her eyes, and when she opened them, there was despair reflecting back at me. "Someone has laid claim to your future child."

Chapter 2

"What?" I cried, clutching my stomach. "No. You've made a mistake. This can't be possible." There was no way I wouldn't have noticed a curse. Especially one with black magic. And how would Zoe know? She had magic, thanks to her new soul, but she wasn't yet fully trained as a witch. Not in anything as advanced as black magic, anyway. She was wrong. She had to be.

Bea tightened her grip on my hand, her cold fear sending a shiver up my spine. I knew right then whatever Zoe was talking about was the truth. Beatrice Kelton rarely let her emotions get away from her. She had an uncanny ability to hide them from me. Only something as awful as black magic could tear down her defenses.

"Bea?" I forced myself to my feet, doing my best not to panic.

She turned, her shoulders rigid, and tried to smile, but it came off more as a grimace. "We'll figure it out, Jade. I promise."

My heart sank to my knees, leaving a hollow ache in the middle of my chest. "I don't understand how this happened. No one cursed me."

Bea glanced at the spot Zoe had been sitting in, but the new witch was already headed toward the door. "Zoe!" Bea called in her teacher voice, the one that made everyone stop and listen. Only Zoe didn't get the memo and kept right on going out the front door of the house.

"I'm sorry," Lailah said as she rushed after her.

Kat appeared beside me and wrapped her arm around my waist. I leaned into her, grateful for the contact.

The front door slammed behind Lailah, the sound echoing through the silent room. Most of the guests were clumped together on the far side of the room, keeping as far away from us as they could get. Or, more to the point, as far away from *me* as they could get.

Rosalee and Dani were off to the side, separate from the group. Dani stood completely still, her face stark white, while Rosalee performed a cleansing spell, no doubt to make sure my black magic hadn't tainted her sister.

"We should go," Bea said.

I nodded but said, "Not until we're sure Dani's okay. Rosalee's spell is probably sufficient, but I'd feel better if *you* checked her for any dark spells."

Bea glanced between us, and I could tell she was fighting with leaving my side.

"Go," I said. "I'll be all right."

"Okay, but don't go anywhere. I want to explore the spell attached to you and see if we can find a magical signature that will point us to the witch responsible for this."

"I didn't think that was possible. When Lucien was cursed, we never did that."

"Of course I did, dear." Bea gave me an odd look. "It was there, but was so old it was too faint to identify. Yours has to be fairly recent. We have a much better shot of tracing it."

I nodded, forcing down the unease trying to choke me. Could someone I knew actually have done this? I'd made a few enemies over the past year, but most of them were demons or black magic users who'd been neutralized or incarcerated. Had one escaped? I wrapped my arms around myself and shuddered.

Whoever it was, the person must've wanted my future child for his or her power. Kane was an incubus, and I was a white witch. The chances of having a mundane child were almost nil. "I'm yours when you're ready."

Bea touched my hand in a motherly gesture and then took off across the room.

I slumped into a chair and picked up the nearest drink.

"I wouldn't if I were you," Pyper said.

"Huh?" I froze, my lips inches from the straw.

"The last thing you need is a penis in your mouth." She smiled gently and took the drink from my hand and replaced it with a highball glass. "Vodka with a twist. I think it's clear you could use something a little stronger."

"Where did you get this?" I eyed her. "The bar is serving wine and daiquiris."

She shrugged and patted her bag. "I brought backup, just in case."

I let out a sad chuckle and forgot I'd sworn off alcohol as I took a sip. The liquid hit the back of my throat and burned pleasantly as it went down. My nausea from earlier had vanished. Thank the gods. I drained the glass and smiled lazily at Pyper. "Thanks. That helped."

"Pyper to the rescue." She held a small flask up. "More?"

"Yes."

She mixed me another drink, and then another, both gone seconds after she'd handed them to me.

I slammed the glass down on the table, relieved the panic that had been trying to seize me had been buried by the booze buzz.

"You okay?" Pyper asked.

"As okay as can be expected, I guess."

Kat sat next to me, and the three of us watched Bea talk with Rosalee and her sister.

"It's not your fault, you know," Pyper said.

I turned to meet her gaze. "No? Maybe not, But I always seem to be the catalyst when this stuff goes down."

"You know why," Kat said. "Dark forces seek out power. But that still doesn't make any of this your fault. It's just a fate you were born into."

I nodded because I knew that was what was expected of me. But her words made my heart sink. Could I bring a child into the world knowing what she was going to be subjected to? Suddenly I understood why my mother had kept my power from me for all those years. If I'd stayed in Idaho and continued to live my quiet life, would any of this have happened?

Maybe not, but it was clear darkness would've found me anyway. And then I wouldn't have Kane. I straightened, putting my shoulders back. Second-guessing my choices would get me nowhere. What I needed now was a plan.

I stood, swaying a little, as Bea made her way back toward us.

"You ready to go home?" Pyper asked me. We'd ridden to the blessing together in her car.

I shook my head. "Not yet."

"We're headed to my shop to see if we can pinpoint who cast this spell," Bea said to her. "You and Kat are welcome to come with us if you want."

"I would, but I need to pick Lucien up across town. His Jeep is in the shop," Kat said.

"And I have a body-painting job I have to get to," Pyper added, glancing at her watch. "I assume this means you'll be riding with Bea?" she asked me.

"Yes," Bea said before I could answer.

Instead of leaving, both of my friends stared at me, their emotions conflicted. Their unease crawled over my skin, making me itch. They were worried, probably not happy about leaving me after learning about the curse. I backed up, putting distance between us. "It's fine. Bea and I can deal with whatever we find out, and then I have to get home. Kane will be waiting."

We had a date set for seven. Between his demon-hunting commitments and the shadow walking I'd been doing for Chessandra, we'd spent very little time together lately. Even Christmas Eve had been interrupted by the Brotherhood. Kane had been called to deal with a demon who'd been playing Santa down in Jackson Square. Talk about a nightmare before Christmas.

"All right. If you're sure," Kat said, her expression skeptical.

"I'm sure."

They both gave me a hug and made me promise to call after Bea and I were done with the testing.

I waved as they reluctantly left. Bea crossed the room to let Rosalee know we were going, and I sat at the table by myself, watching the dwindling blessing party. All the remaining guests were alternating between staring at me and pretending I didn't exist, trepidation streaming off them in waves. Sighing, I picked up Pyper's abandoned daiquiri and took a long swig. If everyone in the room was going to treat me like a leper, then I was going to need copious amounts of alcohol.

After I'd finished Pyper's drink, my vision turned fuzzy and I no longer cared what anyone thought. I was the one cursed, not them. And it wasn't like black magic was contagious.

The room was spinning by the time Bea came for me. "Jade?" she asked. "Ready?"

"Absolutely," I slurred and got to my feet, stumbling sideways. Giggling, I clutched her arm. "I probably shouldn't drive."

"That's obvious," she said dryly. "Come on. Let's get you out of here."

Bea wrapped her arm around my waist and guided me out of the lavish house. The late-afternoon sun blinded me, and I stumbled once more, crashing into the railing. At least I hadn't flailed down the porch steps.

"Oh, boy. I think maybe you need a restorative."

"Why? I feel great." I tilted my head up, enjoying the warmth of the day.

"You won't when that booze wears off. If the left side of your body isn't bruised, it'll be a miracle."

I waved an impatient hand. "I'm perfect. For once, all this witchy B.S. isn't bothering me one bit."

"How could it? You can't feel a thing." She tightened her grip on my arm and carefully tugged me to her silver Prius. "Get in."

I slid into the passenger's seat and glanced around. "Where's Pyper? I came with her."

Bea started the car and shook her head. "She left already, remember?"

I blinked, hard. "Um, yeah, I guess." But I didn't. The day's colors were blurring together, and I wasn't even sure where we were anymore. "I might be a little drunk."

"You don't say." Bea patted my leg. "Don't worry about a thing, Jade. I'll have you fixed up in no time."

I sat back and closed my eyes, only to have my world spin out of control. Renewed nausea made bile rise up to the back of my throat. My eyes popped open, and I grappled with the door, looking for the window button.

"Oh, goddess above," Bea mumbled.

My fingers finally found purchase, and the window lowered. Cool air rushed in, settling me.

"If you get sick, you're cleaning it up," Bea said, her voice harsh.

"Don't worry," I forced out between gulps. "I won't."

"I've heard that before."

I turned to squint at her but couldn't focus. "We'll be to your house in a sec anyway."

"No. We won't. I'm taking us to my shop. That's where my potions are."

"Oh, crap." My world tilted as she took a sharp turn, and I had to grip the door frame to keep from slumping over.

She chuckled. "Keep it together, Jade. We'll be there in a few."

I concentrated on breathing. In. Out. In. Out. Time got away from me, and I thought I might have blacked out for a moment, because all of a sudden we were parked in front of her shop, the Herbal Connection.

My door swung open, startling me. I glanced up into Bea's exasperated face.

She held out her hand. "Let's go, party girl."

I clacked my tongue on the roof of my mouth and let her pull me from the car. "I'm not feeling so great."

"No kidding." She deftly unlocked the front door of her witch supply store.

The scent of fresh rain and sea-salted air washed over me. It was Lailah's spell on the shop that put all patrons at ease by triggering their favorite scents. My stomach settled just a touch, the spell working its magic.

"Take a seat." Bea deposited me on the stool behind the counter. "I'll be right back."

I did as I was told, trying my best to keep my eyes from crossing. The air conditioning blew down, and gooseflesh popped out over my arms. Suddenly everything came into focus, the wooziness vanished, and my alcohol haze fled.

Bea stood in front of me, holding an empty glass vial, a self-satisfied smile claiming her lips.

"What was that?"

"Elemental magic. It's something I'm experimenting with. Looks like it worked."

I raised one eyebrow. "Healing air?"

She nodded and held up the small vial. "I prepped a ginger bath, spelled the steam, and then trapped it in here. All I had to do was ask it to encircle you, and there we have it."

"So air and water?"

"Actually, air, water, earth, and fire. Each was present. The ginger for earth, and the fire to heat it."

I slumped back on the stool, my energy completely gone, and stifled a yawn. "That makes sense. So simple."

Bea smoothed her elegant sheath dress. She looked so conservative standing there in her New Age shop. Had she ever looked the part? Not since I'd come to town a year and a half ago. She was always dressed in classic styles as if she was ready for tea at any given moment. The one exception was when she was digging in her garden. Then she wore overalls and cotton button-down shirts.

"I'd love to experiment with the elementals with you." I grimaced and waved a hand at myself. "I mean, once we get past my current personal crisis."

She patted my hand patiently. "I'll get you my notes. Now, let's go into the lab, where we can get down to business."

I followed her through the tight rows of merchandise and into the back room that she'd turned into a research lab. There were two stainless steel workstations, both orderly, with hardly a thing out of place. Shelves of potions and herbs lined one wall, while leather-bound books lined another.

Bea snapped her fingers, her magic lighting the candles nestled in the wall sconces. The warm light glowed in the small room. She walked to the middle of the lab. "Stand right here while I get the potion ready."

Nervous apprehension ate away at my stomach. My energy and ability to shield myself from outside forces had disappeared. Faint traces of excitement seeped in through the walls, no doubt from the tourists walking the streets of the Quarter. At least Bea was once again able to mask her own emotions from me. Because even though I no longer felt her concern, her short, jerky motions told another story. She was worried.

"Okay, I've got it." Bea had a mortar and pestle in one hand and a bag of herbs and a potion in the other. "It's not going to taste very good, but it'll do the job."

I gritted my teeth. And just when I was feeling better, too. No potion in the history of the Craft had ever tasted decent.

Bea eyed the potion and gave me an unconvincing smile. "It probably won't be that bad."

"Probably? You're joking, right?"

"Okay. It's going to taste awful, but it won't hurt you. And by the end of it, we'll have an image of whoever spelled you with black magic."

A wave of exhaustion hit me, and I settled on a stool, ready for the day to just end. "Let's get this over with."

Bea nodded and went to work. In no time, she handed me the pea-green potion. I took the cup and stared down at the sludge that was roughly the same thickness as clam chowder—complete with herb chunks.

"This looks disgusting," I said, my nose crinkled.

She raised her eyebrows. "Do you want to know who cursed you?"

"Yes."

She waved to the cup. "Here's your shot."

"Crapballs," I muttered and then chugged. The bitter sludge hit the back of my throat, and I forced it down, struggling to not gag. Good gods. Bea had lied. It was more than bad. It was horrible. I clutched my stomach and glared at her, grimacing.

"Give it a moment," Bea said softly.

I would've sent back a snarky remark if I hadn't been afraid I'd yak right there in her lab. Instead, I closed my eyes and mentally counted to ten. Slowly the nausea faded, and all I was left with was the rank aftertaste of dandelion and garlic. "Can I rinse my mouth out?"

Bea shook her head and handed me a thick white pillar candle, the flame already flickering. "Not yet. Suck in a deep breath and blow this candle out. The smoke will tell us what we need to know."

At least that part was easy. I held the candle with both hands, filled my lungs with air, and then blew. The candle winked out, leaving only the blue-tinted smoke. As I continued to blow, the smoke thickened, rolled, and stretched in and out into unidentifiable shapes.

Bea and I both held perfectly still, waiting.

The smoke turned and twisted, then materialized into something that might resemble a human form, but before any features could be identified, it folded in on itself again, hovered, and then shot across the room and back again. It pinged off the walls, crisscrossing the room.

Bea frowned and pursed her lips.

"It didn't work," I said.

She shook her head and raised her hands toward the smoke, her lips moving in a silent chant. I was dying to ask her what she was doing, but I didn't want to interrupt. If she was in the middle of a spell, any sort of distraction could cause an issue.

The smoke started to slowly drift toward her, but then it stopped, balled up, and shot away from us both, straight to

Lailah's workstation. Tendrils spilled off the ball and wrapped around a medium-sized vial full of red liquid.

"Bea? Is that a fertility potion?" I asked, watching as the smoke solidified back into the putrid green potion I'd swallowed and covered the bottle, forming a small pool on the counter. "Disgusting."

She grimaced and glanced away, hitting a button on her phone. "Yes. It was."

"But why—"

"Lailah? I need to see you right now," she said into the phone. Gesturing to me, she headed for the door that led into the shop. "No. It's an emergency…okay. See you in ten."

Bea closed the lab door behind us, while I headed straight for the bathroom.

I could not go one more second with the vile taste in my mouth. I took my time rinsing with water and then again with the mouthwash I found in the cabinet. Once I felt like I wasn't going to gag, I rejoined Bea in the shop. "All right. Lay it on me. What happened back in the lab?"

A muscle pulsed in her temple. The cold, hard expression on her face was almost terrifying. If I didn't know her so well, I'd be convinced she was ready to spell me into next week.

"Bea?"

Her jaw tensed and her voice rasped as she ground out, "That was a bottle of fertility potion. The spell indicates that's what was used to curse you."

Shock turned my limbs to ice. I stood there, totally confused and at a loss for words.

Bea waited, her face set in stone.

I shook my head, logic winning out over fear. "That's impossible. I haven't even taken any. The bottle you left me is tucked away in a drawer in the bathroom until we decide what we want to do."

A few months ago, after Bea had made the suggestion that Kane and I might want to start thinking about a family, she'd discreetly left a bottle of it on my nightstand. Instead of finding her meddling invasive, I'd thought it sweet. She knew firsthand how being a powerful witch could take over one's life. I'd decided it was her way of letting me know I had options.

Bea's brow furrowed. "I didn't leave you a potion. Did you get some from the store?"

"No. I found it on my nightstand a few days after we talked about it. I assumed it was from you."

She shook her head. "I didn't put that there, Jade. Someone else did that."

"Who?"

We both glanced at the fertility potions lined up on a nearby rack. Then we looked at each other.

"My spell didn't identify any of the other bottles in the lab," Bea said. "Only that one...on Lailah's workstation."

Chapter 3

"What?" I said stupidly, my brain refusing to register what she'd just said.

"Lailah—" Bea started.

I held my hand up. "Like I said, I haven't taken any of that potion. Besides, Lailah would never curse me. Just like she didn't curse you…dammit." The light bulb clicked on as I remembered the time Lailah had been unwittingly forced to poison Bea. "You think she's been compelled to harm me? Or possessed? No." I shook my head. "That's ridiculous. I know her too well now. I'd have been able to tell."

Bea raised one skeptical eyebrow. "Really, Jade? You think that's how this works?"

All the righteous indignation left me and I slumped. "No. It's just not probable that she'd be targeted again. I mean, why would she be possessed?"

"To get close to you, of course," Bea said.

"Of course." My voice was flat. If that was the case, I was going to get Lailah a freaking magical bodyguard. It was one thing for some asshat to come after me, but to use my friends to do it was beyond low.

The door burst open, and Lailah rushed in, her breath coming in short bursts. Her long blond hair had been piled into a haphazard bun, and she'd changed into olive-green cargo pants and a white T-shirt. She stopped inches from me. "What happened?"

I stepped back, putting space between us.

She frowned and turned to Bea for an explanation.

"Come with me." She slipped her hand through the crook in Lailah's arm and guided her toward the lab. I moved to follow, but Bea paused and put her other hand up. "Wait here. We'll be right back."

I opened my mouth to protest, but the image of the potion flashed in my mind, and I closed it. "Fine."

The pair disappeared, leaving me alone in the dark shop. I could either sit there stuck in my own head, or I could do something. Anything. I stared across the store at the fertility potions Bea had for sale. The little red bottles seemed to call to me. I stood and shuffled across the hardwood floor. Packages of dried herbs fell to the floor when I brushed against an aisle display, but I didn't stop to pick them up. I was on an involuntary mission, completely transfixed.

My brain had short-circuited, and even though I knew I shouldn't touch anything in my current state of mind, that I should wait for Bea, I couldn't stop myself. My hand rose, and the next thing I knew, I had one of the bottles cradled in my palm. The cool air of the shop caressed my skin, soothing me, as I undid the top.

A sweet wisteria fragrance permeated the air. The stress of the day faded away, and I could no longer remember, nor care, why I was at Bea's shop. The only thing that mattered was the potion. A thirst overwhelmed me, and my mouth watered. Nothing had ever smelled so good.

Just one taste. That was all I needed.

Tipping my head back, I lifted the bottle to my lips and—

"Jade!" Bea's stern voice echoed through the shop.

I jerked, spilling the contents down the front of my dress. The fog clouding my judgment lifted, and I shook my head, trying to get my bearings.

Bea stared at the bottle still clutched in my hand. "What were you doing?"

"I…" I glanced around, frowning. Then I focused on the potion bottle and dropped it as if it had burned me. The remainder of the liquid splashed onto the floor. "Omigod. I'm sorry. I don't know what happened."

Bea's eyes narrowed. "You were spelled?"

"Maybe." My hands shook, and it pissed me off. I was stronger than that, dammit. "I was intent on drinking the fertility potion, but I don't know why."

"It's the curse, most likely," Lailah said as she crossed the room with a roll of paper towels and floor cleaner in her hands. "It wants your child, and the potion is a way to speed up the process."

My heart stuttered in my chest. "You mean I'm going to start doing things that will result in a pregnancy, even if I want to avoid one?"

"It's possible," Bea said, her tone raspy as if she hadn't slept the night before. She cleared her throat. "Lailah didn't cast the spell on you. At least there's no evidence to support that theory, since the potion on her lab table has no traces of black magic."

Too afraid to help Lailah clean up for fear I'd go into another potion-drinking trance, I frowned and joined Bea near the counter. "Then why did the spell target the potion?"

"It's angel magic," Lailah said.

"What?" I spun around and stared at her open mouthed.

"The curse. It's angel magic." Lailah stood up, clutching the wet paper towels in one hand. "I bet you anything that's why it went after the last thing I worked on."

I braced myself against the counter, clutching the edge so hard that pain seized my fingers. "Angels use black magic?"

She pursed her lips. "Only as a last resort. If one is that desperate, the angel usually ends up falling, you know? But the remnants of the revelation spell Bea cast are still in there. I felt it clear as day. There's a pureness to it that could've only come from an angel."

Well, wasn't that just the cherry on this shit show of a day? I was already a slave to the high angel, at her beck and call, and now one of her minions had cursed me. Wanted my child for some nefarious activity. "Can you tell who?"

She shook her head. "No. Someone who wants power, though, that's obvious."

Bea reached behind her desk and pulled out a notebook. "Is there dissent among the council?"

Lailah shrugged. "No more so than usual as far as I know. But if anyone else is investigating Chessandra, then maybe."

A heavy foreboding weighed in my soul. Chessandra was the high angel, and for months she'd been overstepping her authority. In addition to almost getting her sister killed while trying to seal a demon portal, Chessandra had sent a group of angels on a dangerous mission to the shadows, and Lailah suspected she was the reason another angel, Avery, was missing. For the past two months, Lailah had been looking for the missing angel while investigating Chessandra. So far no luck.

No one had dirt on the high angel. But if someone else was going after her, they'd need all the power they could get. I ground my teeth. "You don't think Chessandra did this, do you?"

"Why would she?" Bea asked.

I shrugged. "I don't know. Why does she do anything she does?"

"But she's mated to your father." Bea looked anything but convinced.

"That doesn't mean anything," Lailah said, echoing my thoughts. "But no. I highly doubt she did this. Her magic is barely detectable. I wouldn't have felt any at all."

Of course. She was the high angel. Her magic was strong but subtle. She didn't leave traces. "Then the angel who did this either is an idiot or is deliberately trying to piss her off."

Lailah nodded. "Or both."

I worked closely with Chessandra. When she found out someone had targeted me, she was going to see it as a personal betrayal by one of her own. The thought should've helped put me at ease, since she likely wouldn't let this go until the traitor was found. Instead, it just made me feel worse. I didn't trust her. No one ever knew what she would do for "the greater good."

"I have to go." I got up from the stool. "I have to tell Kane, and then I need to request a meeting with Chessandra."

Bea put her hand on my arm. "I don't like this."

"Me neither," Lailah chimed in. "Would you consider letting me investigate a bit first?"

I hesitated. I had a serious curse threatening not only me but my future child. Every instinct told me to run to the high angel and demand she do something about it. Force her hand in some way.

"What if she keeps you there for safekeeping?" Bea asked.

"Oh, son of a…" She could very well put me in the room where time stood still. Or brush me off. Only goddess knew what she'd do to further her agenda. I wouldn't even put it past her to lay claim to my unborn child in order to keep him or her safe.

I met Lailah's clear blue eyes. "You think you can find anything out?"

She hesitated then gave me a curt nod. "I've got an appointment with one of the former council members tomorrow for the Avery case. I can do some poking around then."

"All right. In the meantime, I'll retrace my steps and see if I can figure out when this happened." At that moment, all I wanted to do was go home and fall into Kane's arms. "Give me a call me tomorrow. And we'll see if either of us has news."

"You got it." Her eyes turned soft, and for a second, I thought they misted.

"Lailah? You okay?"

"Yeah. I'm…oh, dammit." She reached out and pulled me into a fierce hug, nearly knocking the breath out of me.

"Whoa." I automatically hugged her back, my emotions warring with shock and tenderness. Lailah and I had history. And while she was my friend now and we both trusted each other, we weren't besties in the strictest sense of the word. We didn't hug. Ever.

"Sorry." She pulled back and wiped her eyes. "It's just not right what's being done to you. And I'm more convinced than ever that my kind are gearing up for some sort of war."

"With whom, though?" Bea clutched one of her leather-bound books. "The demons?"

That was the natural guess. Demons and angels had been in a struggle to control souls since the beginning of time.

Lailah let out a frustrated grunt. "Maybe. But there's no noise on that end other than the usual grumblings. If there was an epic battle coming, you'd think we'd hear something. Only we haven't. That just leaves an internal battle in the angel world, which isn't out of the realm of possibility."

My soul guardian heaved a heavy sigh. "A lot of the angels I've spoken to are unhappy with the leadership. Only they're quiet about it because no one can pinpoint a specific thing they dislike. There's a high amount of distrust and unease. A feeling if you will. But that's hardly a concrete reason to revolt. Still, I don't disagree with them. And because of that, if a rebellion starts, I have no idea which side to support."

Bea put her hand on Lailah's arm. A small spark of magic lit under her touch. Probably a comfort spell. "Try not to be so quick to jump to conclusions. Everything is still speculation."

Lailah looked away and took a deep breath. "You're right. But something's coming." She turned to me, worry clouding her eyes. "I can feel it. Especially when I look at you."

"Because you think whoever did this is trying to put me in the middle of it?"

"They already have, haven't they?"

I sighed. "I guess so."

Chapter 4

Lailah's fears weighed heavily on my mind as I walked the eight blocks through the French Quarter toward the home I shared with Kane. What if the angel realm really was gearing up for some rebellion? What would that mean for everyone else? They were soul guardians, charged with watching over the most vulnerable souls. If they were to fight each other for power, certainly some people would fall through the cracks and be lost. Or, worse, swallowed up in Hell.

I shuddered thinking about it. Both Pyper and I and even Lucien had been saved because of a soul guardian. Specifically Lailah. She was a true hero. What would happen to her? No doubt she'd be in the middle of the fight one way or another.

Fear for her overshadowed the unease of the curse I knew I carried. As long as I wasn't pregnant I was okay…for now.

The shotgun double I shared with Kane came into view, and the weight on my heart lessened a bit. The gaslights hanging over the porch flickered invitingly against the light breeze. Artificial light illuminated the curtain-covered window, and I imagined Kane lounging in the loveseat in the living room, a glass of wine in his hand while he waited for me.

I quickened my pace, running up the wooden steps to the front door.

But when I stepped through, he wasn't in the living room. And the rest of the house was dark. "Kane?"

No answer.

"You home?" I made my way down the hall toward the kitchen, flicking on lights as I went.

Again no answer. I bit down on my bottom lip and scouted the kitchen. Kane had said he was going to make dinner tonight, but there wasn't one dish out of place. My chai tea mug was still sitting in the sink exactly as I'd left it this morning. I let out a deep sigh.

He wasn't here.

Just to be sure, I checked the hallway. A soft glow of light shone underneath the door to our master bedroom.

Maybe he was home.

"Kane?" I said again and pushed the door open. The bedside table lamp cast a soft glow over a tray filled with cheesecake and fresh strawberries that had been left on the bed. A pair of wine glasses and a single lit pillar candle completed the scene.

"Have a good day?" Kane asked, leaning against the bathroom doorframe. His hair was damp from the shower, and his jeans hung low on his hips. No shirt in sight.

On any other day, if I'd walked in on this scenario, I'd be wiping the drool from my chin. But today all I wanted to do was cry. I didn't, though. Taking a deep breath, I forced myself to smile. "Not exactly, but it looks like it's about to improve."

His lips turned up into that slow, sexy smile that always made me melt. Even now. My balled-up tension turned to desire as his dark eyes smoldered with intensity.

Dammit, my libido was already in overdrive, no doubt because of the curse. Sucking in a breath, I slammed the door on my lustful cravings. We couldn't do this. Not now. We had to talk.

I cleared my throat and walked to the bed, needing the cheesecake more than I ever had. Reaching down to pick up one of the plates, I glanced over at him. "Do you mind? It's sort of a cheesecake emergency."

All the heat vanished from his gaze. "What happened?"

The fact that I hadn't waited for whatever he'd had planned told him something was very off. A half-naked Kane and cheesecake was just about my favorite combination. The last time we'd had dessert in the bedroom…well, let's just say both of us had been a little sticky the next morning.

Kane sat on the edge of the bed and pulled me down into his lap. "All right. Spill it."

I swallowed the small bite of cheesecake. There was no sugarcoating this one. "I've been cursed."

Both of his eyebrows shot up as he scanned my body, obviously looking for any signs of damage. Frowning, his grip on my waist tightened. "I can't believe you were attacked at a blessing. What happened? Are you hurt?"

I shook my head. "No. That's the thing, I wasn't attacked at all. I have no idea how it happened." I explained Zoe's outburst and relayed Lailah's information. "So apparently some angel cursed me and our—" my voice cracked "—future child."

Every muscle in Kane's body tensed. Then a storm rolled through his eyes. Without saying anything, he lifted me off his lap and got to his feet. "An angel cursed you?"

I nodded. "That's what Lailah said."

Kane crossed the room to our armoire and pulled out the first shirt he found. He had it over his head and was stuffing his feet into his shoes before I could even register what he was doing.

"Where are you going?" I asked, already knowing the answer.

"Chessandra needs to fix this. Now." His body vibrated with so much anger I felt it as my own. The rage took over, consuming me, and my promise to Lailah to let her investigate first flew right out the window. His emotional energy had infiltrated mine, pushing me so far over the edge that I didn't even experience any guilt that I was about to break my word. Lailah would be pissed, but I couldn't seem to find the will to stop myself.

Kane's hand tightened over mine as he tugged me out of the bedroom and into the front of the house. We stood in the middle of the living room, both of us looking up at the ceiling.

Normally one had to be invited to the angel realm in order for the gates to open, but because Kane and I worked for Chessandra, we had a direct line to her, so to speak. She could hear me when I called for her. And with the amount of irritation streaming through me, there was no way she could block me out.

"Open the gates, Chessandra," I ordered. "It's urgent we see you tonight."

Kane's frustration intensified, nearly knocking me over with the weight of it.

"Come on, Chessa. We need to see you. It's an emergency." Power tingled under my skin. And because the high angel was ignoring us, I did nothing to hold it back. "I said, let us in!"

A shot of pure white magic burst from my fingertips at the same time a searing flash of pain just above my left eye blinded me. My knees gave out, and had Kane not been hanging on to me, I would've crumpled to the ground.

"Shit!" I clutched my head, focused on the pain trying to break me, and said, *"Evanesco."*

The pain escalated, consuming me as the magic pulsed with ever-growing intensity.

"Jade?" Kane's concerned voice pushed through the pain.

I let out a loud roar as my power broke through a barrier and rushed to the throbbing claiming my head. Cool relief doused me, and all the pain vanished, leaving me almost numb with relief. I glanced up at Kane with squinted eyes. The light from the angel realm shining behind him blinded me. I blinked rapidly, trying to keep my eyes from tearing.

"Let's go." I straightened, my voice all business. "We don't want to miss our window."

"Are you all right?" Kane's arm tightened around my waist.

"I am now," I said, full of confidence. Whatever had been plaguing me, I'd neutralized it. I felt powerful and in control for the first time all day.

The world spun, blurring white as our bodies were pulled through the veil into another realm. A second later, our feet hit the gold-and-white tile of the angel world's version of Saint Louis Cathedral. It was exactly the same, except everywhere there should be color was now white and gold, including the murals on the walls.

We stood at the back of the empty sanctuary. An ominous cloud settled over me, leaving me uneasy. It was as if we were breaking and entering. "Where is everyone?" I asked.

Kane shrugged. "Out partying?"

I snorted out a laugh. "Please." But then I sobered. "It's weird, right? Usually they're here with buckets of judgment and disdain."

"Not to mention we basically broke through their wards. You'd think an alarm would sound or something."

He was right. "Something's wrong."

"More wrong than one of them cursing you?" His eyes were narrowed again and full of contempt. Then he shook his head. "Never mind. You're right. They should be here with pitchforks by now."

I slipped my hand into his and sighed. "Come on. Let's go find out what the issue is this time."

Kane and I made our way up toward the dais unimpeded, but as soon as we turned left down the hall that headed toward Chessandra's office, their alarm finally sounded, echoing through the building. Within seconds the noise abruptly stopped, followed by rapid footsteps.

We glanced at each other then retreated into the sanctuary to wait.

"I guess we have our answer." I sat down in the front pew as if I belonged there. Kane stood beside me, no doubt feeling like he had to protect us. I wasn't that worried, though. Chessandra was too fond of forcing us to do the work she deemed too dangerous for her minions.

A half dozen security guards ran out of the hallway, each one with a different weapon. The leader had a sword brandished in one hand, while the one right behind him had an amulet sparking with magic.

Kane stood his ground, while I leaned forward and said, "We need to see the high angel. It's important."

Sword Guy came to a stop a couple of feet in front of us and glared. "How dare you invade our inner sanctum without an invitation?"

Kane stiffened, and his indignant irritation crawled all over my skin.

I placed a soft hand on his arm while I spoke to the guard. "My apologies for arriving unannounced, but I assure you we're here on official business."

Okay, so that wasn't exactly the truth, but it would be when I demanded she let me out of my contract.

The short, dark-haired guard moved forward, pointing his amulet at me. Without him saying a word, magic shot from the stone and hit me straight in the chest.

Red-hot bolts of fiery pain erupted above my heart, paralyzing me for just a second. I opened my mouth, trying to form words, but none would come. Rage boiled in my gut, eating me from the inside out. I sucked in a shallow breath and then called on my own magic once more. It rose up instantly and squashed the fire in my chest. Only a small ache remained where the magic had entered my system. I rubbed at my breastbone, glaring. How dare this jackass unload his amulet on me when all I'd been doing was sitting there? Freakin' angels.

Kane's outrage filled the space between us, and right before he lunged forward, I stood and gripped his arm.

"No, Kane," I demanded through gritted teeth and stepped in front of him, staring the angel down. "I don't know what you think you're doing, but that spell was completely unnecessary. We told you why we're here. Attacking me was uncalled for."

Kane stepped up beside me, and in a low, dangerous voice, he said, "Do not attack my wife again, or you're going to have a very unhappy demon hunter on your hands."

"You dare to threaten us, incubus?" Sword Guy thrust his weapon toward Kane.

Kane didn't even flinch. "You're damn right, I am. Hurt her again, and we're going to have a problem."

The other four guards fanned out, brandishing daggers, an ax, and two other magic-wielding stones.

Power shot from my center to my hands, making sparks of magic crackle in my palms. Even though we were in the angel realm, that didn't mean everyone was aboveboard. I'd be damned if I sat back and let a six-on-one fight go down. "Back off, assholes."

Amulet Guy chuckled. "Look, boys. The white witch is white as a sheet. Any bets on how much effort it'll be to take her down?"

No doubt I was pale from the magic I'd already expelled. But if he thought that made me weak in any way, he was an idiot. White witches had legions of power.

I sent the guard a twisted, saccharin-sweet smile. "You can test my abilities now or you can take us to Chessandra. If you choose the former, you'll also have the privilege of explaining to the high angel why her shadow walker kicked your ass. Because I will. Trust me."

My power intensified, consumed my hands, and climbed up my forearms. I raised my hands, ready to blast them if they struck a blow.

Kane laughed, but it was humorless as he pulled out his Brotherhood dagger. It had a special stone that would not only stave off their magic but would absorb it, making him that much more powerful in a magical battle.

Realization dawned in Amulet Guy's eyes. He muttered an oath and pocketed his weapon. The others with magical stones did the same.

"What are you doing?" Sword Guy demanded, glaring at them. "They can't take all of us."

"Yes, they can. Especially the incubus. That dagger, it's a game changer," a familiar deep male voice boomed from the back of the sanctuary.

I twisted to see Drake, my biological father, making his way toward us.

He met my gaze and frowned. "What's wrong, Jade?"

"We need to see Chessandra," I said, lifting my chin.

"Fine. I'm sure that can be arranged. But why are you so pale?"

"I had a migraine. It's gone."

His eagle-eyed gaze turned to Sword Guy. "Retreat. Now."

"But—"

"I said retreat. Do you have any idea who this woman is?" Drake took two steps toward the guard, his frame appearing to grow larger with each movement.

"Yes, sir. She's the New Orleans coven leader, but I thought—"

"I don't give a damn what you thought. Drop your weapon and get the hell out of here."

"I'm under orders to apprehend any intruders," Sword Guy said, his chest puffed out in defiance.

Drake narrowed his eyes and glared at the guard. "Did you realize that not only does she work for Chessandra, but she's my daughter?"

"No." Sword Guy's tone was clipped, full of righteous indignation as he sheathed his blade. Fuming, he closed the distance between them and stood defiantly in front of Drake. "That's not my concern."

"It should be," Kane said mildly.

Drake turned to the other guard standing off to the left and pointed at Sword Guy. "Apprehend him. Then wait in my office."

The guard gave Drake a curt nod. "Yes, sir."

"Hey!" Sword Guy struggled as two of the guards pulled his hands behind him and bound his wrists with plastic ties they'd pulled from pockets in their tunics.

I sucked in a breath, barely able to contain my impatience. "Can we go see Chessandra now?"

Drake pointed to the guards holding Sword Guy. "Take him to the holding tank. I'll be there to deal with him when I'm ready."

I had to hold back a smirk. Even though my daddy had come to my rescue, so to speak, I still took great pleasure in the incredulous look on Sword Guy's face.

"Let's go." Drake gave me a tender look I'd never seen before.

"Thanks," I said awkwardly. Drake and I didn't have much of a relationship, much less a special father–daughter one. "For taking care of the guard. You really didn't have to. We could've—"

"Yes, I did. You're my daughter. As your father, one of the perks is that I get to protect you. But since you're so strong, that's not something you need often. So don't try to deprive me of my parental right. I've already missed too much."

I stared at him, stunned. Drake was my biological father, but neither of us had known it until recently. We weren't close and had almost no relationship outside the fact that I worked for Chessandra, who happened to be his significant other. I swallowed. "Okay."

He gave me a faint smile and then shooed the guards away. Once they were gone, he turned to us. "Follow me."

I relaxed my hands, trying to let go of some of the overflowing frustration, but failed when I fell into step beside Kane. He was still wound tight, his mood overtaking mine. I didn't even have the will to erect my imaginary glass walls to block his emotions out. I was too exhausted to care. By the time we were outside Chessandra's office, we were both on edge.

But instead of opening the door, Drake paused with his hand over the knob. "Why are you here?"

Kane pressed his lips together in a tight line, clearly not willing to answer him.

"Does it matter?" I asked, genuinely curious. He'd stepped up and gone to bat for us before with Chessandra just as he had back in the sanctuary with the guards. But he was still Chessandra's partner. I was pretty certain they could communicate telepathically. I wanted to see her face when we told her what had happened. Having her know beforehand would ruin that.

"Yes. Of course it does." Drake's expression turned exasperated, but he said nothing else. With a shake of his head, he turned and pushed the door open.

Chessandra was reading what looked to be a report while sitting on the edge of the desk. She was wearing a silky red satin negligee, her chestnut hair pulled into an elegant twist, as if she were waiting for her lover to come take her off to bed.

"Drake. There you are. I—" Chessandra's head snapped up, and she scowled. "Why did you bring them here? They haven't been invited."

Kane pushed past us both and glared at her. "So you can tell us why one of your angels has cursed Jade and our future child."

Chapter 5

She dropped the papers onto her desk and then, with the grace of a dancer, she uncrossed her legs and stood on silver high heels. "Excuse me?"

Drake glanced at me. "Is that true? That you've been cursed by one of us?"

I nodded, staring Chessandra in the eye.

The high angel stood before us, her expression skeptical. "And what makes you think one of my angels would curse you?"

I refrained from rolling my eyes at her superior attitude. She might be the high angel, but I wasn't impressed. If she'd ever shown one grain of empathy, I might've felt differently. But she was so cold, impassive. Just about the only time I'd seen her show any emotion was when her sister had been trapped in a void world. And even then she'd been restrained.

Brushing past Drake, I walked over to a chair and sat, crossing my leg over one knee. It had been a long day. "I did a fertility blessing today, and instead of my friend being blessed, the magic targeted me and revealed a black-magic curse."

Chessandra lowered her lashes and gave me a dry, impatient look. "Witches are the ones who dabble in black magic. Not my angels."

I crossed my arms over my chest. "Not according to Lailah."

"And how would that lower angel know? Such a major disappointment, that one."

"You can't be serious?" I jumped to my feet, unable to stay seated in the face of her ridicule. "Lailah's the best damn angel out there. A major reason the magical community of New Orleans is still intact."

"And yet she can't seem to find one missing angel." Chessandra spat the words out, venom poisoning her tone.

The magic pulsing in my chest intensified. If I'd let my guard down, I'd have strangled her with the sheer will of my power. "And Avery is missing because you sent her on a mission she wasn't equipped to handle."

"You know nothing of the situation, witch. Now leave my office. You're not welcome here."

"She'll do no such thing." Hatred streamed off Kane in the form of a red cloud. "You're going to find out who did this and reverse the curse."

Chessandra straightened her back, seeming to grow at least two full inches. "How dare you order me to do anything, incubus? You work for me, remember? You'll do as I say, not the other way around."

Kane's pupils dilated, and I started to fear he was going to wring the high angel's neck.

"Chessa," I said.

She whipped her head around and glared at me. "It's Chessandra."

"Right." I swallowed a snarky reply and said, "Beatrice Kelton cast an identification spell, but the test was inconclusive. Apparently that spell doesn't work on angel magic. Only we didn't understand the problem until Lailah arrived and said she felt an angel signature. There's no reason to doubt this, but feel free to cast your own spell or whatever you need to do. Because we're not leaving here until this is resolved."

"No angel would—"

"Chessa," Drake said quietly.

She cast him an irritated glance. "What?"

He held up his hand in a wait motion and then studied me, his expression contemplative. A tickle of air brushed over my skin, followed by a dull ache in my abdomen.

I pressed a hand to my gut and let out a small moan.

"My apologies," Drake said as the feeling vanished. He frowned, his eyebrows pinched. "Jade's telling the truth. The signature's too faint for me to place, but there's no doubt an angel did this."

Chessandra's mouth worked, and an array of emotions passed over her face. Disbelief, irritation, anger, and, finally, acceptance. "I see. Well, this is a problem."

"You don't say?" I gritted my teeth, totally disgusted with her attitude.

She ignored me and crossed the room to a small closet. With swift movements, she pulled out her white angel's robes and tugged them over her slinky lingerie.

"It's about time," I mumbled just to piss her off.

I was rewarded with a death glare.

"All right," Drake said, eyeing us both. "Let's focus on a solution."

"This way." Chessandra pressed a button, and a hidden door in the white paneling slid open.

Kane's eyebrows shot up as he glanced at me with a silent question.

I shrugged. The door wasn't something I'd seen before.

Drake swept his arm out, inviting us to go ahead of him.

Kane slipped his hand into mine, and together we followed the high angel through a stark white hallway. There weren't any doors or windows. Just white tile and white walls. If I didn't know better, I'd think she was taking us into a mental ward. Or maybe she was.

Son of a... Was she taking us to the room where time stood still? Lailah had speculated that she might. But with Chessandra in front of us and Drake behind us, there wasn't anything to do but follow.

Within moments, we came face to face with an ornate walnut door. Chessandra strode through, leaving the door open behind her. I stood in the threshold, taking in the rich, warm tones of the hardwood floors and the creamy walls. Bouquets of red and orange daisies graced a side table. And right in the middle of the room were two stark white couches that faced each other. Chessandra had already taken her place at the far end of the one facing us.

"Well?" she said, that signature impatience etched in the lines of her face.

I snapped out of my paranoid trance. Who knew there was a place like this in the cold confines of the angel realm? If it hadn't been for the white couches, it would've been downright inviting. Perhaps it was her private study.

Kane and I sat together across from Drake and Chessandra. Drake leaned forward, his long white-blond hair brushing his clasped hands. "Do you have any idea how this happened?"

I shook my head, keeping my gaze on Chessandra. She stared across the room at nothing, appearing to be lost in thought.

"You don't remember any sort of odd magic at all that could've been the cause of this?" Drake asked.

"Nope. Nothing." Turning my attention to my father, I waved a hand at Chessandra. "What's she doing?"

"Concentrating." Drake rose and disappeared into another room off to the left.

Kane and I glanced at each other. His eyes narrowed, and that tension that always seemed to pulse beneath my skin when I was in the angel realm intensified.

I stood and placed my hands on my hips. "I don't know what's going on, but we need to get down to business here."

Chessandra turned her head slowly, her eyes flashing pure white.

Whoa.

"We're waiting for the angel who cursed you to arrive." Chessandra's voice was far away, detached.

"I see." Only I didn't. Was she able to call angels to her side? Did she have some weird dark-mark-type magic that plucked angels out of thin air?

"Chessandra?" Kane called, his tone hesitant. "What do you see?"

Her pupils turned black again, but her irises stayed white. The only thing that would've made her look more evil is if her eyes had turned red. I shivered, wanting to get as far away from her as possible.

"Bad things," Chessa said in an ethereal voice. "Not safe. Dark forces are coming."

A ripple of fear ran through me. Not because I was afraid of dealing with dark forces. We'd done it before and we'd do it again. But because of the creepiness rippling from her.

She stood abruptly. "This way." Her white robes sailed out behind her as she hurried off into the room Drake had disappeared into.

Kane and I didn't hesitate to follow. Had the angel responsible for this shown up? I could only hope. Whoever it was, he or she was going to regret ever messing with my uterus.

We crossed into the second room, and I stopped dead in my tracks. I recognized it. White furniture, overstuffed chairs, and couches filled the living room. There was a fully stocked kitchen and four connecting bedrooms. Poppy-colored pillows were the only color to break up the stark room.

There weren't any windows and no other exits. My heart started to pound against my ribs.

The room where time stood still.

Dammit! How stupid could I be? Lailah had warned me, and I'd let Kane's anger drive me to force my way into the realm, right into Chessandra's clutches. Again.

I spun, intending to retreat into the first room, but the door had already vanished. All that remained was a smooth sheetrocked wall.

Slowly, I turned, my fists clenched in tight balls. "Why are we here?"

"Jade," Drake started, his tone meant to soothe me. "Please understand."

"No. I don't have to understand anything." I strode across the room and jabbed him in the chest with my forefinger. "What the hell? I can't believe you were in on this."

"You've been cursed. Don't you understand what will happen if someone takes your child? We have to protect you until we can figure out who's behind this spell."

"I thought Chessandra was waiting for the angel to show up."

"She is. But it can sometimes take a while. She's put the spell in place. When the angel lets his or her guard down, we'll know it."

"What does that mean?" Kane demanded, his gaze trained on Chessandra. Her head was tilted up and her eyes were closed as if she were worshiping the sun.

"Her magic is powerful, but angels have guards to keep their souls protected. All it takes is for them to relax for just a second, and then Chessa will have them. Sometimes it happens instantly, sometimes it takes a while. That's why we've decided it's best if you both wait here until we can contain the angel who's cursed Jade."

"Stay here? Contained in this room?" Kane shook his head in disgust. "You're out of your mind. We both have jobs to do. There's no way we're waiting around here for an unspecified time."

I nodded and walked to his side to present a united front.

"Mr. Rouquette, you're welcome to go. You're not the one in danger. But I'm afraid we're going to have to keep Jade here until the threat passes." Drake ran a hand over the plush white sofa. "Do not worry. Every comfort will be provided for her."

"No one is staying here," Kane ground out. "Open the door. We're leaving."

"It's not safe. Danger is coming," Chessandra repeated.

"It's your choice, Kane," Drake said as he crossed to Chessa. He wrapped an arm around her waist, cradling her against his body. "Let's go, love."

Chessa turned her head, her gaze focusing on him. She frowned, seeming confused.

"I've got you. Everything's going to be okay," he crooned and brushed a lock of her dark tresses from her forehead.

"Everything is not fine!" I stood in the middle of the room, vibrating with magic. "Let us out, or I'll blast my way out of here."

Drake's expression turned curious. "Now that would be impressive if you could. You're welcome to try. So far no one has managed it, though." He tilted his head, studying us. "But together you might have a shot."

I scowled. "This isn't a joke."

"No, Jade, it isn't." Drake stood up straight, his eyes piercing me. "Like I said before, it isn't often I get to protect you, but I'm doing it now. It's my job. I won't let some rogue angel hurt you or my grandchild."

"Future grandchild," I corrected. "I'm not even in danger... yet."

"If you're cursed, you are. This is the best possible solution."

Kane stepped in front of me, his dagger in his hand. Only the stone wasn't glowing with magic as it usually did. "We're leaving. Together. Now open the door, or we're going to have this out right here."

Drake shook his head. "I'm sorry, but that's not possible."

Kane's muscles bulged under his T-shirt. He rocked forward on the balls of his feet, and just when he was about to pounce, Chessa and Drake faded translucent.

Drake's eyes met mine. "I'm sorry to force this on you, but I don't see any other way. I'll be back once you've seen reason."

I gaped then shook my head, dislodging the jumbled thoughts in my brain. "See reason? You can't—"

The pair of them vanished, leaving me and Kane in the room where time stood still.

Chapter 6

"Are we where I think we are?" Kane asked, his voice unusually controlled.

"Yes." I flopped down on the oversized couch and closed my eyes. I was exhausted, too empty to care about much of anything. My father had just locked me away in a dungeon disguised as a fancy apartment.

He scanned the room. "Do you know where the main door is?"

I waved a hand toward the plain wall to the left. "That's where it was last time. But my magic wasn't able to penetrate it at all."

When my soul had been compromised, the angels had locked me and Lailah, along with another angel, in this prettied-up hellhole. I'd spent hours trying to blast my way out. Nothing had worked. I didn't see why it would now.

"You didn't have a demon hunter's dagger." Kane pulled his blade from the sheath and held it out in front of him. The stone on the hilt glowed eerie red and then winked out.

I raised a curious eyebrow. "What happened? I noticed the stone wasn't lit before when you showed it to Drake. Is the room making it faulty, or did you shut it down on purpose?"

"No, I didn't shut it down. I'm not sure what's happening." He pressed his lips together in a thin line as he inspected it. After running his hands along the edge of the blade, he glanced up at me. "It didn't exactly fail. It's more like it's weak, as if it needs a power source."

"It won't take it from you?" I sat up, concerned. "Or has it already taken too much?" My fingers dug into the couch cushions. This was crazy. Kane was an incubus. Incubi maintained power through sex. If Kane was weakened, he'd need me. And the last thing I wanted to do was get busy in the room where time stood still. Who knew who was watching us? Not to mention being a prisoner was about the least sexy thing on the planet.

He put the blade on the table in front of us and closed his eyes. After a moment, he nodded. "I still have plenty of power. The stone won't take it from me, though." Glancing around, he frowned. "Does this place have wards?"

"I'm sure it does." My steps were silent as I floated over the plush carpet toward the door I knew was concealed in the smooth white wall. I placed my palm straight out and ran my hand over the light texture. A faint ripple of magic tickled my hand. "Yes. They're there."

Kane nodded, picked up his dagger, and crossed the room to stand beside me. The stone in the dagger remained dark and lifeless. Then he pressed the hilt of the weapon to the wall and turned to me. "I need your help."

I nodded, casting him a curious glance. "Sure."

He gestured to the hilt of the dagger. "I need you to pull the magic from the wall into the stone."

Surprise stirred my magic coiled in my chest, followed by determination. That stone collected magic to neutralize enemies. If it could steal the magic from the wall, we might have a chance of breaking out. I placed my hand over the dagger and focused on the tiny thread of magic pulsing from the core of the stone. A small burst of my own magic shot into the hilt.

The moment my magic connected with the power of the stone, a wave of warmth slammed into me, and something inside me connected to the ancient magic. I closed my eyes and sucked in a deep breath. As I slowly let it out, I tugged, pulling on the magic from the stone.

My body went rigid and vibrated from the first jolt of mixed magic, and then everything came to an abrupt stop as if the power had collided with an invisible wall. My mental hold struggled to maintain the connection, and sweat broke out on my brow.

"Jade?" Kane asked, his voice sounding a million miles away.

I shook my head. I had to focus. Losing concentration for even one moment meant the connection would be lost. Something told me if we didn't break out of there, we'd be in there for years. Chessandra wasn't stupid. She knew if someone had control over our future child—who no doubt would hold considerable power—she'd be screwed. This was our one shot. And between the two of us, we had to get it done.

"Put your hand over mine," I ordered Kane.

I felt his movement beside me and then the brush of his flesh against the back of my fingers. "Pull the magic with me."

"On three?" he asked.

I nodded and counted. When it was time, a blast of his magic pinned not only my hand but my forearm to the wall. Our streams of power mixed, and the spell embedded in the wall slowly began to move.

The effort was so great I felt as if we were pushing boulders uphill. But it was moving, and as I watched the wall, a faint outline of the door flickered into view.

"It's working," I assured Kane.

He let out a grunt and increased the pull on the magic.

A dam burst, and just like that all the magic that had been collecting into the stone shot into my hand, up my arm, and straight to my heart.

My body convulsed, and all control of my magic vanished. Sparks of power and remnants of the spell shattered through me. I saw nothing but the horrified expression on Kane's face as I rose in the air, floating at least a foot off the ground.

The spasms in my muscles vanished, and I hung there serenely as if I were a fairy godmother come to grant Kane a wish.

"What the hell?" I asked, glancing around.

Kane stared up at me in awe.

"Snap out of it, dude!" I reached for him, but my hand slid right through his arm. "Oh my God." I stared at my hands and arms. They were solid just as they'd been before. What was happening?

Kane's surprised expression turned to one of determination. He reached a hand out to take mine, but again when we tried to connect, his hand passed right through me.

"Jade!" Kane took a step forward, both arms raised, and grabbed for me, but he came up empty. "Goddammit! That went all wrong."

"Not completely wrong." I waved a hand at the now-visible door. "At least now we know where it is."

The stricken expression on his face told me he couldn't care less about the stupid door. "Jade, you're translucent."

"I am?" I held my hands out in front of me, not seeing anything different. "That's not what I see."

"Well, I do, and I can see right through you." A muscle at his temple pulsed.

I shook my head, unwilling to entertain the implications of what he was saying. "Where's your dagger?"

He jabbed his head off to the side. "Why?"

"Get it. This happened to me when you took the magic into the stone."

Kane hesitated for a fraction of a second, then he snatched it up and held the blade so the stone was facing toward me. A wave of calm washed over him and his eyes turned almost black with concentration.

With the first pull of magic, ice filled my veins, making me shiver. My entire body shook, and I felt like I wanted to crawl right out of my skin. I couldn't wait until the foreign magic was expelled. I writhed and twisted, unable to stay still.

Everything started to hurt. A dull ache filled my chest, making it hard to breathe. And then a sharp pain stabbed me in my solar plexus. I gasped. "Stop!"

Kane dropped the dagger and stepped forward just as I fell from my suspended spot in the air. I landed, crumpled in his arms, exhaustion keeping me from finding my feet. "I guess I'm solid again," I said, out of breath.

His arms tightened around me. "Yes, mostly. But the door is almost gone, too."

Mostly? That wasn't a good sign. I glanced at my feet, noting they were in fact planted on the floor, but I couldn't feel them. There was a shimmer just below my knees, and even though I looked solid to myself, I guessed to him my shins and feet were still part of the "other world."

"What do you want to do?" Kane's voice penetrated my haze.

I jerked my head up. "About my feet?"

"And the door. Whatever we're doing to bring you back is hiding it again."

I cast a glance at the barely visible outline on the wall. Anger consumed me from the depths of my soul. It was raw and resentful and full of a hatred I'd long ago buried. I wasn't a ward of the angel realm. They'd have to work a hell of a lot harder at keeping me locked up.

"Unload the magic on the door," I said and twisted out of his hold. A surge of power shot up from my toes as I once again rose in the air. Fiery magic spilled from my fingertips, blasting the seams of the door. It crackled and caught on, creating a ring of magic fire around the frame.

Kane turned and unleashed the power stored in the stone of his dagger. His red stream of magic collided with my flames. The inferno escalated, the flames licking their way up the door, turning the wood a deep orange as the fire penetrated to the center and burned from the inside out.

"It's working," Kane said.

Intense magic streamed from my fingertips as I remembered how I'd been trapped in this place for more than two months. How the angels were always manipulating everything, how they thought they owned us.

I unleashed every last bit of anger and frustration at the door until the structure seemed to moan under my ministrations. Then the wood expanded in a surreal state of slow motion until it burst, the explosion knocking us both backward.

Splinters of smoldering wood flew past my face as I crashed against the side table. Pain slashed through my back, knocking the air out of me.

Kane grunted and moaned about five feet from me. He was splayed out on the floor, his arm twisted at an odd angle.

I sat up, rubbing at my eyes, trying to clear my fuzzy vision.

"Hurry," an unfamiliar voice called. "Before they arrive."

I blinked again. A jean-clad male angel stood in the doorway. He had copper-colored hair and couldn't have been a day over twenty. "Who are you?"

"I'm the one who's going to get you out of here. Come on. The guards will be here any second now."

I pushed myself up, my head spinning, and was relieved by the wave of Kane's faint smoky fresh-rain scent. He wrapped his arm around my waist. I pressed into him, needing his comfort, but pulled back slightly when his skin nearly seared mine with his heat. I glanced up to see him gritting his teeth. "You're hurt."

"I'll be fine. Let's go."

We hurried to the door. Anxiety gripped me. The angel stood just on the other side of it, and I was certain there would be an invisible barrier. If I was making wards, that was what I'd do. I reached out a tentative hand. Just as my fingers crossed the threshold, a sharp jolt of pain raced up my arm. I jerked my hand and winced.

"It's best if you jump through it quickly to get it over with."

Kane pulled away from me, cradling his hurt arm to his body.

Dammit! Jumping through the spell was gonna hurt like a bitch.

"Let's go." Kane gave me a small nudge, and I jumped. An invisible vise crushed me from all sides, and a cry got caught in my throat as I crossed the barrier into the hallway. I slammed into the opposite wall, trying my best to not crumple into a heap right there at the angel's feet.

Kane followed me, landing with much more ease and grace than I did. But the twist of his face told me it hadn't been pleasant.

"This way." The angel took off down the hall without waiting for our response.

Kane and I glanced at each other, then with a silent nod of agreement we followed.

We rounded a corner and suddenly the world swirled and shifted, throwing us into a pixilated world of confusion, almost as if we were barreling through television static.

My feet hit the earth, jarring me, and it took a moment to catch my breath. Kane crouched beside me, his dagger held out with his good arm, ready to battle.

"There's nothing here to attack you, Mr. Rouquette," the angel said mildly.

I glanced around. We were standing on the banks of the Mississippi, the French Quarter to the one side and the river to the other. Only there weren't any people but us in sight. And the world was monotone. No life. No color. No energy. It was exactly like the void world Mati had been trapped in a few months back.

"Why here?" I asked, accusation lacing my tone. Had we left one prison for another? Mati hadn't been able to leave. I could've tried to jump back into our world right then, but I needed answers. Who was this angel, and why had he helped us?

I took a moment to get a good look at him. He was tall, almost as tall as Kane at six foot two. But he was lanky, hadn't yet grown into his frame. He had dark, almost black eyes and unruly hair that curled at the top of his ears. If he hadn't been an angel, I might've mistaken him for a beach bum type.

Kane slowly straightened and sent the angel a narrowed gaze.

"Because the other angels can't follow you here," the angel said, answering my question.

"And you can get here because…?" I asked.

He shrugged. "It's my gift. I can jump worlds. And ever since Chessandra's sister stayed here, once she was freed, I've been able to jump in and out. I don't know why. But it seemed the safest place to talk."

I crossed my arms over my chest. "About what?"

The angel swept his gaze over us as if sizing us up. A nervous energy streamed from him, but if I hadn't been an empath, I'd never have known. He appeared as calm and cool as could be standing there in the presence of a white witch and a demon hunter. I had to give him credit for that, considering either one of us could've likely taken him with one hand tied behind our backs.

He took two steps and turned to face the mighty river. "If it's known I'm helping you in any way, I'll be punished to the highest degree. I need your word you'll keep my confidence."

I opened my mouth to agree, but Kane said, "Not until you tell us who you are and why we should trust you."

The angel shifted, staring straight at Kane. "I'm the high angel's assistant. I'm privy to a lot of information. Information I think you want. But unless I get a clear agreement from you that not only will you keep my confidence but you'll also protect me from her potential wrath, I'm leaving now and you'll never see me again."

Kane's gaze met mine. Interest and a sense of excitement danced in his eyes. I nodded, sure he saw the same in my expression reflecting back at me. This was our break. The one we needed to get to the bottom of Chessandra's deception.

I stepped forward and held my hand out. "Deal."

He stared at my hand and shook his head. "This isn't a gentlemen's agreement. If we move forward, the spell will be binding."

Oh, son of a… I did not want to be bound to this dude. I didn't even know him.

"Fine," Kane said.

I gaped at him.

He shrugged. "He's not going to budge on this. If this is the cost, then so be it."

"How can you be sure?"

"By his body language." Kane swept his gaze over the man from head to toe. "Go ahead. Read him. Tell me what you think."

I sighed. "You know I try not to do that."

"Do it," the angel said. "If it builds trust, then do what you have to."

Fatigue weighed on me, and all I wanted to do was sit down to rest. Doing a reading wasn't going to help my lack of energy. But I had no choice, really, other than just leaving, but I couldn't pass up the opportunity.

"Fine." I sucked in a breath and probed lightly at the angel's energy. Cold determination and pure nerve met me in the form of a steel wall, followed by light shocks of anxiousness. Closing my eyes, I probed deeper, sending my magic past his barriers and straight to the depths of his soul. Love, righteousness, and fear swarmed together to create the kind of man willing to put everything on the line for what he believed in.

The emotions gripped me, spun me up, made me want to do everything in my power to help his cause. I pulled back, the shock of losing his energy leaving me numb. "Yeah," I choked out, hardly able to form words from the intensity of it all. "We'll complete the binding."

The angel sent me a grateful smile, raised his arms, and called, *"Witch, incubus, angel, one of three and three of one, may the alliance binding be done."*

Three separate bolts of magic shot out of the sky and struck each of us in the neck at the same time. Only a tiny pinch of discomfort radiated over my skin before it vanished as if nothing had happened at all.

Kane and I stood together, watching the angel.

He stared back, a look of satisfaction on his face.

Foreboding curled in my gut. He was entirely too pleased by this outcome. I pursed my lips and then asked, "What's your name?"

"Jasper." His expression turned cold, hard, angry. "And Avery, the angel who's missing? She's my fiancée."

Chapter 7

Understanding crashed through me, and my heart went out to the young angel standing in front of us. Avery had been sent into the shadows under Chessandra's orders during a time when it wasn't safe, and she'd just disappeared. The high angel had tasked me and Kane with finding her, but we hadn't even had any leads, much less any luck.

Lailah was now on the hunt for the lost angel, but despite all her research and investigating, she wasn't doing any better. If I'd been in Jasper's shoes, I'd have blown up the angel realm a long time ago. Figuratively and literally.

"I'm so sorry," I said, my voice soft and full of emotion.

He gritted his teeth, and a muscle flexed in his neck. "You're going to help me find her. And we're going to take Chessandra down in the process."

Kane nodded. "You got it."

"No question about it," I said. I'd offered Lailah my help before, but so far she'd said she didn't have enough to go on, and the only thing she could think of was breaking into Hell. But with no assurances or even a hunch as to where Avery might be in the underworld, that was a suicide mission. With Jasper on our side, we might be able to glean more useful information.

"Good. I'll be in touch within forty-eight hours." Jasper turned to go.

I held my hand out. "Wait a minute."

He paused and glanced back at me, his black eyes piercing me with his gaze.

I found him interesting. An enigma for the angel realm. Most angels of the realm lived with single-minded determination. One goal: to save souls any way possible. They were almost emotionless about it. But there was plenty of emotion consuming this young man. He was drowning in loss, need, and revenge. And ever since the binding, it was all right at the surface, easy for me to read. We were connected now, and hiding his true feelings would be harder for him.

"Why didn't you come to us sooner?" I asked, genuinely curious.

"I didn't have enough leverage then."

I frowned, confused. "We would've helped you anyway."

"Even without the binding spell," Kane said, his tone neutral.

The kid shook his head. "I couldn't be sure of that, and I'm not taking any chances. Now, no matter what, because of the spell, you'll be compelled to help me, and you can't lie like everyone else I've gone to for help."

"Wait, what does that—?"

Jasper took a step and vanished from the void world.

"Dammit," Kane muttered.

That foreboding came rushing back. Exactly what kind of binding spell had he used? Binding spells usually meant the parties were magically bound to protect each other. That confidences couldn't be betrayed. But compulsion? That wasn't standard. What had we gotten ourselves into?

I blew out a breath and met Kane's troubled gaze. "Let's go home."

He nodded and wrapped his hand around mine.

Together we took a step and found ourselves in the middle of his club. A half dozen patrons were lounging in the blue-velvet–covered seats around the stage while one of the regulars danced to the latest Meghan Trainor song.

Charlie, the club manager, glanced up and startled when she saw us. She rushed over, typing on her phone as she went.

Kane jerked his head toward his office, indicating for her to meet us in there.

She quickened her pace and met us at the door. "Where the hell have you two been?"

My eyes widened in surprise, and before I could answer, Kane pulled me into the privacy of his office. Charlie followed, her mouth rigid and her body stiff with tension.

"Well?" she demanded, standing with her fists at her waist.

Kane sat in his chair behind the large banker's desk. I leaned against it and picked up his office phone to call Bea. While it rang, I said, "In the angel realm, dealing with Chessandra."

"For two weeks?"

Kane muttered another curse. That dammed room. I'd never understand how so much time could go by when it felt like only minutes.

I echoed Kane's curse just as Bea answered.

"Jade?" She sounded wary and hopeful at the same time.

"Yes, it's Jade. Kane's hurt. Broken arm, I imagine. Can you meet us to check it out?"

"Where are you?"

"His club."

"I'm on my way." The line went dead.

Charlie still stood in the middle of the room, her face turning red with anger. "Do you have any idea what you put us through? The police were called. Lailah and Bea had the entire Witch's Council out looking for you. And Pyper—"

The door burst open, and the woman in question stormed through, her electric-blue-streaked hair flying behind her. "Holy fuck on a throne of dildos. Explain yourselves." Without waiting for us to say anything, she bombarded me, wrapping her arms around me in a tight hug. "Don't ever do that to me again," she said into my ear. Then she kissed my cheek and ran to Kane's side, kneeling near him as they talked quietly.

I turned, and instead of explaining anything to Charlie, I walked over to her and gave her the same kind of hug Pyper had just given me. "I'm sorry," I whispered. "We'd never leave y'all on purpose. We were held against our will."

Her posture relaxed as she sank into the hug. "Jesus, we were worried." She pulled back and searched my face. "Are you both all right?"

I nodded. "Except for Kane's arm, I think so."

"We're fine." Kane gave Charlie a look of gratitude. "Thank you. I'm sure it's you who kept this place running."

"And Pyper." She waved a hand. "You know that one could take care of anything even if she was on her death bed."

"You're right about that," Kane agreed.

I sat in a chair, utterly exhausted.

Charlie glanced around the room, her gaze lingering first on me and then Kane. The thick wave of her relief was so strong it nearly suffocated me. She made her way to the door, and just before she slipped through, she turned and said, "You have no idea how glad I am to see both of you."

She'd been more than worried. My heart squeezed for what Chessandra had put our friends through. Two weeks we'd been gone. Cripes. Kat was going to be a mess as well.

"I think I might have a clue." I sent her a ghost of a smile.

She let out a small chuckle. "I guess you do." With a nod, she strode back into the club.

While Pyper and Kane talked, I picked up the phone and called Kat. No answer. I tried Lucien and ended up leaving a message. The same with Lailah. "Damn, where is everyone?"

"They're with the coven most likely," Pyper said.

"For?" I asked, curious.

"They've been looking for you. With no luck, I might add. Apparently the angel realm is impenetrable."

"Even Lailah didn't know?" How could she not?

Pyper shook her head, a lock of her blue hair falling into her eyes. "Nope. If she did, she didn't tell anyone. But I don't think so, because she's been worried sick as well."

"Damn Chessandra. And Drake too." He was just as much to blame as she was. Maybe more. Wasn't he the one hell bent on protecting me?

I clutched the arm of the chair, hatred forming a ball in my gut. They were both way over the line. Stealing two weeks of our lives in that room when we hadn't committed any crimes. Keeping us locked away because someone had cursed me wasn't any kind of acceptable.

"We should go stop them. There's no need for them to keep this up." I stood, ready to head to the coven circle.

"Don't worry, dear," Bea said from the door. Her salon-dyed auburn hair was pulled back into a low ponytail, and she was dressed in a full-length, form-fitting, shimmering, pink-beaded dress. She was truly the bell of the ball. Whoa. Where had she been? "In about five seconds you'll be speaking with them anyway," she added.

"Why? Are they coming here?"

"No. You'll be going there." She gave me a patient smile and then it hit me. They were summoning me.

Of course. I shook my head, trying to clear the cobwebs as my body started to tingle with a soft caress of magic.

Bea was already inspecting Kane's arm. He grimaced in pain as she tested his movement. I raised a hand, trying to get his attention, but my arm was transparent...again. I let out a tiny gasp. I was fading into the ether.

My world turned to dark shades of gray, and static filled my ears. Chaos seemed to be my now-normal state of travel. So when I appeared in the middle of the coven circle, I was barely fazed at all.

My eyes adjusted, and instead of the moonlit night I'd expected, I was in a bubble of color. The circle's ground was lit with electric blue. Beyond the circle was an opaque sheet of green, blocking out the trees I knew resided there. But most interesting was the fact that Lailah glowed with traces of lavender, while all the witches were tinged red. All except one. Zoe was the only colorless soul in the clearing.

"It's working, keep chanting," I heard Lucien call from his spot on the northernmost point of the circle. But I only had eyes for Zoe.

Her head was down, her arms out and hands clasped with fellow coven members. But the only magic coming from her was the magic passing through her from the other members. She wasn't tapping her magic source. Why?

"Zoe?" I said.

The witch's head snapped up, and her mouth dropped open in shock. "How did… Uh, I mean, you're here."

I tilted my head to the side. "You weren't expecting me."

It wasn't a question.

Her mouth worked, but before she could get anything out, Lucien called, "Jade!"

I gave Zoe one last look and then turned to face my second in command. Lucien had the brightest red light of them all, no doubt because he was the most powerful. But he was also haggard. His weariness slammed into me, making me want to sit down right there in the middle of the coven circle.

"Thank the gods," he said.

I shuffled over to him in my translucent state.

"Where are you?" he asked.

Truly touched at his concern and how hard he'd worked to find us, I gave him a small smile. "Right now, I'm here, but my physical body is in Kane's office. We just escaped from the angel realm."

He sucked in a sharp breath. "Escaped?"

I nodded. "We can talk about it more later. But for now, Kane and I are both safe."

The tension in his jaw eased, and the red light morphed into a soothing blue. "First thing in the morning? Coffee?"

"Yes. At my place."

"I'll be there at eight." He unlocked hands with the two witches on either side of him, and when he did, all the color faded, and my spirit snapped back into my body. The blood rushed to my head, making the room spin.

I came to lying on my back in the middle of Kane's office. His face swam into view, his brow pinched with concern. A soft, cool hand brushed over my forehead. "Bea," I said, recognizing her light vanilla scent.

"Welcome back." Her faint Southern drawl coaxed a smile from me.

"Did you get Kane's arm working again?"

She chuckled. "Yes, dear. He's as good as new."

I stared into her hazel eyes. "Was it broken?"

She shook her head. "Hyperextended elbow. A little magic fixed it right up."

"Good." I closed my eyes, exhaustion taking over. "Can I go home now?"

"Of course you can," she said warmly. "Kane?"

His fresh rain scent overpowered everything, and the next thing I knew, I was cradled in his arms, snuggled into his chest. I wasn't sure if I blacked out or if he shadow walked us home, but the next thing I knew, we were standing outside the front door. Kane was propping me up with one hand while trying to unlock the door with the other.

I put my hand over his on the door knob. "Let me."

Kane kissed the top of my head. "I wasn't sure how aware you were."

"I'm fine." I straightened and squared my shoulders as I sent a bolt of magic into the lock. A soft click sounded, and the door swung open. I leaned into Kane and whispered, "Take me to bed. I hear it's been at least two weeks."

Chapter 8

Kane carried me to our bedroom and carefully lowered me to my feet. I made a short stop into the bathroom, emerged a few minutes later, and climbed into bed.

As soon as my head touched the pillow, I closed my eyes and reveled in the comfort of everything around me. Even though it hadn't felt like we'd been gone for more than a few hours, my body seemed to know that wasn't the case as it melted into the soft pillow-top mattress.

The sound of Kane's footsteps echoed on the hardwood, followed by the faint click of the bathroom door. I must've dozed off, because the next thing I knew, Kane was back, nudging me. "Jade?"

"Hmm?"

His warm lips brushed over my neck, just below my ear. "Are you awake?"

I turned my head, blinking. "I am now."

Smiling, he trailed more kisses over my jawline.

I curled my fingers into his short dark hair, enjoying the warmth of his lips on my skin.

"I don't know why—" his tongue darted over my pulse "—but it feels like I haven't had you in months."

"It's the... Oh."

His left hand cupped my breast, his fingers squeezing my nipple beneath the silk nightie I'd changed into before sliding into bed. He chuckled at my reaction, his chest reverberating against my side. "What was that you were saying?"

"Uh...I think—" I sucked in a breath as he ran his hand between my breasts to my abdomen and down to the edge of my matching silk panties "—that you might have expelled too much power."

"Could be," he said, his voice low and full of desire.

We'd been together the night before...or what was actually two weeks ago on New Year's Eve. And since Kane was an incubus, he gained magic through sex...meaning me. For us, time had stood still, so that shouldn't have been a factor in his depleted power, but the amount of magic he'd dispelled certainly could've contributed to his hunger.

Kane's demanding hands slid the nightgown up, exposing my bare breasts to the cool air. He suckled one nipple while kneading the other. Desire and need shot through me and coiled deep in my gut. With each movement, his touch became more and more impatient, demanding.

I arched into him, moaning. "I don't think I can wait."

He crushed his lips to mine, his tongue invading my mouth with a demand I knew all too well. His familiar weight resting on top of me heightened my need for him. He was mine. Tasted of mint and man and desire. Both of us were on the edge of losing control. My hands found his boxers, and a second later, he was bared, his muscles rippling under my touch. I wiggled out of my panties and was opening to him when a thought slammed into my brain so hard, I stiffened and pushed him away, scrambling to sit up.

Kane froze. "What's wrong? What happened?"

"The curse," I whispered, my voice trembling. "We can't do this."

He frowned.

"If I get pregnant..." I couldn't complete the thought. I didn't want to think about what could happen.

Kane propped himself up beside me, pulling the covers over us. "But you're on birth control still, right?"

I nodded and shifted away from him, the mood completely broken. The realization of our situation had zapped all my pent-up desire. "I don't know if the curse affects it…or God, the fact that we were in the room where time stands still. What if I'm two weeks behind on my pills? I'm probably not, but we can't take any chances. As much as I want your child, we just can't."

Kane stared at me for a moment, then he cupped my cheek with his palm and leaned in. "It's all right, Jade. We don't have to do this now. After we break the curse, we'll revisit the idea of starting a family."

Tears filled my eyes, and I was powerless to hold them back. Just a few days ago we had been all but ready to give the baby-making thing a try, and now we were sitting naked in the bed, with me too terrified to get intimate. "I'm sorry. I know there are other ways to replenish your power, but—"

He pressed his fingers to my lips. "Shhh. We can wait. I'm not in any rush."

"I love you," I whispered.

He kissed me gently. "I know, pretty witch."

I stood in my bathroom, towel drying my hair, trying my best to work past the sleep haze clouding my brain. I'd slept like the dead the night before and had woken up twenty minutes before eight. Twenty minutes before Lucien and Kat were supposed to arrive.

A knock sounded on the door, followed by a hand snaking in that held a paper cup from the Grind. I recognized the agate and silver ring on the hand's middle finger. Pulling the door open, I smiled at Kat and took the cup.

"Chai tea for my missing friend." She smiled and blinked back the moisture forming in her eyes. Her bright-red curly hair fell in haphazard waves around her face, softening her angular features. She usually spent more time taming her curls, but it was obvious she hadn't put much effort into getting ready either. Only while she looked adorable, I was fairly certain I resembled a zombie bride with my limp strawberry-blond hair and dark circles under my green eyes.

"Thank you." I put the cup down and wrapped my arms around her. We both held on tightly to the hug for a long moment. And when we separated, she turned away to wipe her eyes.

I grabbed the chai and headed back into the bedroom to give her a moment. If she'd been missing for two weeks, I'd have lost my mind. It was no wonder she was overcome with emotion. Sitting on the bed, I pulled my bright pink-and-white–striped socks on and stuffed my feet into a pair of tennis shoes. I'd already dressed in dark jeans and a long-sleeved, hot-pink tee. No makeup, and I just couldn't be bothered to try to do anything with my hair. I didn't have the energy.

If I had my way, I'd stay curled up on my couch, mainlining chai tea and stuffing my face with cupcakes. *Mental note: send Kane to the café to pick up a dozen chocolate cream cheese cupcakes.*

I grabbed my phone and sent him a text, even though I knew he was just in the other room, so I wouldn't forget.

He texted back immediately. *Kat already brought them.*

I let out a loud squeal and ran into the bathroom. "Cupcakes!"

She turned around, grinning. "I figured you deserved them."

Grabbing her hand, I tugged her out of the bathroom into my room and all the way out into the kitchen, where we found Kane and Lucien devouring the cupcakes. My ghost dog, Luke, sat near them, drool forming an imaginary pool under the chair. Goodness. Thank the gods I was the only one who could see him.

Only two cupcakes remained in the box Kat had brought. I set my chai on the counter and glared at both of them.

"What?" Kane said, mumbling through the cupcake filling his mouth.

I raised one eyebrow and cut my gaze to the now almost-empty box.

"We saved you some." Lucien wiped his mouth with the back of his hand, leaving the chocolate evidence still clinging to his lips.

Kat laughed. "So predictable." She walked to the fridge and pulled out a white pastry box. "That's why I brought extra."

"That's my girl." I plucked out the two left in the opened box, strode over to Kat and handed her one. I glanced back at the table. "I think you guys have had enough."

"Where'd those come from?" Lucien asked, eyeing the second box. "You only had one when we left the shop."

She cast him a flinty glance and shrugged.

Laughing, the pair of us sat at the table, careful to keep the new pastry box close to us.

Kane's lips twitched.

I couldn't help but melt under his gaze. He knew I'd share with him. But it was fun to watch Lucien squirm. He and Kat hadn't been together as long as Kane and I had. Cupcake sharing appeared to be something they hadn't yet worked out.

Lucien took a long sip of coffee and turned his attention to me. "All right. Let's have it. What happened?"

I quickly explained our time in the angel realm and ended with, "So now we have an ally. I need to notify Lailah as soon as possible, since it appears Jasper might have some clues that could help us find Avery. Or at least figure out what happened to her."

Lucien jotted some notes down in his notebook. When he glanced up, his expression was troubled. "Tell me more about this binding you have with Jasper."

I frowned. "It was weird. We consented to it, thinking it was a normal binding, you know, but then bolts of magic shot from nowhere and jolted us in the necks. It didn't hurt, it just surprised me."

"Then he said we were compelled to do as he said," Kane added with a heavy dose of irritation.

Lucien's expression turned to one of anger. "That's a shitty thing to do."

I raised both eyebrows. "Does it mean we're literally compelled to do what he says?"

"No, he can't compel you to do something you really don't want to, but he did tie himself to your power and might be able to force your magic from you. Meaning he could tap into your power source if he needs to in order to complete a spell… or a curse."

A chill ran up my spine. Jasper might have been an angel, but that didn't mean he always had good intentions. If he was angry enough at Chessandra, who knew what he'd try to do? "We can't ignore this. It's too dangerous."

Lucien nodded. "Agreed. You and Kane are both far too powerful to let anyone have access to your magic. I suggest you break the spell as soon as possible."

"And how is that done?" It rankled that I had no idea how to do that. I was more of a "throw magic at it first and research later" kind of witch. I'd been studying up the last few months, but I'd been focusing on potions and healing herbs, the same sort of thing my mother and Bea specialized in. It was clear I should've been brushing up on defense and reversal spells for dark magic.

I'd have to make that a priority just as soon as we caught a break.

"I have a few spells I know, but I doubt they're powerful enough," Lucien said then frowned. "Come to think of it, they're for spells cast by witches, not angels. I don't think you're going to be able to break it at all unless you have his cooperation. Angel magic is tricky like that."

"Crapballs. Of course it is," I said.

Lucien scribbled something else down in his book. "Maybe it's not what we think. If he's really in this fight to just find Avery, I'm sure he'll drop the binding as soon as we have answers."

"I hope so." But somehow I wasn't convinced. Nothing was ever that easy.

Now—" he glanced up "—tell me about Zoe. What was going on with her last night?"

"You noticed then?" I asked and took a big bite of the cupcake, feeling better now that I had at least the start of a plan. It didn't involve doing anything about the curse still plaguing me, but I'd get to that next.

"The fact that you were studying her like a microbe under a microscope? I think we all noticed."

I put the cupcake down on the table. "She wasn't actually participating. Not with her own magic, anyway."

He frowned. "What does that mean?"

"She was used as a conduit for the other witches."

"That's impossible." Lucien closed his notebook. "Otherwise we wouldn't have been able to summon you. It takes all participants for that spell to work."

I shrugged. "I'm just telling you what I saw. You were all bathed in magical light. Every one of you except Zoe—witches in red, Lailah in lavender, and Zoe in nothing. She wasn't actively using her magic while I was there. Maybe she was before I appeared. Or maybe you were able to summon me because I was close. We were already at Kane's club by then."

"We should talk to her about that. If she'd dropped the spell, it could've failed miserably." Lucien sat back in the chair and shook his head. "She's not adjusting well, is she?"

"Zoe? Not as well as we hoped, no. But I'm not sure what to do about it." I stared at the paper cup in front of me. Most of Zoe's spirit had been stolen at the same time as her soul. She'd been given another soul, but there was nothing to do about her spirit other than pray that it would heal itself. I often wondered if that meant she was damaged beyond repair.

"She probably just needs time," Lucien offered.

"Probably." I stood. "I'm going to call Lailah. The sooner we can meet up, the better."

Kane stood too. "Anyone need more coffee?"

"Yes, please," Lucien said.

Kane and I moved from the table into the kitchen. I grabbed my phone from the charger and hit Lailah's number while Kane poured more coffee. But as soon as he put the carafe back on the warmer, the stone on his dagger strapped to his belt glowed bright red, indicating he was being summoned. He turned to me. "Sorry, Jade. I can't ignore this."

"I know." I gave him a light kiss. "Go kick some demon ass. Lucien and Kat can chaperone me."

"Yeah, we got this," Kat chimed in from the table.

"Thanks," Kane said to her, grabbed the hilt of his dagger, and stepped through the fabric of our world into the shadows.

Kat got up and joined me in the kitchen, the pastry box in her hand. "Ready to do some ass kicking of our own?"

I laughed. "Always."

She winked, nodding to the pastry box. "For reinforcements."

"I like the way you think."

Lucien appeared behind us. "Just what we need. The evil-fighting, chocolate-cupcake-toting duo."

My eyes widened in excitement. "That's a great superhero team name. I'm getting that tattooed on my ass."

"Me too," Kat said and pointed to her left butt cheek. "Right here."

Lucien shook his head in mock exasperation. "Come on, we have work to do."

"I don't think he's amused," I stage whispered to Kat.

"Oh, he's amused. He just doesn't want you to know how turned on he gets by tattoos."

Lucien let out a loud groan as we dissolved into giggles.

Chapter 9

Kane

Walking through the shadows was second nature. Ever since that day I'd been turned into an incubus, moving through worlds took zero effort. I simply thought about where I wanted to go, and I stepped through the fabric of each dimension. Or in this case, the Brotherhood called, and it was more like I was pulled through.

In a blink of an eye, I went from standing in my kitchen to crouching in what appeared to be a warehouse of some sort. Dim light glowed from the windows high above, casting long shadows over the crates stacked neatly against the walls. Dust filled the musty air. No one had been here in days, maybe weeks. I held the smooth hilt of my dagger in one hand as I scanned the darkness for demons.

A sense of awareness that four of my demon-hunting brothers were nearby settled any apprehension I might have felt. Whatever I'd stepped into, I had backup.

I held perfectly still, waiting in the ice-cold building. There was no sound, no movement, just dead air and nervous anticipation that was always present in the space just before a battle.

Then I heard it, the faint hiss of a demon off to the right. I pivoted, balancing on the balls of my feet as my muscles clenched with tension. I felt rather than heard the other demon hunters move in behind me. And then, without any forewarning, all the crates lining the walls crashed to the cement floor.

The Brotherhood fanned out, each of us charging forward as more crates from behind us splintered and flew through the warehouse seemingly on their own.

I spun, adrenaline coursing through my veins, and spotted a demon. His bright red eyes glowed against his gnarled olive-green skin. Talons the length and shape of steak knives slashed through the air with each swipe of his claw.

Jesus, he was an ugly bastard. Smelled like a shithouse, too. "Ever hear of a shower?" I taunted.

He snarled, yellowish goo dripping from one fang.

Disappointment shuddered through me. "Such a cliché. Damn, man. Couldn't you have tried a little harder? No one is impressed with your total lack-of-effort, B-movie-rated persona."

The demon stopped slashing at nothing and closed his maw, his red eyes piercing me with irritation.

"Show me what you've really got," I ordered.

The demon clacked his talons together and then morphed into a taller, wider version of himself, only this time with an extra set of fangs.

"No imagination," I muttered and wasted no time in chucking one of my throwing darts right where his black heart would be. The poisoned blade hit its target with amazing accuracy, burying itself all the way to the hilt.

The demon froze for just a second, glanced down, and then ripped the dart from his chest. That same yellowish goo oozed from his chest wound, no blood in sight. Interesting. A lesser demon, one of the third string. They were ugly, huge, and full of nasty. But they were also slow, simple, and easy to take down.

I could throw my dagger and end him with just the one blow, but then I wouldn't get any answers. So I grabbed another dart and flicked it at his head. The dart landed in the side of his face, making the demon roar with indignant rage.

"What do they call you?" I asked him.

His eyes turned a brighter shade of red as he flailed his arms in the air, aiming at nothing. I took half a step back, studying him. That was odd. He wasn't in attack mode. Not even a little bit. All he was doing was making noise and taking up space.

I cast a quick glance at the demon hunters behind me. The two I saw were actually battling with their much more sophisticated demons. One of them breathed fire, while the other emitted what looked like poisonous gas. Tricky.

But Miles, an older hunter, was dealing with the gas by sucking up the poison with his dagger. If that stopped working, he'd be in deep shit. The fire was currently not being dealt with, as Ashton was too busy bouncing around, ensuring he didn't get burned.

And what did my demon do while I was battle gazing? He sat down on one of the remaining crates and drooled. Disgusting.

Sucking in a deep breath of clean air, I walked over to the demon, expecting he'd attack the moment he saw me move. But he didn't. He tracked me with his eyes, breathing heavily. I frowned. This didn't make any sense. He was winded but hadn't even exerted much effort. Why would anyone send this sack of uselessness into a battle with the Brotherhood?

"Why are you here?" I demanded.

The demon tilted his head to the side and studied me. His long talons now gleamed in the tiny stream of light illuminating him. He crooked one, indicating I should come closer.

I stood my ground. Just because I was certain I could take him out with minimal effort didn't mean I was an idiot.

The demon narrowed his slanted eyes and then swung his trunk-like arm out to the side, decimating a pile of debris. With an unexpected quickness, he reached down and picked up a wide-eyed young man—no... make that angel—by the neck. The faint white glow surrounding the man indicated he was, in fact, an angel. It was something we demon hunters could see when we were tapped into our magic.

A few of the demon's talons sliced the angel's neck, and blood seeped between his fingers.

Anger made my blood boil. His quick movement and heightened coordination meant the demon had shifted into one of the third string, pretending to be an easier mark than he really was. It was a trap. I held perfectly still and met the demon's now neon-green eyes. "What do you want from me?"

"Your soul," he ground out and shook his hostage. "Or I'll take this one's life and then go after everyone you love, including your future child."

His mention of my child sent a chill straight to my heart while cold rage infiltrated every molecule of my being. The demons knew about the curse. They had to. It was too specific a taunt. The family Jade and I wanted to start would be in mortal danger from all sides. I had to do something, anything, to send the message I wasn't going to let anyone threaten my family.

If it hadn't been for the angel lying limp in his grasp, I'd already have ended the demon. Possibly with my bare hands. The angel wasn't dead yet, but if those wounds weren't tended to, he would be soon, judging by the amount of blood staining his shirt.

Son of a bitch. This battle just went from routine to majorly fucked up in a nanosecond. If an angel was killed, it would be a tragedy. But if it was known it had happened in the presence of the Brotherhood, relations with the high angel would deteriorate even further between the two groups. Chessandra would stop at nothing for revenge, and the simmering war between the angels and the demons would likely erupt into a full-on battle. Then no one would be safe. Innocents would surely be caught in the crossfire.

And after learning everyone had an interest in my future child in an obvious quest for power, I'd had enough.

"Let him go," I said. "Then we can have a one on one for my soul."

The demon snarled, revealing a third set of fangs.

I stared at him, my jaw set. "Drop the hostage or lose your chance for a sanctioned battle."

A tiny voice in the back of my head whispered, *What are you doing? You already know he's not the simpleton demon he's pretending to be.* But I ignored it. It was too late now. I'd already offered. There was no taking it back. Besides, I was sending the message that Kane Rouquette wasn't taking anyone's shit.

Pure hunger rippled over the demon's expression. A sanctioned battle meant we'd fight one on one, and the victor had the right to determine the other's fate: a permanent stay in Hell, an informant, or something worse, like instant death. Offering a sanctioned fight was almost unheard of. And if I wasn't mistaken, a demon who brought in a demon hunter, one who was the husband of the most powerful white witch in the south, would earn himself a lifetime of cachet with the leaders of Hell.

"Deal." The demon sent me a twisted smile and dropped the angel in a heap to the concrete floor. The creature shimmered and shifted into a leathery red form, his head thick and full of pointed horns. The kind of demon who'd been around for not only years but millennia. There was no doubt he was a badass of epic proportions.

But I didn't care. Adrenaline and raw determination had taken over. This demon would never talk about my unborn child again, nor would he take the life of an angel.

Leather Head let out a loud cackle of glee and spread his arms wide. "Stop!"

The word reverberated through the warehouse, the effect instantly halting the fighting.

"A challenge has been issued. I, Malstord, second to Vallencino, have been challenged to a sanctioned fight by the demon hunter Kane Rouquette. You all are compelled to witness."

A shocked murmur passed among my fellow demon hunters, while the demons shouted in pure glee for Malstord to rip me to shreds and tear my head off.

I blocked it all out, focusing on the swagger of Leather Head. He seemed more than a little confident. Good. That'd make it easier to find his weakness.

"I have a few conditions," I said.

"No conditions, incubus. The challenge has been made. I've accepted. It's done."

I didn't break my hold on his defiant gaze. "Terms have not yet been set forth."

"The terms are that we fight. You either die or surrender, and I take you to Hell as an offering to my superior."

"And my terms are one, you let one of my brothers take the angel for medical care before we fight. And two, either we fight to the death or when you surrender you'll return to Hell, where you'll be confined for the rest of your demon existence." Because I wasn't one hundred percent sure I could kill this bastard, but knew I could inflict considerable damage, sending him back to Hell to lick his wounds might've been my only way out of this mess. It was a gamble but one I had to take.

"The angel stays."

I'd known he would say that, but I had to open a negotiation. "Then one of my brothers shall be allowed to treat his wounds."

Malstord growled again and then waved a large hand, indicating his acceptance.

My fellow hunter, Ethan, went to the angel's side immediately. I breathed a little easier. Ethan had medical training and knew what he was doing. If the angel could be saved, Ethan was the man for the job.

"The terms have been set," Malstord called. "No one is to interfere on either side. If they do, their life will be forfeit."

There was an uproar of protest from my brotherhood, but I held my hand up. "I've agreed to the terms. You have to do the same. There's no choice."

They grumbled but ultimately consented.

The demon jumped off his makeshift crate podium and landed in front of me, his eyes flashing gold and his eagle-like talons extended and ready to fight.

I reached a hand out toward one of my fellow hunters. In the next second, I had not only my dagger but a second one as well. I grasped one in each hand and circled the demon.

It was game on.

Chapter 10

Jade

The weak mid-morning sun shone down on Lucien, Kat, and me as we stood on the doorstep to Lailah's pale-pink single shotgun home. She lived three blocks off Bourbon Street in the quieter residential part of the French Quarter. To the right was a two-person turquoise swing covered in white daisies that was starting to look weathered. I imagined her sitting in it, her feet tucked under her as she sipped her tea.

I longed for a life that included quality time in swings. But between my job at the café, the coven, and my work for the high angel, my life was more often one blur of crisis after crisis with small breaks for chai tea and cupcakes. I didn't even want to think about my glass bead making. My small online business had taken a major hit over the last year. I was lucky to get into my studio once a week.

Kane's time wasn't any better. When he wasn't taking care of stuff at the club, he was fighting demons or dealing with a few of his financial planning clients.

I touched the slender glass bead I wore on a silver chain and mentally vowed to make more time for swings and bead making. Just as soon as we finished navigating the latest catastrophe.

Lailah's door swung open, and she stood in the threshold of her century-old home glaring at us in her faded olive camo pants and a white T-shirt. It always amused me that she dressed in such drab colors when her house was a rainbow of brightness.

"Well, hello, sunshine," I quipped.

She pointed her finger at me, nearly poking me in the chest. "I can't believe you. I had to hear from Lucien that you were back. A phone call would've been nice, don't you think? Considering I spent the last two weeks doing nothing but trying to hunt your butt down."

I frowned. "Didn't you check your phone?"

She rolled her eyes. "Of course I did. Do you think I'm an idiot?"

"No. I'd never think that." I searched my brain. I *had* tried to get in touch with her, right? Yes. I had. "I called last night. From Pyper's phone. Right after I'd left a message for Kat."

She slowly lowered her hand and frowned as she pulled her phone out. She held it out to check. There were no calls from Pyper's phone in the last twenty-four hours.

"That's strange. Maybe I misdialed." But that couldn't be right. I remembered hearing her message on her voicemail.

Lailah closed her eyes, took a deep breath, and put her phone back in her pocket. "Probably. Sorry. It's been a stressful two weeks."

I placed my hand on her arm. "I'm sorry."

Her eyes flew open. "You should be. I told you not to go to Chessandra until I spoke to her. Now not only are you on her most-wanted list, but I've been blacklisted. I can't help you if I don't have contacts. I can't help anyone. The search for Avery is all but dead in the water. Too much time has passed. For all we know she's fallen demon already."

She spun, her long blond hair flying out behind her as she stalked back into her house.

"Well, that went well," Kat said.

I glanced over my shoulder and cast her an irritated look.

"Sorry." She grimaced. "Just trying to lighten the mood. Clearly too soon."

Lucien chuckled and stepped by both of us into Lailah's house. "She'll get over it. Especially after she hears the news."

"What news?" Lailah called from the house, impatience in her tone.

Lucien grinned. "See?"

"Just get in here and fill me in." Her impatience turned to exasperation.

My mood lightened. "That's the Lailah I know and love."

Kat chuckled while Lucien led us into her small house. Lailah's living room was an explosion of color. There was a pink shag carpet and a bright-red couch, with yellow- and poppy-colored pillows. Vibrant paintings depicting the French Quarter hung on the walls in varying shades of blue, turquoise, and green.

Lailah was perched at the end of her couch, tapping her fingers on the armrest.

"Wow," Kat said turning around in a circle. "This is gorgeous." She stopped and eyed Lailah. "I never would've guessed you love color so much."

She shrugged. "In my line of work, it's not good if one stands out. So I do my best to blend in. At home I get to be me."

I glanced around. "Where's Zoe?" The newish witch had been staying with Lailah while she got used to her new soul and abilities.

"She's at the Herbal Connection. Bea's been giving her lessons."

Good. That meant Bea could keep a close eye on her. She'd know if the young witch was struggling.

"Have a seat." Lailah stood. "I'll get tea."

"Coffee?" Kat asked hopefully.

"And a cup of coffee," Lailah said and disappeared.

I sat in a red armchair across from the couch and closed my eyes as I waited, trying not to think of Kane and what he might be fighting right at that moment. He hardly ever came back with even so much as a scratch, but that didn't keep me from worrying about him. At the thought of Kane, a nagging thread of fear worked its way into my subconscious, and my eyes flew open. Pain shot through my abdomen, and I grunted as it left me winded.

"Jade? What's wrong?" Lucien appeared by my side, his touch vibrating with magic just waiting to be unleashed. "What happened?"

I shook my head. "I don't… Oh." I clutched my stomach and bent over, trying not to vomit.

"She's sick," Kat said. "We need to get her to the bathroom."

"No. I don't think I can…" I took quick, short breaths, trying to work my way through the pain. Was it the curse? Was the black magic poisoning me?

"Here." A white bucket was put on my lap. "Just in case."

I glanced up at Lailah. A hundred questions ran through my mind, but there was only one I cared about. *Is this about my future child?*

"Take this." Lailah handed me three green capsules. "They'll dull the pain and your anxiety."

Without hesitation, I popped the pills in my mouth and washed them down with the water she offered. It only took a moment for the pain to subside, though a dull ache lingered as if I'd been sucker-punched.

"Better?" Lailah asked.

I nodded. "Thank you. Bea's herbs?"

She shook her head, "No. I got them from your mom, actually. I've been studying healing herbs, and she was gracious enough to send me some to deconstruct."

"You're thinking of trying your hand at them?"

"Yeah." She gave me a shy smile—one very out of character for the Lailah I knew. "When Bea retires, I want to take over her store. But I don't just want to copy everything she's done. I want to understand it and make my own mark."

"That's great, Lailah," Lucien said, taking a seat on the couch once more.

"Definitely," Kat added.

"Thanks." She disappeared back into her kitchen and returned with the tray of tea and a mug of coffee for Kat. She set it on her intricately carved coffee table and took a seat in the pink-striped armchair next to mine. "All right. Enough about me." Lailah turned to me. "Want to explain what that was about?"

"I don't think I can." I took another sip of the tea and sat back, totally exhausted. "I was just sitting here when it felt as if I was being attacked—as if I'd been punched in the gut."

She shared a look with Lucien.

I bit back a heavy sigh. They were always doing that when something hinky was going on that they didn't want to tell me. "What? Spit it out."

Lucien lifted his hands, palms up. "It could be the curse. Your body could be trying to repel it."

My heart plummeted to my feet.

"Or an echo," Lailah added. "Something that's happened to you before that you don't remember."

"You mean like my subconscious trying to tell me something?"

"Yes," she said. "Or it could be a vision. Something that could happen in the future."

I stood on wobbly legs.

"Where are you going?" Lailah asked.

"I don't know. I… Crap on toast. This *can't* be happening to me." Kat gave me a pitying look, and I just about lost it. "Don't look at me like that. Jeez."

"Sorry," Kat said.

I flopped back into the chair, too frustrated to do anything else.

"Okay, just relax," Lailah said. "It's probably the curse. Once we figure out how to get rid of it, you'll be fine."

"And how are we going to do that? We have no idea who cast it."

"We know it was an angel, and that's a start. Now, why don't you tell me exactly what happened in the angel realm?"

"What do you know?" I fingered the piping on the armchair.

"Not much. Once you went missing, I stormed the angel realm to talk to Chessa, but she wouldn't see me. And when I insisted, she spelled me back to earth and banned me from the realm until further notice."

"What a bitch," I said without any heat. I was beyond being outraged by what the high angel did.

"Pretty much." Lailah shrugged and poured herself a cup of tea. "But I'm dying to hear what happened."

I sat back and explained how my own father had insisted we be kept in the room where time stood still and how it had felt like we'd only been there for minutes before we busted out, presumably with the help of Jasper.

"Jasper is Chessandra's assistant?" Lailah's light eyebrows shot up her forehead. "You're kidding."

I shook my head. "Nope. That's what he said. Why?"

She chewed on her lower lip. "Well, she's usually really particular. I've never known her to choose a male assistant, either, since she forces them to do everything, including help her get dressed. It's unusual is all."

"Do you think he's lying?"

"Probably not." Lucien added, "It would be too easy to check. I'll do it now." He got up, whipped his phone out of his pocket, and disappeared into the kitchen with the phone pressed to his ear.

"Who's he calling?" I asked.

"Chessa's office, I suppose," Lailah said.

"He can do that?" How come I hadn't known that?

"Only through the Witch's Council. He has connections there." Lailah rose from her chair, crossed the room, and dug out a notebook. "What else did Jasper say?"

"He thinks Chessa's up to no good and wants to be our informant with the understanding that we help him find Avery. She's his fiancée."

Lailah's eyes gleamed as she scribbled something down. "You know what this means?"

I shook my head.

"We just got our first lead."

Chapter 11

Kane

Malstord lunged forward, swinging wildly. I jumped back, gratified when he fell off balance and stumbled headfirst right into my path. With a quick jab, I slashed, leaving a deep cut across his ribcage.

He let out a loud roar, the sound echoing through the warehouse.

"Is that all you got, crater face?" I taunted, referring to the deep wrinkles of his leathery skin.

Green fire danced in his eyes as he circled me. Then he balanced on the balls of his feet and reached out an arm with lighting speed, his talons slicing through my shirt and the skin beneath. I barely felt it with the adrenaline fueling me and twisted, catching him just above the hip with one of my daggers.

Despite the hit he took, the demon twisted with me and clamped his claw down on my forearm, yanking my arm behind me, no doubt attempting to either break it or bring me to my knees. But instead of fighting, I went with it, throwing both of us to the floor. Limbs flew, each of us receiving our share of blows.

By the time I scrambled away from him enough to get back on my feet, blood was pouring into my left eye and pain pounded in my right knee. There was no time to regroup.

The demon came at me, his arms out as he reached for my neck. I feinted left, ducked, and gave him everything I had with both daggers right into his gut.

His eyes widened and he froze.

I kept a tight hold on the daggers and, while staring him right in the eye, I said, "Poison from the well, end this demon, save him from Hell."

Magic shot from the stones of my daggers down into the blades still lodged inside Malstord.

"No!" His horrified denial drowned out the shouts of the onlookers.

And as his talons dug into my shoulders, I doubled down, pushing the daggers in even farther, and twisted. Those sharp talons dug so deep into my shoulders, I was certain he'd hit bone. We were locked in a battle of wills more than we were one of strength. Each of us had the other one skewered. It was only a matter of waiting to see which one of us would break first.

"Bastard incubus," he said, more yellow pus bubbling at his lips. "You have no idea what you've just done."

"I think I do," I said through the pain, trying to fight the fog claiming my brain. If I passed out now, I was a dead man. I'd never see Jade again. There'd never be a family.

My resolve strengthened. I would not let this be the end. "Give up, demon. You can't win this. The magic is already taking you down. If you surrender now, you'll heal. Wait any longer, and you'll be dust."

Blood so dark it was almost black mixed with the pus on the demon's lips. He tensed, spit the disgusting mixture right in my face, and released me.

I wasn't expecting the abrupt movement and jerked back as his fluids dribbled down my forehead. Shuddering with disgust, I sputtered and regained my footing just in time for the demon to repay my actions by burying one of his claws in my gut. Fire sluiced through my torso, and sweat ran down my face, stinging my eyes. Agony engulfed me as a collective gasp went up around us. I was impaled, unable to move or even breathe.

The demon moved in a few more inches and whispered, "You might have won this round, but rest assured if you survive, one way or another I'll find a way out of Hell. And when I do, you're dead."

He released me with a howl of frustration, took one step, and vanished back to Hell where he belonged.

I clutched my middle, my warm blood seeping between my fingers, and fell to my knees, not even noticing the heavy impact against the concrete floor.

Chaos erupted around me, but I heard nothing as white noise filled my ears and my vision narrowed to one person—the angel. He was propped up against the wall, staring at me with curious eyes. Ethan had saved him.

The faint hum of machinery filled my senses as I struggled to wake. My confused world was dark, permeated with flashes of light and full of unidentifiable sensations.

"Kane?"

I heard the call of my name but couldn't register who was speaking.

Jade? The word wouldn't move past my lips.

"Mr. Rouquette? Do you know where you are?"

That voice. It was deep. Belonged to someone I knew.

"Blink if you can hear me."

I felt my eyelids follow his command, and my vision started to clear. The outline of a man in all white hovered over me.

"He's awake," the same voice called, but it wasn't coming from the man standing next to me.

"Yes, but he's not out of the woods yet. I'm going to sedate him again, let his body heal a little more before we wean him off the meds."

"But we need to—"

My world faded once again into the deep slumber of nothingness.

Jade

"I'll have the crab cake to start, the shrimp and grits, and a diet soda." Lailah handed her menu to the waiter.

"The same," I said, snapping the menu closed. It was just after six p.m., and we were at the Crescent City Brewery trying to do whatever it took to take my mind off all the crap going down in our lives right then.

"I thought you were having the duck." Lailah tore off a piece of bread and popped it in her mouth.

I shrugged. "Decision making seems like too much effort."

Her lips quirked into a small, ironic smile. "It sucks to always be at the center of the battle of good and evil, doesn't it?"

"Yes." I picked up my water glass, desperately wishing I'd gone with wine instead of diet soda. "Only this time I have no idea who's on what side."

She clinked her water glass to mine. "You said it, sister."

Lailah had asked me out to eat under the guise of discussing Zoe, but I knew she was secretly trying to keep my mind off the curse and the fact that Kane had been gone for hours without any word. It wasn't necessarily unusual for him to not call when out on a mission. And for the most part I was used to it. Except I couldn't shake the nagging doubt that something was wrong.

"Maximus would get in touch if anything had happened," Lailah said, leaning forward on her elbows.

"I'm sure he would. I... Man, I don't know. It feels like something is way off. I don't know how to explain it."

Her expression changed from mildly amused to concerned, and worry radiated off her, brushing my skin.

A tiny shiver ran up my spine at the look on her face. "What?"

She shook her head. "I don't know. Not really. But I have learned to not ignore those feelings."

I let out a deep sigh and grimaced at the twinge of pain still plaguing my abdomen. "Yeah. Me, too. After we're done here, I'll call Maximus just to put my mind at ease."

"It can't hurt."

"Other than Kane being annoyed that I can't even go twelve hours without checking up on him." I spread a thick layer of butter on my bread, not caring in the least how many calories I was consuming.

Lailah raised an eyebrow. "That's a lot of butter."

I fixed her with a defiant stare. "So?"

She held both hands up and laughed. "Nothing. Nothing at all."

I nodded as I chewed. That's right. I was entitled to a little butter therapy. "Tell me about Zoe."

Lailah sat back in her chair and crossed her arms over her chest. "She's been doing really well. I bring her to the Herbal Connection with me, and she spends her day helping either me or Bea with various things. We started slowly, you know, having her wrap sage bundles and stocking candles, things like that. But now she's able to do intention spells with great accuracy. Her specialty is in metals. She's working on a line of necklaces called Dream Makers. People custom order them from her and then she spells them. All they have to do is wear them and speak their intentions for the spell to work. They have to mean what they say, though, otherwise the necklaces fail."

"That's pretty cool. Like when people put intentions out into the world? The necklace helps reaffirm their commitment to their goals?"

"Exactly. So when someone says they want to find love and get married within the next year, Zoe spells one of her necklaces with that specific goal, and while the person is wearing it, they're more likely to engage in behaviors that lead them to their goal. In the case of finding love, the spell may help nudge them into being more open to people, accepting more dates, making the first move, that kind of thing."

"I like it. Maybe I should get one that says I intend to stay out of trouble."

Lailah laughed. "I said she was pretty good, not a miracle worker."

I frowned. "I still don't understand why she wasn't participating in the summoning spell at the coven circle, but maybe she was just overwhelmed or afraid she'd do it wrong."

"Maybe." Lailah nodded to the waiter, who set our drinks on the table. "I'll talk to her about it tomorrow. It might be something like the chorus singer who's too self-conscious to sing in front of everyone else, so she mouths the words."

I hoped she was right. Because if Zoe really hadn't wanted to find me—No. I wasn't going to second-guess everyone I knew just because a few were playing dirty. Silence fell between us as we both got lost in our own thoughts and were interrupted only when our food arrived.

Shrimp swam in the rich sauce surrounding a mound of grits in the center.

"This looks amazing." I took a bite, and my whole body relaxed with pleasure.

"It always is." Lailah held her full spoon up in a small toast. It was then I noticed the sparkling blue sapphire on her left ring finger.

"Lailah," I said, teasing suspicion in my tone. "When did you get that gorgeous ring? And more importantly, who gave it to you?"

She sucked in a breath and choked on a mouthful of grits.

"Oh, jeez." I reached over and patted her back as she proceeded to cough up a lung. Her face was so red she resembled a hothouse tomato. "Here." I passed her my full glass of water. "Try this."

She took it and sucked down half the contents before she was breathing normally again.

"Okay?"

"Yeah…" She cleared her throat. "Food went down the wrong way."

"Clearly." I laughed, enjoying watching her squirm. It was so rare to see Lailah vulnerable, I couldn't help it.

She was very tight lipped about her private life after having an on-again off-again affair with Philip for years—another angel who'd been mated to someone else. Granted, his mate had been a demon at the time, so it wasn't a cheating situation, but Philip had never been able to fully commit to Lailah. She'd cut him off last year when Meri, his mate, had returned to our world as an angel. I wasn't sure if the two had gotten back together or not, but for Lailah, that didn't matter. The possibility would always be there, and she couldn't keep letting herself be hurt by Philip.

"So?" I stared pointedly at the ring. "Got a new man in your life?"

She shook her head as her face burned a deeper shade of red, if that was even possible.

"Philip?" I heard the incredulity in my voice and cringed.

"No, no. I haven't heard from him in months." She picked up her soda and sipped slowly.

I raised a curious eyebrow. "You don't mean Jonathon?"

She grimaced guiltily as she put her glass down. "Please don't think I'm a terrible person."

My teasing humor fled. How long had she been holding on to that secret? Guilt blossomed in my chest and ate away at my conscience "Of course I don't think that. Dang, am I really that judgmental?"

She glanced down at her abandoned food and gnawed on her lower lip. "No. But he was pretty awful when he was here. I figured no one wanted anything to do with him. So that's why I haven't said anything."

She was right, of course. The first time I'd met Reverend Jonathon Goodwin had been on an airplane ride when Kane and I had been headed home from Idaho. He'd been offensive on many levels—so offensive, in fact, that he'd been taken into custody by the air marshals.

Imagine my surprise when I later learned he was an angel who had a vendetta against witches, and me in particular. It had been mostly for show to raise money for his evangelical church, but he'd been pretty nasty.

Turned out he'd only gone into ministry after his mate had left him at the altar. Weird thing about angels: each of them had one fated mate, unlike the rest of us. And Goodwin's mate happened to be Lailah. She swore he'd been very different when they were together as teenagers, that he'd been nothing like the douche-canoe persona Goodwin had taken on. She just hadn't been ready to make that final commitment. It had crushed him.

Everything had changed for him, though, after the Angel Council had decided he was harming more souls than helping them and forbade him to continue his ministry. Since then, I hadn't seen much of him, but it appeared Lailah had.

"I can't say he was my favorite person, considering all that went down, but I assume he's had some major adjusting to do," I said.

She glanced up at me, hope filling her big blue eyes. Then she laughed. "You could say that. He's working at a nonprofit shelter, where he has access to the most vulnerable souls around. He's doing some good work. Really important work." She lowered her lashes and in a soft voice said, "He's changed, Jade. Become a person I can be proud to know."

I reached across the table and squeezed her hand. "That's good, Lailah. I'm really happy for you."

"Thanks." A genuine smile spread across her face and she glowed with joy, looking positively radiant.

"So, the ring? Do you have news?"

"Oh." She laughed. "No. It was a Christmas present. Considering our history, we're taking things slow."

I stared at the gorgeous princess-cut sapphire and then added, "I can see that."

She rolled her eyes and dug into her dinner.

We were almost done when my phone rang. I glanced at it, expecting to see a call from Kane, but the number was blocked. I frowned and picked it up. "Hello?"

"Ms. Calhoun?"

"Yes?"

"It's Jasper. I'm outside the restaurant and ready to talk."

Chapter 12

Kane

Bright florescent lights blinded me, and my eyes watered. I threw my hand over my face and groaned, doing my best to ignore the plethora of aches in my battered body. Jesus. My shoulders, left leg, and hip. But most of all, every time I took a shallow breath, pain shot through my gut. "What the hell?" I croaked out in a raspy voice, the stench of disinfectant stinging my nasal passages. "Someone turn the lights down."

"Welcome back, Mr. Rouquette. You had quite the rough day."

I moved my arm just enough to eye the tall, dark man scribbling in a chart. "Who are you?"

"Rhodes. I'm the healer."

The healer wore a white lab coat over his black T-shirt and jeans. He was older, with gray hair, but fit, as if he'd spent his life a regular at the gym. Only I knew that wasn't the case, because I felt a whisper of the Brotherhood connection. He was a demon hunter. Likely a retired one who now spent his days in the infirmary patching up fallen hunters like myself.

"How long—" I cleared my throat, trying to unclog my words.

"Here. Drink this." Rhodes handed me a plastic cup with a straw.

I sucked down the water, reveling in the cool liquid on my tongue. When the straw made a gurgling sound, Rhodes took the cup and placed it on the side table.

"How long have I been here?" I tried again, glancing around at the sterile white room full of medical equipment.

"About fourteen hours. You were in pretty bad shape when you arrived."

I grunted. Of course I was. I'd been gutted like a pig. "And now?"

"You'll survive. But you'll carry the scars with you for the rest of your life. Demon scars are permanent."

I closed my eyes, not caring in the slightest. As long as I was with Jade again—My eyes popped open. "Is my wife here?"

Rhodes shook his head. "No. This facility is not open to visitors the likes of her."

"Not open to witches, you mean," I said, my tone full of irritation. A surge of disgust rippled through me, and if I hadn't been beat to shit, I'd have stalked out right then.

"It's not my policy." Rhodes flipped his chart closed. "I'll be back in an hour to check on your pain dosage."

"Wait. Has my wife been notified I'm here?"

The healer paused at the door and shrugged. "I doubt it. The hunters who brought you in went right back out on another run."

"I need a—"

The healer left before I could finish my sentence.

"Son of a bitch!" I had no idea where my clothes were, much less my phone.

"There's a phone at the front desk," a male voice said from the corner of the room.

I jerked, trying to sit up, but was thwarted by the stabbing pain in my gut. "Holy fuck."

I heard the slow click of footsteps on the tiled floor a few moments before he came into view. It was the angel the demon had almost killed. "It's you," I said.

"It's me." He sat in the chair beside my hospital bed, his dark blond hair sticking up all over the place. There was a deep purple ring around his neck as well as three rows of fresh stitches.

I studied him. He was vaguely familiar, and I wondered where I knew him from. His clothes were dirty, but they were definitely designer quality. He was young, late teens or early twenties. Tall with an oversized frame that hadn't yet filled out. And the way he sat, shoulders straight, one leg draped over one knee, his gaze never leaving mine, left me with the impression he'd been raised in a privileged environment. Confident and self-assured, even though he'd just had his ass whupped.

Of course, I was the one lying in a hospital bed. Talk about an ass whupping. At least Malstord was magically bound to Hell for the rest of his days. It was something. "What's your name?"

"Ezra."

"I'm glad to meet you, Ezra. Mind telling me how you ended up in that warehouse with the demons?"

He averted his eyes. Maybe not as confident as I'd thought. He cleared his throat. "I was abducted and taken to Hell about nine months ago."

Son of a… "Why?"

He turned his steely blue gaze on me. "I'm the high angel's son."

This time I gritted my teeth through the pain and really did sit up so I could get a good look at him. Damn. Chessandra had a son? "You can't be serious."

He leveled a flat stare, almost daring me to challenge him.

It was the same don't-fuck-with-me look Chessandra sometimes had. Double damn. That's why he looked familiar. Was he Drake's? Was this kid Jade's half brother?

Jade.

She must've been worried sick. I pulled the blanket off, realizing I was in a flimsy hospital gown. But I didn't give a shit. I had to let her know where I was.

I glanced at the kid. "Help me up, would you? I've got to call my wife."

He just sat there, keeping his gaze trained on my face.

"What?"

"You're not fazed by my revelation? No one knows I exist. You know that, right?"

"No, I'm not fazed," I lied. The implications of what this could mean were huge. "But I am surprised no one knows you exist. Why?"

"I was an inconvenience to my mother. She sent me away, and now that she's made enemies, I've become the leverage for the other side. I want to do something about it."

My feet hit the cold tiled floor. "And what's that?"

"Take her down. And you're going to help me."

Jade

I left Lailah at the table and hurried outside onto the brick sidewalk, shivering from the chill in the night air. Jasper leaned against the wall under a flickering gaslight, an unlit cigarette hanging out of his mouth. He was dressed in dark jeans and a black henley, with a knit hat covering his unruly hair.

He spotted me and jerked his head, indicating he wanted to head toward Canal Street. Holding the cigarette with two fingers, he said, "Let's go."

I stood my ground. "Wait. I was having dinner."

"It's over. We need to talk, and not here."

I bristled at his pushy demand. "I'm not leaving Lailah. You can either come inside and sit with us, or you can wait for us."

His eyes narrowed, and I could swear I felt a hint of rage boiling beneath his I-don't-give-a-shit demeanor. The feeling vanished as fast as it had appeared, and he leaned against the wall once more, stuffing the cigarette back into his mouth. "Hurry up. I don't have much time."

Pushy little bastard. I was starting to regret aligning myself with him. But he had information we needed. "I'll be back in a minute."

Irritated impatience swirled around him like storm clouds. I resisted flipping him off and mentally gave myself a medal. He was the one who'd interrupted my dinner without any warning. He could wait a few minutes for me to pay my bill. I hurried back into the restaurant, only to find Lailah had already taken care of the check and was on her way to catch up with me.

"Thanks," I said. "How much do I owe you?"

"Don't worry about it. You can get it next time."

I smiled, enjoying our easy friendship. It wasn't that long ago neither of us would've been caught dead having dinner together, much less paying for each other. I fell into step beside her. "He's kind of being an ass. So fair warning."

She glanced over at me. "I might be an ass if my fiancée was missing, too."

"Maybe. But not like this. You'll see."

We reemerged on Decatur to an empty sidewalk. "Dammit." I frowned. "Where is he?"

Lailah glanced up and down the street, then she grabbed my hand and pointed across the busy street.

Jasper was sitting on top of a cement barrier between the parking lot and the sidewalk, barely visible in the darkness. I shook my head and led the way down the street to the crosswalk. "What's he up to?"

"Showing us who's in charge, I imagine." She seemed unconcerned with his antics. Or maybe she sympathized.

I had no such compunction. If Kane was missing, I'd go after him with both barrels raised. No games necessary. But then, I was a white witch and leader of the New Orleans coven. I had a lot more resources than this kid did. My irritation with him all but vanished. How long had Avery been missing? Three, four months? However long it was, it was entirely too long. I had to give the kid a break.

We crossed the street, the wind off the Mississippi River whipping my long hair across my face. I pulled it up into a haphazard bun and crossed my arms against my chest, trying to stave off the cold. When we were about ten feet from Jasper, he hopped off the cement wall and walked toward Canal, not acknowledging us.

"He's making sure he can claim plausible deniability. If anyone spots him and this gets back to Chessandra, he'll want to make sure he's not seen walking or talking with us so he can claim coincidence," Lailah explained.

"But we talked outside the restaurant."

She lifted one shoulder. "I'm sure he has his reasons."

I cast her a side-eye glance. "You're being very diplomatic."

She laughed. "Yeah, probably. I'm trying to reserve judgment until I've spoken to him. Chessandra is a total bitch to work for. He probably trusts no one. I guess I'm willing to give him the benefit of the doubt."

Shame wound its way through me. She was right. The kid had lost someone important to him, and he had to work for the woman who was responsible for her disappearance. It was enough to break anyone.

We followed Jasper down North Peters and up Bienville, weaving between the tourists, until he abruptly ducked into an old brick warehouse that had been recently turned into luxury condos. Lailah and I strolled into the building's lobby, chatting away as if we were oblivious to the world around us. But in reality, we were both on high alert.

Lailah glanced quickly at the ornate door off to the right and then back at me.

I'd heard it click closed only a second ago. If we went through it, I had no doubt we'd find Jasper waiting for us.

Lailah continued to chat about a purse she'd seen at the Coach Factory that she'd talked herself out of buying. By the way she was going on and on, you'd think she'd formed an unnatural attachment. Considering I'd never once seen her carry a designer purse, I had to deduce she was making it all up off the top of her head.

It was impressive.

Finally she paused for a breath, and I said, "Let's go up. I'll show you my collection."

She nodded, and I rolled my shoulders, expelling some of my tension. This undercover stuff was for the birds. I was more of a take-a-stand-and-deal-with-the-repercussions-later type of girl. Probably not always the best course of action, but so far it had worked for me.

The moment we stepped into the stairwell, Jasper snapped, "This way." He ran up the steep wooden stairs, taking them two at a time.

"Let's do this," I said to Lailah.

Jasper didn't slow down once on the four-flight climb, and by the time I stepped into the condo, I was sucking wind like a pack-a-day smoker.

Lailah had barely broken a sweat, and Jasper was standing near a full-length window, that cigarette back between his lips.

"Do you ever smoke those, or is it just an oral thing?" If he really was a smoker, I was going to feel even worse about myself, because, really?

He ignored my question and flipped a switch.

I froze, my heart pounding as I stared at the sight in front of me.

"Whoa," Lailah said softly.

One full wall was full of photos, graphs, notes, and diagrams. In the middle there was a picture of Chessandra. Tacked to the wall around her photo was her sister, Mati, and the date they'd tried to close the demon portal, the date Avery had gone missing, a couple memos, a picture of a demon, and a young boy with a shock of blond hair.

I turned back to Jasper. "How long have you been researching this?"

"Since about a week after Avery went missing."

Lailah turned and made eye contact with him. "Does anyone else know you're doing this?"

He shook his head.

"Why?"

I highly doubted Lailah didn't know the answer to her question. It was likely she just wanted to hear him say what she was thinking.

He let out a humorless chuckle. "Because no one wants to believe the high angel is corrupt. Or that she's the real reason Avery's gone."

Lailah and I shared a glance. He was right. No one wanted to hear their leader was as shady as a New Orleans politician.

We both turned and studied the wall once again.

Lailah reached out, pressing her palm to the photo of Avery. Then she turned to Jasper. "I believe you."

Chapter 13

Kane

The walk down the dimly lit hall took every last bit of strength out of me. I'd put Ezra's revelation aside for the moment in order to focus on the phone call I had to make. If I went missing, who knew what Jade would do to find me? By the time we got to the deserted desk, I was clutching Ezra's arm so tight, I was surprised I hadn't fractured it.

Leaning against the wall because I was certain I couldn't sit down, I gritted my teeth against the pain and asked, "You all right, man?"

Ezra wiped the sweat from his forehead. "If I can survive a demon attack, I can sure as hell manage getting you to the phone."

"Fair enough. Do me a favor, will you? Dial this number for me?" The phone was on the other side of the desk. I'd never reach it without inflicting more damage on my slaughtered abdomen.

Ezra picked up the phone and dialed as I rattled off the number.

It went straight to voicemail. I bit back a curse and left her a vague message about how I was okay and I'd get in touch the next day.

Ezra hung up the phone and raised a curious eyebrow.

"There's no need for her to worry. I'll survive."

He gave me a dubious look and then helped me back to my room. By the time I collapsed in the hospital bed, I was sweating and more than a little pissed off.

"Looks like you could use an hour or so with a sex witch," Ezra said, his tone snide.

I fixed him with a hard stare.

"What? Isn't that how you get your power? You're an incubus, right? And a sex witch would likely fix that shit going on with your gut. I mean, dude, the fact that you were walking at all is hardcore. But it obviously hurts like a bitch."

"Drop it."

"I'm just sayin'."

"I said drop it," I all but growled. The last thing I wanted to do was think about being with anyone other than Jade. And thinking about her, well, I'd give just about anything to be curled up next to her while my body healed itself.

"Sorry." Ezra slumped back in the chair, watching me.

I wanted to throw his ass out. Call the doctor and ask for more pain meds. Because this was bullshit. If Bea had been here, she'd have me on some special pain-reducing herb, and I'd likely be walking out of here in the morning. Or maybe I was giving her too much credit. I had been thoroughly gutted.

But as annoying a presence as Ezra was, he had questions to answer.

"Tell me about your mother. Why do you think we need to take her down?"

His brown eyes flashed with fury as he stood and paced the room. "She's a traitor. Has demon connections. If she had her way, you and your wife would be locked away in Hell right now."

I frowned. Chessandra was no saint, but his statement felt off. For Christ's sake, she'd even tried to close portals in the past. "I've never gotten that impression."

He stopped his incessant stalking. "She's nothing like who she pretends to be."

"Enlighten me, then." I propped myself up on the pillows, ignoring the ever-increasing sharp stabs in my gut. Whatever drugs I'd been on must've been wearing off. Fuck, if I hurt this much medicated, what would it be like completely sober? I shuddered thinking about it.

He moved slowly back to the chair beside my bed and sat, his elbows resting on his knees as he leaned forward. "Do you know what it does to a kid who's told he isn't wanted?"

"I might know something about that." My parents had never been cut out for child rearing. They never pretended they were, either. In fact, I'd heard more than once from my selfish mother that I'd been a mistake. That did something to a kid. Something almost beyond repair.

"I doubt it," Ezra said.

"That's your choice." I saw no reason to participate in his indulgence. If he wanted to believe he was the only kid with fucked-up parents, he could. I wasn't his freakin' therapist. I only wanted to learn what he had to say about his mother.

Ezra cast me a nasty look.

I ignored that too and did my best to keep him talking. "Did you grow up in the angel realm?"

"No." He bit the word off.

That made sense. If he had, it was likely everyone would know about him. "Boarding school?"

He shook his head, his anger getting more and more pronounced by the second. "Foster care. In the fucking system if you can believe that."

Now that was a surprise and completely opposite of my earlier assessment. Sometime in the near past, he'd been exposed to privilege, though, and perhaps that was where most of his anger came from. Knowing what he missed out on as a kid. "Where was your dad?"

He shrugged. "Don't have one."

"Don't have one, or you don't know who he is?"

"Both." Ezra rubbed his left temple as if to ease a headache.

I couldn't get past the foster care remark. "So you're saying your mom, the most powerful and certainly well-to-do angel in the angel realm, put you in the system instead of raising you herself?"

"That's what I said, Rouquette. Keep up."

My irritation was growing by the second. I'd had enough. I'd saved his ass from certain death. I didn't need this crap. "So you had a shitty childhood and your mother is a piece of work. Welcome to the club. Get over it. Get a therapist. Find a girl to lose yourself in. Do something other than whining about it."

His light-brown eyes narrowed, and his lips formed a tight line. "You don't know what you're talking about."

There it was. The cold hatred I knew was lurking under his tough-guy attitude. The kind that if tapped would show someone's true colors. "I'm listening."

"My mother didn't just not want me, she threw me away, sent me to live with mundanes who had no idea I was an angel. They weren't equipped to deal with anything magic related. When I was six and learned I could control birds just by talking to them, that was cool. But later, in school, when I could sense things about people, see their auras and know when they were suffering, do you know what that does to a kid? I had no idea what any of that meant. No idea how to handle it."

My irritation with him eased. His experience sounded similar to Jade's when she was a kid, learning to deal with her empath gift. At least in her formative years, she'd had her mother around to help her through it. How tough must it have been to be a kid and be subject to the massive amounts of suffering in the world without any coping skills?

"And if that wasn't enough," he continued, "I was constantly being shuffled around. Corruption, divorce, drugs. You name it, I've been subjected to it. I've lived on my own since I was sixteen, and the day I turned eighteen, I went looking for her."

"How did you find her?" That seemed difficult at best. Chessandra lived most of her life in the angel realm. Getting to her was almost impossible.

"I tracked down her sister."

"Mati?" That would do it. Chessandra's family lived across the river.

"Yeah." He let out a humorless laugh. "Imagine my surprise to find out my family was less than ten miles away living an upper-class lifestyle while I was scraping by in the slums most of the time."

"It's bullshit, man."

"Tell me about it." He snorted and winced when he jerked his head, stretching his new stitches.

"What happened after you tracked Chessandra down?"

His expression clouded with cold fury. "She gave me money."

That in and of itself wasn't a terrible thing. But I could only imagine the way the exchange had gone down. "A payoff?"

He nodded once. "She doesn't want anyone to know I exist. I'm her dirty little secret."

Ouch. I'd never liked the high angel, but this wasn't something I'd have expected from her. She was righteous and the height of propriety. Maybe that was the problem. She couldn't afford to have anyone questioning her judgment. So fucked up. "And now you want to expose her? Is that what you're saying?"

He nodded. "And I want you to help me."

I frowned. As unsettling as it was that Chessandra had forsaken her own child, it wasn't for me to second-guess her choices. Judging by his age, she must've been pretty young when she'd had him. A teen, really. It wasn't out of the realm of possibility that she'd thought she was doing what was best for him. "I'm not sure what exactly you're trying to achieve. To humiliate her? Revenge? Is it worth that?"

A deadly calm washed over him as he pierced me with a cold stare. "This isn't some childish scheme to get back at a shitty mom. I want to claim my birthright. I should be one of the players in the realm. But more than that, she's dangerous to everyone. The angels. The witches. The mundanes. The things I've learned in the last six months… They're unconscionable."

He had my attention now. We already suspected Chessandra had dirty dealings. Did this kid have the answers? "You're saying she's corrupt?"

"Yes." He sat back in the plastic chair, gripping the armrests. "And I'm going to bring her down one way or another. What she's done to me pales in comparison. You in?"

I mulled his words over, then asked, "Do you have any proof?"

A slow, self-satisfied smile claimed his lips as he pulled a piece of paper out of his pocket. "How does a signed contract with a demon sound?"

I raised an eyebrow. "Contract for what?"

He handed me the paper. "Read it."

A strange mix of apprehension and excitement slammed into me. Whatever that paper said, I was certain this was the catalyst that would change everything. A battle would be waged and, good or bad, nothing would be the same. The only question was, could we survive it?

Ezra sat back, watching me.

Scanning the document, I noted it was dated five years ago. I glanced up at Ezra. He nodded, indicating I should read on.

I lowered my gaze, skimmed all the legalese of the contract until I got to the meat of the document.

> *I, Chessandra Ballintine, high angel of the angel realm, hereby formally grant a full pardon to the demon Wes Lancaster in exchange for his silence regarding the incident in question. He shall be cleared of all wrongdoing with the understanding that neither party shall ever speak of said incident again.*

Running a finger over the two signatures, I felt the faint trace of magic. This was indeed a magically binding contract.

"What incident?" I asked Ezra.

He shrugged. "It's only referred to as a case number. I have to guess it's in the files in good ol' Mom's office. But I've been told it was an attack on a human who died and that this demon,

Wes Lancaster, has something on Chessandra she doesn't want to get out. What I've heard is that he had a safeguard in place so that if he died, someone else would expose the secret. So she bribed him for his silence in exchange for his life."

I narrowed my eyes. The only entities that should have those kinds of records were the angels, the Brotherhood, and Hell itself. One would need high clearance to get their hands on it. "And you know this how?"

His smile vanished. "I had an interesting visitor last year."

"Someone who knows Chessandra's secret?"

"You could say that." He blinked once and then stared me in the eye. "The demon Wes Lancaster."

Chapter 14

Jade

Jasper let out a long sigh of relief. And I couldn't blame him. Avery had been missing for months without any real help from anyone to find her. Now he had the New Orleans coven leader and an angel on his side.

When looking at things from his point of view, I couldn't even blame him for the binding spell. I didn't like it, but at least I understood the desperation behind it. Even the seemingly crazy conspiracy theory evidence covering his walls seemed reasonable. What else was he going to do?

I took my time studying the various photos and facts he'd assembled. There were a few photos of Chessandra speaking with other council members—something she did on a regular basis—a phone bill with a number circled and a question mark beside it, a couple snippets of conversation he'd had with her that seemed meaningless, and a timeline of dates. All of it was minor, and when you added it all up, there was nothing substantial to go on.

All of it except one thing. I pointed to a piece of paper that read *Last location: Lakeshore.* "What's this?"

Lailah glanced at the paper, and then we both turned and looked at Jasper expectantly.

His brow pinched in confusion. "Exactly what it says. Avery's last known location before she went missing."

"Is that the information Chessandra gave you?" I asked Lailah.

She shook her head. "No. I was told she went into the shadows and never returned."

"Me too."

Jasper pulled the knitted beanie off his head and ran a frustrated hand through his wild hair as he muttered something about evil bitch angels. "Of course that's what she told you. She didn't want anyone to know what she was doing. Couldn't let you in on her dirty dealings, now could she?"

"You're saying Avery was actually in Lakeshore when she went missing? Not the shadows?" I asked for clarity.

"Yes." His voice was clipped. "She was meeting a demon."

Lailah and I both let out a gasp.

"You can't be serious?" Lailah said, her eyes wide.

"Oh, I'm serious. It's not the first time, either. For the past year, Chessandra has been sending Avery out to the same spot once a month to deliver communications. Avery would take a package to the same spot, wait in her car for the demon to pick it up, and then drive off after she was sure he got it."

Holy crickets on a cracker. Chessandra had dealings with a demon, and she'd sent her assistant to do the dirty work. I opened my mouth to speak, shook my head, and then met Lailah's gaze, not sure what to say. This couldn't be real.

"Are you one hundred percent positive the contact was a demon?" Lailah asked, getting down to brass tacks.

Jasper shoved his hands in his pockets, making the chain clipped to his belt loop clatter. "Yes. Avery broke down and told me about it. She was scared because strange things were happening. But she felt like she couldn't say no to Chessandra."

"Why?" I said, forcing the word out. If everything he was saying was true, there was no excuse on the planet that would justify Chessandra sending an angel to meet a demon. There just wasn't. Even if she was waiting in her car. It was too dangerous.

"Because Chessandra threatened to fire her if she didn't do it. She said running errands was standard, and if Avery couldn't handle it, she was welcome to leave."

"So she chose to deal with a demon rather than just quit?" I asked. That would've been a no brainer for me.

"You don't understand." Jasper paced the apartment, the sound of his heavy footsteps echoing off the hardwood. "Avery came from a poor family. They're bayou witches. Very little money. And she has a younger sibling with health issues. The kind that magic doesn't help. So she was sending most of her money to them. Admin work for the high angel pays considerably better than any other admin job she might get. Besides, even if she hadn't been engaged to me, she wouldn't have left the realm to make a go of it in this world. No angel who works that closely with the high angel would do that. It's too dangerous. If anyone were to find out the knowledge she had, it would've been disastrous."

Family. More often than not, that was what got most of us in a bind. I couldn't say I'd never made questionable decisions when it came to taking care of someone I loved.

Lailah raised her eyebrows and cast him a side-eye glance. "Looks like the pair of you weren't exactly hurting for money." She waved a hand around the luxury condo. "Places like this in the French Quarter aren't cheap."

His posture stiffened. "No. It isn't. This place belongs to a buddy of mine who's out of the country. He asked me to keep an eye on it since I've been spending so much time in this world looking for Avery. And I am."

She crossed her arms over her chest and blinked at him. "That's…convenient."

"Jeez. You want his number?" Jasper pulled out his wallet and started fishing through a small stack of cards.

I reached out and stopped him, hating that our default for every explanation was distrust. I cast Lailah an exasperated glance. "He doesn't have to prove anything to us."

She shrugged while Jasper shoved his wallet back in his pocket.

"Okay, then," I said. "Based on this new information, I'd like to do a calling over in Lakeshore. Jasper, do you know the exact spot Avery met with the demon?"

He nodded.

"Good. I'm going to call in the coven. We're doing this tonight."

I stared at my phone, willing Kane to call. When I'd gone to contact the rest of the coven members, I'd realized my phone had somehow gotten turned off. And of course there was a message from Kane. I was grateful to hear from him, but his voice had sounded scratchy, worn out, as if he was either sick or hadn't slept in days. But it was more than that. There was a wariness in his tone that set my alarm bells off. It didn't matter that he said he was all right; he certainly didn't sound it, and I couldn't stop the worry clouding my mind.

"Ready to do this?" Lailah asked.

We were standing next to Kane's Lexus in the parking lot next to a park on the shores of Lake Pontchartrain. The wind had died down, but there was still a bone-deep winter chill in the air, and I wished I'd remembered to bring my scarf.

"As ready as I'll ever be." I grabbed a backpack full of candles and herbs, while Lailah held the salt and Bea's truth potion just in case we needed it for something.

"I want to try Bea one more time," I said, already hitting her name on my phone.

It rang three times, then she answered. "Jade?" Her tone was jubilant, and upbeat jazz music blared in the background.

"Bea. Can you talk for a minute?"

"Sure," she yelled into the phone. "Give me a sec." There was a rustling as if she were holding her hand over the phone, and then everything went quiet. "I'm back. What's wrong?"

"Nothing really. We've got a lead on Avery, and we're doing a calling. I wanted to ask if you wanted to be here for this, but it sounds like you're busy."

"Oh, dear. Well, yes. I'm the hostess of a fundraiser, but I guess I could—"

"Never mind. Lailah and I are on it," I said quickly, even though a pit was forming in my stomach. We could potentially be calling a demon, and that scared the crap out of me. Not so much for myself. I could deal with one. I had before and I undoubtedly would again. But with my coven here, it was hard not to worry for their sakes. When dealing with demons, one never knew what to expect. "Didn't mean to bother you. We've got it. Enjoy your party. I'll talk to you tomorrow."

"Wait. Jade?"

"Yes?"

"You really can handle this, you know. But if you need me for any reason, send me a text. I'll keep the phone on vibrate so I'll feel it."

"Sure," I said, relieved to know she'd be around if the worst happened. "Thanks."

"I mean it. Don't hesitate to send me a message."

I chuckled at her no-nonsense voice. "Yes, Mom. I'll text."

"You'd better."

I slipped the phone into my pocket, and took a deep breath not sure I was ready for this.

"She's not coming, I take it," Lailah said, pulling her wool coat tighter around her slim frame.

"Nope. Some fundraiser. But she's on call if we need her."

Lailah nodded, and the pair of us took off across the grass to meet up with the rest of the coven members who'd already arrived.

Lucien, wearing a suit, stood in the middle of the group, trying unsuccessfully to answer questions.

I grimaced. I'd pulled him out of work. He'd had a gallery showing and had left early. Everyone else was dressed in normal casual wear. I only hoped I hadn't ruined their plans as well.

"Listen up, everyone," I said over the chatter. "The angel Avery has been missing for months. It's come to our attention that this was the last place she was before she disappeared." I met Jasper's gaze as I relayed the information he'd disclosed earlier. "It's possible she was with a demon."

Small gasps and whispers erupted among the members.

"I don't have to tell you this is a potentially dangerous situation since this place has a history of demon activity. If another one shows up, the most important thing is that you don't panic. Don't break the circle. And under no circumstances do you engage the demon in any way. Let Lucien and I deal with it. Understood?"

There was a murmur of agreement, but tension hung in the air, and I couldn't help the weight that settled over my shoulders from potentially subjecting my coven to demons. But we had to do the calling here. It was the last place Avery was seen and the most likely place the spell would work. If all went according to plan, Avery would show up in spirit form and we'd be able to get information about what's happened to her.

I nodded to Lailah. She nodded back and enlisted a couple of the members to help her form a thick salt circle. It was always dangerous to deal with demons, but since we weren't at the coven circle, we had to make one, and a strong one at that. Salt was the first line of defense.

Rosalee took the candles and went to work placing them on the circle. Her hair was tied back in a ponytail, and she wore skinny jeans with a tight V-neck sweater. She looked about twelve. My nerves took over, sending me into a jittery state. Damn. I needed to calm down.

Moving away from the group, I headed toward the shore, where the lake water was lapping gently against the manmade beach. I concentrated on the sound, letting it soothe me.

"I can't believe someone is finally doing something," Jasper whispered.

I jerked, surprised he'd followed me.

"Sorry, didn't mean to startle you." He gave me a half smile, appearing grateful.

My heart pounded. It wasn't often anyone could get that close to me without me noticing. I was too sensitive to human emotions. However, Jasper was an angel. It was possible he was hiding them from me. But he hadn't been back at the apartment. His frustration and pain had been clear as day. Was there something different about him? Me? Or this place?

I couldn't tell. And I didn't want to try and probe his emotions. If he was concealing them from me—which he had every right to do—he'd feel me intruding. I shook off the thoughts. My empath ability was more of a burden anyway. I should've been grateful I wasn't listening in on him.

"It's all right," I said. "I might be a little nervous, but as soon as we start up, I'll be fine." That was true enough. When I wielded power, everything else faded away, and it was all I knew.

He smiled and tossed a small rock into the dark lake.

I heard the faint plop when it entered, and that was when I felt it. Another presence. Someone…no, something other than the two angels and group of witches waiting to start the spell.

I spun, my breath coming in quick gasps.

Right there about two feet from Lailah was a creature with electric-green eyes glowing in the darkness.

A demon. One was here.

Chapter 15

Kane

Two seconds after Ezra dropped his bomb of meeting the demon in question, the healer arrived with a dark-haired, petite female in tow.

"We're going to need to ask you to wait outside, son," my original healer said, gesturing for Ezra to leave.

He grumbled something about them needing better chairs in the lobby and then shuffled out.

"All right, Mr. Rouquette. This is Healer Haymoore. She's going to fix you up enough so that you can get out of here."

I let out a sigh of relief. Home would be infinitely better than this stark cinderblock room.

"On a scale of one to ten, how much pain are you in?" Haywood asked in a husky voice. She had a small penlight in her hand and was staring at me expectantly.

"Six?"

She chuckled softly. "Tough guy, huh? Seems to me since your meds are all but worn off and you were walking around, you'd be closer to an eight or nine. But I guess if you had any power reserves, it might not be that bad."

I'd lied. My power was completely depleted, and it was getting hard to breathe. But I'd suffered through a lot worse situations. So a nine on the pain scale would be one step from death. Which might have been more accurate.

"All right, then. I think after we're done here, you might have a new understanding of just how bad this was."

I didn't need a new understanding. If I hadn't been an incubus with power streaming through my veins, there was no doubt I'd have died. "Just go ahead and do your thing, doc," I said, closing my eyes.

"Healer," she corrected.

"Whatever you say."

Her warm hand pressed against my forehead, and just for a second, I felt a tingle of magic ghost over me. My entire body relaxed, the pain subsided, and then everything turned fuzzy and my world faded to black.

I woke, groggy and more than a little achy. The kind of ache that came after lying in the same position for too long. Shifting in the unfamiliar bed, I stretched my legs out in front of me and groaned with pleasure. Damn, that felt good. And more importantly, there wasn't any pull in my abdomen.

The healer had really worked some magic. I glanced around the dark room, trying to make out my surroundings. I'd been moved, that was certain. I was no longer in the hospital bed surrounded by beeping machines. No, the bed was a high-quality queen with thick, warm blankets, and beside it there was what appeared to be a wood nightstand with a digital clock. Four a.m.

I wondered how long I'd been out. Six hours? Or twenty-eight? There was no way to tell. I sat up, pleased I only had to deal with some stiff muscles, and swung my feet out of the bed. My hospital gown was gone, replaced with a T-shirt and sweat pants.

A vague unease rippled through me at the thought of not remembering someone changing my clothes. But I put it out of my mind. My body had been healed, and that was all that mattered. Except getting home. I'd shadow walk if I had to, but first I needed to find out where I was and if Ezra had tagged along.

In my bare feet, I slipped out of the room into a hallway lit with wall sconces. Medieval paintings depicting angels and demons in battle lined the walls. Walking soundlessly over the hardwood floors, I made my way to the end of the hall, where a light shone under a closed door.

Before I could knock, it opened on its own, and Maximus, the leader of the Brotherhood, glanced up from his desk. He was a tall, dark-haired man, with a powerful presence even when he was sitting down. He smiled. "Good morning, Kane. It's good to see you awake."

I cleared my throat. "How long have I been here?"

Maximus turned his head toward the clock and said, "A few hours. The healers needed your bed. So they brought you here."

I rubbed the stubble on my jawline. "Ah, well, what I really want to know is how long have I been unconscious? Just one night? Or multiples?"

"Oh, I see. Just one." He stood and waved toward a comfortable-looking leather chair. "Have a seat. I'll have food brought up."

"Thanks." My stomach rumbled at the thought of something to eat. "I haven't eaten since breakfast yesterday."

He nodded. "Sounds about right." After picking up the office phone and ordering enough food for the entire Brotherhood, he sat back down. "I hear you met someone interesting yesterday."

My eyebrows rose. Was he talking about Ezra or the demon? "Someone or something?"

"Someone."

"Yes. I did. Any idea where he is?"

"In another one of my guest rooms."

I glanced around the book-lined office, noted the old leather-bound books, bronze statues, and more medieval paintings. It was nicer and more personal than any of the rooms I'd seen at the Brotherhood, including Maximus's main office. "Is this your private residence?"

He nodded. "It's not often I have guests. I hope the accommodations were adequate."

I swallowed a laugh. "Adequate? You could say that. Much better than that hospital bed, that's for sure. Though I haven't seen much of it."

"I'd give you a tour, but I imagine you're probably not up for it at this hour."

I shook my head and then ran a hand down my face, unable to shake the fatigue plaguing me. My wounds had healed, but it would obviously be a while before I was one hundred percent. "Maybe another time, but I do need to talk to Ezra before I leave."

He leaned forward, his elbows on his desk. "There's a lot to discuss before you go home, but first, breakfast." Gesturing to the door with his chin, he said, "Just put the tray on my desk, Victor. Thank you."

The aging man's hands shook as he placed a large tray of metal-covered plates on the desk. Another younger servant followed him with a silver serving tray of what I assumed was coffee. I'd never known Maximus to be a tea drinker.

When they were gone, Maximus lifted two of the covers. One had an omelet and the other French toast. "Have whatever you wish."

I knew I should go for the omelet but caved and devoured the French toast with the hunger of a starving man.

When I was done, Maximus gestured to the other plate. "Have more. You need the calories to rebuild not just your strength but your magic as well."

His words triggered two thoughts. My dagger and Jade. Both would help my powers faster than an egg-and-cheese mixture. I glanced down at my bare feet and began to feel uncomfortable. What was going on here? I was eating breakfast in Maximus's office at four a.m., barely dressed, while Maximus himself was perfectly groomed in his Brotherhood robes, two daggers strapped to his waist and an amulet around his neck.

I cleared my throat. "Excuse me if this is a rude question after your hospitality, but why didn't the healers just drop me off in the dorms at the Brotherhood?"

Irritation flashed over Maximus's face before he could mask his emotions. He forced a patient smile. "I thought after your ordeal, this would be more comfortable."

I stood, ready to shadow walk right out of there. He wasn't being truthful. I could tell by the unnatural hitch in his voice and the way he wasn't quite meeting my gaze. "Tell me what's going on, Maximus."

My leader rose, his posture tense as if he was ready to battle. "Sit down, Rouquette. We have things to discuss."

I stared him down, acutely aware I was weaponless and not likely to be able to shadow walk out of his office. No doubt he had wards, and that was the reason I was here and not with the others. After a moment, I stretched my neck in a show of dominance and reclaimed my seat in the leather chair. I poured myself a cup of coffee and raised the carafe in offering, trying to be civil.

He lowered himself into his chair and gave me a short nod. "Thank you."

Neither of us spoke while we doctored our respective coffees. To say the tension in the air was thick would be an understatement.

Finally I set my cup down and leveled my gaze at him, waiting.

It was then I noticed the fatigue lining his eyes. How long had he been awake? Twenty-four hours? "Let's have it, then," I said, breaking the silence.

Maximus took another long sip of his coffee, and I swear he was dragging out the moment. For what? To make me squirm? Wasn't happening. Maybe to gather his thoughts? Whatever it was, he had about five seconds to get on with it.

And just as I was about to get up again, Maximus spoke. "You issued a sanctioned challenge to a very powerful demon yesterday."

"So?" I asked defiantly. I was part of the Brotherhood, and Maximus was our leader, but I was still my own man, made my own decisions when it came to challenges. There weren't any laws on the books that said I couldn't.

"You made a very powerful enemy."

I shrugged. "Not my problem. He'll be stuck in Hell, where I don't intend to be."

Maximus abruptly slammed his fist down on his desk and stood, leaning toward me as his entire body vibrated. "It is your problem. Just like it's my problem and that of every other hunter in the order. Don't you get it? In your quest to prove something today, you created a situation that could turn into a major war. Malstord will not sit idly by and let his banishment to Hell go by unnoticed. All his minions will be after you, and we'll all get caught up in the crossfire."

Anger exploded in my chest at his outburst, and I leaped out of the chair, unwilling to take his shit sitting down. "And how exactly is this different from any other day of the week? We're demon hunters. Demons show up all the time, and we battle them by either destroying them or sending them back where they came from. I do this willingly to be part of something greater than myself. But when it threatens my family, that's when it becomes personal. The challenge I issued yesterday was about protecting what's mine. Specifically Jade and our future."

His brows pinched in confusion. "What are you talking about? What did Malstord have to do with your wife?"

I took a deep breath and let it out, trying to dispel some of my frustration. Having a shouting match with Maximus wasn't going to change anything. Even if it would make me feel better to tell him to join Malstord in Hell. "Jade has been cursed with a black magic spell that lays claim to our future child. Apparently the curse comes from an angel, but Malstord knew about it. I have a hunch he's either controlling or working with the angel who cursed her. And I'm telling you right now, Maximus, no one messes with my family. No one."

"Son of a... Christ." Maximus kicked his chair out of the way and paced his office. "Your child?"

I nodded and clenched my fists into tight balls to keep from hitting something. Specifically Maximus.

He stopped pacing abruptly and turned to me. "I don't have to tell you what the odds are of you two having an extremely powerful child and what that would mean if a demon had control over him or her."

Murder. It actually crossed my mind. If I were to end him right now, would any jury in the world convict me? Here he was talking about the implications of power dynamics instead of being horrified someone had essentially already laid the plans for kidnapping my child. My body pulsed with hatred. When had Maximus turned into a calculating bastard?

He was behaving just like Chessandra. Thinking of the greater good instead of an innocent child. It took all my willpower to force out, "I'm well aware, but I'm much more concerned with the actual safety and well-being of my family than I am anything else."

Maximus's expression turned to one of horror, and then he took a step back as he glanced at the ground. Was that regret? Shame? But then he looked up again, and his expression was blank, void of any compassion. "Of course you are. I'd expect nothing else."

That was it. I was done. Done with being expected to sacrifice everything I had for the cause. Done with Maximus and his condescending tone. He and Chessandra could have each other. "Excuse me. I think I'll be going now."

Maximus grabbed a dagger from his belt and shot a stream of magic at the door, leaving the frame sparking with magic. "Not until we're done with this conversation."

I took a step forward, my fists still clenched. "You're the worst kind of bastard."

Shifting, he pointed his dagger at me. "Move one more step, and I'll lay you out flat."

The desire to tear him apart with my bare hands was there, coursing through me with unimaginable force. But I knew better. If I went after him, even if I won the battle—which, considering his advantage, was highly unlikely—this would end badly for me. I had to take a moment and reevaluate my options.

There was nothing to do but hear him out. I stepped back and rolled my shoulders, doing whatever I could to calm myself. "I find it interesting you think you need to keep me unarmed in order to have a conversation."

He ignored my statement and sat back down in his chair, his shoulders back and feet planted on the floor. Very formal. "Now then. As I was saying about the demon you challenged."

"Yes."

"While I still maintain it was poor judgment, I understand you managed to stop him from killing an angel. That will help us in relations with the Angel Council."

I said nothing, no longer giving a shit about Chessandra and her ilk. My only concern was Jade.

"But this is going to increase the demon attacks. And you'll be a target."

"Fine."

His eyes narrowed, and he shook his head. "You have no idea what this means."

"I think I do. I also believe that because my wife is already a target, something like this was going to happen anyway. If I were you, I'd learn to accept this as a new reality and then get some sleep, because you need it." I waved a hand toward the door. "Now, can I go check on my wife? It's been a long night."

He snapped his fingers. The magic vanished.

I turned, heading for the door.

"Rouquette?"

"Yes?" I said without turning around.

"Take the angel with you."

Of course he'd demand that. The Brotherhood's relationship with the angels was strained. He wouldn't want anyone here who might try to report back anything we did. Too bad Maximus had been such an ass. I'd never gotten around to telling him what I'd learned about Ezra. If he knew, Maximus wouldn't let the kid out of his sight. He'd use him in some way.

Too late. Ezra wouldn't work with his kind anyway.

"Fine," I said as if it were a huge imposition and then strode out of his office, letting the door slam behind me.

Chapter 16

Jade

"Demon! Stand back!" I ran full out toward my friends. Lailah must have felt the demon behind her, because she spun at almost the exact same time I'd started running. And in her haste, salt sprayed out in front of her from the open container. The bluish-gray demon jumped back, roaring and rubbing at his eyes as he writhed in pain.

"Nice aim," I called as I caught up to her.

She dropped the salt container, because as useful as it was to create a circle, it didn't do anything in a battle other than blind someone temporarily. Magic balled in her palms before the demon could recover, and she started throwing ball after ball of magic at him.

He jumped and lurched, trying to get out of her line of fire, but she hit him almost every time, causing his skin to sizzle with the electric bolts of magic she was tossing his way.

Good—she was keeping him occupied.

I sprinted to Lucien's side. "I'm going to help Lailah. Get everyone else in a circle around us. Fast. Spell the salt if you can, but if you can't don't worry about it. Join everyone's power together, and whatever you do, don't drop it."

"Got it." He took off, running to get the salt, calling orders as he went.

I moved so the demon was between me and Lailah, and I joined her in her assault. When my first stream of magic slammed into him, he turned toward me, his mouth open in a silent objection. His body convulsed under my attack, and a large chunk of blue, leathery skin disengaged and disappeared from his neck, leaving an oozing wound. Disgusting.

Lailah was unfazed and relentless with her magic bombs. I matched her single-minded focus, pouring raw power into him, intending to burn him alive if at all possible. I was taking no chances. Not after what I'd seen demons do in the past.

Only he had his hands stretched out and had managed to form some sort of barrier to keep the bulk of our magic from continuing to burn his wrinkling skin.

He was on the shorter side for a demon, no fangs, over-sized disproportioned head, large ears, and was dressed in contemporary clothes, jeans and a T-shirt. Was he trying to fit in? Usually demons took on some sort of human-looking persona unless they were really old and didn't care about such things. This one either failed or hadn't bothered.

I felt it the moment the coven snapped into place, creating a barrier of magic around us. It solidified my confidence that this demon wasn't laying a hand on anyone. That we'd either end him or send him back to Hell so fast his head would spin.

Then suddenly, Lailah stopped her magical onslaught and stared at the unmoving demon. She held her hand up, signaling me to stop as well.

"Are you mad?" I cried.

She shook her head. "He's not fighting back. I want to know why."

Of course he wasn't. He was too busy holding my power off. Except upon closer observation he was doing that with one hand. There was nothing stopping him from throwing a few curses our way.

I frowned, dropped my magic, and stood perfectly still, ready to attack if he even so much as moved a muscle.

"Why are you here?" Lailah demanded.

The demon cut his gaze to the side and did a slow turn within the circle, eyeing all my members once. Then he met Lailah's pointed stare. "I've been sent with a message."

"Yeah? What's that? You need more innocent souls for your collections?" Lailah practically sneered at him.

He sneered back and scanned the circle with an evil grin. "If anyone wants to volunteer, I'm all too happy to oblige."

I glared at him, noting our magic hadn't really affected him at all. Not one burn mark on his clothes, and his neck had already healed.

"Spit it out," Lailah barked.

The demon rolled his large head and turned his focus to me. "I'm here for your incubus."

Shock rendered me paralyzed, and I stood there saying nothing as I tried to process what he'd just said.

"Why?" Lailah called, her magic building in her palms again.

"He knows why. Tell him we're coming." The demon twisted into a mini vortex and then vanished into thin air.

I took deep breaths, trying to keep myself calm.

Lailah jogged over to me and placed her hand on my arm. "You all right?"

I nodded absently.

"You sure?"

I stared past her to where the demon had stood. "Why did he come here to tell us that?"

She shook her head. "I don't know."

"Kane's a demon hunter. Always going after demons. I don't understand what's different now."

The expression on her face turned to one of sympathy. I was raising questions she couldn't possibly know how to answer, but I had to voice them for my own sanity. Yes, Kane was a demon hunter, but it wasn't like he had demons specifically targeting him. He just fought the ones that invaded our city. Something had happened. I needed to talk to him. I pulled my phone out of my back pocket and pressed his name.

Before it even had a chance to ring, Lailah tugged the phone from my hand. "Not now. We have a calling to do. Remember?"

I glanced around the circle at all the witches watching us intently and took the phone back. "I need to warn him."

"Yeah, okay. But if we want to do this, we should hurry. Who knows when that demon will decide to come back?"

She was right, of course. I turned and met Jasper's wide eyes. He'd never been in a battle before. That was obvious. And he still hadn't, lucky for him. But the demon who'd been here had been scary looking enough to freak anyone out. Instead of calling, I tapped out a quick text to Kane as a precaution to be careful of demons on the lookout for him and hit send.

"Okay. Let's get this done."

"Everyone back on the circle," Lucien ordered. "Quickly."

Lailah and Rosalee rushed around, handing candles to all the coven members. Then, as I took my spot on the northern most point of the circle, Lailah led Jasper into the middle, where the pair of them would act as a catalyst for connecting with Avery, their fellow angel.

"Ready?" I asked everyone.

A subdued murmur of agreement rose from the members.

"Good." I raised my hands out to my sides and held hands with the witches on either side of me. As our hands connected, worry shot through me. The last time I'd done a group spell, the magic had backfired and sucker-punched me in the gut. Would that happen again? Or had it been a one-time thing? There was only one way to find out. Swallowing my nervous energy, I forced myself to focus and said, "This should go quickly. I just ask that you not break the connection until I say otherwise."

More nods.

"Thanks." Closing my eyes, I sucked in a deep breath of the cool air coming off the lake, put everything else out of my mind, and called, "From air, flame, dirt, and sea, hear our call for power, so mote it be."

A spark of magic zipped through each of the witches straight into me. I was filled up with it, almost bursting with their collected power, no pain in sight. It was heady and intoxicating. The kind of magic that could corrupt a weaker individual. The truth was I could probably do the calling all on my own. I didn't want to, and it would suck, but I could. This way was much safer physically but more challenging mentally.

I let go of the witch's hand on my right and then raised my hand palm up, levitating all the candles at once. *"Ignite."*

The candle flames flickered to life, eerily lighting up the faces of all my coven witches.

"With fire, wind, earth, and air, we the New Orleans coven call upon the angel Avery to show us the last time you graced these hallowed shores."

The lake beach wasn't exactly hallowed, but the salt circle and our combined magic had turned it into a workable space.

"Chant with me," I said. "From fire, wind, earth, and air, call upon the angel Avery."

The coven members chanted, louder and louder, until finally I pointed a few feet from Jasper and said, "That's enough."

Everyone shifted to eye the outline of the pretty young woman who I'd only known as Chessandra's assistant. She was standing next to a car, alternating between glancing around and studying her watch. It was obvious she didn't see us. Even in spirit form she should have. Something wasn't right.

Then as she took off toward the lakefront, it hit me—the spell hadn't worked quite the way I'd planned. Instead of summoning Avery's spirit, we'd gotten the memory of her meeting the demon.

Jasper let out a strained gasp as he stared at the echo of the girlfriend he hadn't seen in months.

She had long, dark hair, a tiny frame, and big doe eyes. My hatred for Chessandra only intensified. The angel looked like she could barely handle carrying a multicup coffee tray, much less deal with the evil creatures of the underworld. I was sure she was more capable than my assessment; she just seemed so small, so fragile. As if a demon could snap her in two.

It only made me more determined to find her.

She was carrying a small package, and the boldness in her stride surprised me. She did know she was meeting a demon, didn't she?

Whether she did or didn't, she definitely had a nice dose of self-confidence. Or was that naiveté? Seeing her so unaffected by the possibility of meeting a demon was terrifying.

I ground my teeth together and watched as Avery moved to the edge of the lake and tossed in a pebble. As soon as it plopped in the water, a demon materialized out of thin air.

She smiled and strode toward the clean-cut very human-like demon, who was dressed in a light-gray suit. He was relaxed with one hand in his pocket and the other held out to her in invitation. The only thing about him that said demon was his eyes. They were that same electric green. Not exactly scary.

The two stood together talking for what seemed like forever. But it must've only been a few minutes at best. Then Avery leaned in and pecked him on the cheek.

A kiss? Holy crap. Even if it did stay completely platonic, she'd still kissed a demon. I glanced over at Jasper. He stood frozen, his face twisted into shocked horror as he gaped.

I returned my attention to Avery just as the well-dressed demon morphed into a red, leathery giant. He let out a loud growl. Or was that a mew? Hard to say. The demon had a weird expression on his face. I couldn't tell if he was happy or mildly irritated.

Avery reached a tentative hand up to the demon's face and cupped the sunken area of his would-be cheek. The gesture was so tender. It would've been moving if I hadn't known he was a demon. A true beauty-and-the-beast moment.

"Avery! What are you doing?" Jasper cried from the middle of our circle. I heard Lailah whisper something, but I couldn't make it out. My heart broke for him. To be standing here watching this knowing there was nothing he could do must've been torture.

The demon glanced down at Avery. He let out what I thought might be a moan of frustration and, in one quick movement, scooped her up into his arms. She seemed frozen in the moment, her eyes wide with fear. Then panic set in and she started flailing her arms and legs, punching and kicking as she fought for her freedom.

"You son of a bitch!" Jasper yelled. "Let her go."

I wanted to call out, too, do something to save her, but we were only watching an impression. She wasn't really there, and neither was the demon.

The demon tilted his head down so they were eye to eye. Avery stilled, her fists clenched, ready to strike as she watched him study her. His expression softened, and for a second I thought he was going to put her down, but a fiery pit opened up right there in the sand.

Avery opened her mouth wide, no doubt unleashing a horrified scream just as the demon stepped forward, both of them disappearing into the pit of Hell.

Chapter 17

Jade

"No!" Jasper cried, running into the circle. He slid to his knees at the exact spot Avery had vanished from.

Silence filled the air. No one even moved, too stunned to do anything.

"Why?" Jasper pounded his fists on the earth, gut-wrenching agony pouring from him. His emotions filled the circle, pressing in on me from all sides. Tears filled my eyes as I struggled to erect my barriers to shut him out. But it was useless. The force of his pain was too much for me to escape.

I took a few steps back, distancing myself from him, trying to maintain even a modicum of sanity. But my efforts were fruitless, and no matter what I did, I was trapped in his grief.

Lailah moved forward, bright-white light shimmering around her. When she reached his side, she wrapped an arm around him, rocking with him through the pain. With her help, the intensity of his emotional energy was reined in, and I was able to breathe easier. Thank the gods she was here, or I'd have been sobbing right beside Jasper.

I took a deep breath and turned to address the coven members. "Okay, everyone. I think that's enough for tonight. Thank you for coming. I appreciate it."

Most of them answered with silent nods and then started heading back to the cars. Everyone except Rosalee. She stood on the circle watching Jasper, her posture rigid. Anger and bitter disappointment consumed her and streamed off in the form of red smoke.

"Rosalee?" I positioned myself beside her but was careful to keep my distance. The raw emotions were too much for me to handle. "Are you okay?"

She turned to me, fire blazing in her dark eyes. "No. Not even close to okay. We have to summon her. Avery, I mean. We can't leave her in Hell."

"Yes, we do. But we can't right now. Nor can we do it here. It's too dangerous. We have to do that at the coven circle. You know that."

"But she could fall at any minute." Rosalee clutched my arm, her fierce determination rushing into me, warring with common sense.

I pulled back, fighting to keep from being overwhelmed by her intensity. It was all I could do to ignore my own convictions of what I wanted versus what was safe and practical. If I could, I'd summon Avery right then and there. She was an angel. When angels were trapped in Hell it usually didn't take long before their souls were corrupted and they turned demon. If she'd already suffered that fate, we'd put everyone at risk. I was already acutely aware that what had gone down with the first demon earlier wasn't normal. Not at all. It was clear he'd only been here to deliver a message. If he'd wanted to, he could've caused considerable damage.

A long time ago, my own mother had tried to save an angel from falling by summoning her from Hell. Unfortunately her friend, Meri, had already fallen. The result was that two other witches along with my mom had been taken that day and had gone missing for fifteen years. It was unthinkable to put my coven at that kind of risk. I wouldn't under any circumstances. Precautions needed to be put in place.

"I promise you that tomorrow we'll do the summoning. One way or another. We'll get Bea and Kane and whoever else we need to be on hand in order to safely bring her back. But you have to be prepared for the worst possible outcome. If she's already turned, we can't help her."

Rosalee stared at her feet. Frustration replaced the righteousness that had been overwhelming her. "Tomorrow. What time?"

"I'm not sure, but probably at night. The moon helps." I shifted close to her and squeezed her hand briefly, just enough to let her know I understood.

She glanced up, meeting my gaze head on. "Avery was a friend of mine. Whatever I can do to bring her back I will."

"I understand," I said, blinking back the tears in my eyes.

She nodded once and left without another word.

Weariness washed over me as I watched her go. A lot had happened in the last two days. All I wanted to do was go home, find Kane, and sleep for a week.

Most of the coven had already dispersed, anxious to get away from anything demon related. The only people left were Lucien, Lailah, and Jasper.

Lucien was collecting the candles, while Lailah did her best to calm Jasper. I hesitated and then joined Lucien, grateful for something to do.

"We're going to have to summon Avery tomorrow," I told him.

He nodded. "I figured as much."

"You can't tell Kat."

He straightened, a grimace claiming his lips. "You know that's not going to work out. It never does."

Dread formed in the pit of my stomach. "You're right. But she'll want to be there if she knows. And as much as I hate it, she's a weakness for both of us. If a demon does show up, not only is she at risk, but so are we. You and I both know we'll compromise whatever we're doing to keep her safe."

Kat didn't have magic. When it came to demon battles, she was a liability mostly because she could be used to manipulate me and Lucien.

"Don't you think honesty might work better?" he asked.

I gave him a look. "And how's that worked for you in the past?"

"Crap."

"Exactly." Guilt settled in my gut, and I softened. "Listen, I'm not asking you to lie. Maybe just don't tell her exactly what we're up to?"

His dubious expression didn't do anything to put my mind at ease.

"Okay, fine. Tell her if you must, but be sure to also say that I forbid her to join us for this one."

Lucien snorted, and I knew he was thinking this wasn't a battle either of us would win. Kat was too invested in both of us. It was highly unlikely she would sit around waiting to find out what happened.

"Just do your best."

He saluted me. "Whatever you say, chief." Holding the box of candles, he waved and took off for his Jeep.

Lailah had Jasper tucked under one arm and was walking him toward Kane's car.

I stood on the shore, staring out at the vast lake, feeling small and insignificant against the inky darkness. And utterly alone. It was time to go home. To find Kane. And to settle into his arms and pray the events of the last two days weren't a sign of our year to come.

Kane

I stalked down the hallway from Maximus's office, throwing doors open as I went. His private residence seemed to have more bedrooms than Summer House, my family plantation home in Cypress Settlement. For a single man, his space was somewhat ridiculous.

Grumbling to myself, I reached for the doorknob to the room at the end of the hall, but it swung open, and there was Ezra, his face scrunched up in confusion.

"What's going on?" he asked.

"We're getting out of here." I gestured for him to join me, but he just stood there, blinking. "What?" I barked.

"Where are we?"

"My boss's private residence. And we've worn out our welcome." I jerked my head, and without waiting, I stormed back to the room I'd woken up in. Inside, I searched high and low for my dagger, but it wasn't anywhere to be found. "Son of a bitch."

"Problem?" Ezra asked, sounding much more awake.

"No. Let's go."

He followed me to the stairs, down to the first floor, and out to the grounds. The damp grass was cool on my bare feet, reminding me I didn't even have shoes and pissing me off all over again. Depriving me of my things and my dagger was Maximus's way of showing me who had the upper hand. I didn't much care about my clothes or my shoes or even my phone. The dagger, though, that was another thing altogether.

I'd have to find a way to get another one. Fast. They were assigned, so it'd be tricky, but perhaps I could borrow one from the Brotherhood's arsenal. I glanced to the left at the main house, considering. But then I shook my head. Now wasn't the time. The place was locked up tight for another few hours.

"Where are we going?" Ezra asked, keeping pace with me as we headed toward the gate.

"Home."

He glanced around. "You live around here?"

"Nope." The moment we crossed the property line of the Brotherhood compound, I held my hand out to the angel. "Take my hand."

He stared at it.

"We're shadow walking. Grab my arm if that makes you more comfortable. It's the fastest way to a shower and a hot meal."

After a moment, Ezra finally wrapped his hand around my wrist, creating the connection we needed. With one step, the world twisted into a blur of gray fog. The sensation only lasted a second, and then my feet hit solid ground and the world came back into focus.

Ezra, however, stumbled and fell to one knee upon impact.

"You all right, man?" I asked, pulling him up with one hand.

"Yeah." He got his feet underneath him quickly and shook me off. "Fine."

I started up the stairs to my house but stopped mid-step and glanced back at Ezra. "You coming?"

He shook his head and started off down the street.

"Hey," I called. "We still need to talk about your visit with that demon."

"I'll be in touch," he said without looking back.

I briefly thought about stopping him, forcing him to come into the house to finish that conversation, but the fatigue plaguing me, and the desire to be alone with Jade was far too great. Chessandra and her demon bullshit could wait.

I climbed the last two steps onto the porch and swore, realizing I didn't have a house key. All my personal items were somewhere in the Brotherhood compound. I reached for the door handle on the off chance the door had been left unlocked, but before my fingers closed over the smooth metal, the door swung open, and Jade stood in the threshold, a huge smile on her face.

"You're home!" she cried and launched herself at me.

I caught her, barely keeping from stumbling off the porch. Her legs wrapped around my waist, and as our lips met, I carried her back into the house, kicking the door shut behind us.

Chapter 18

Jade

Kane carried me straight to the bedroom, not breaking his stride once. His mouth was on me, devouring me with rough, insistent demands. A rush of heat sizzled between us as I met his fervor with one of my own, biting, tasting, and claiming him as mine. My entire body hummed with desire while simultaneously melting into him.

He stopped in the middle of our room, turned and sat on the bed with me straddling him. The need in his expression took my breath away. It was raw and powerful and touched me deep in my soul.

"Kane," I whispered.

He met my eyes for just a moment and then tightened his arms around me, kissing me slowly, deliberately, taking his time to savor the love consuming us both.

Burying one hand in his thick hair, I cupped his cheek with the other and pulled back, breathless. "Hey, you."

His lips twitched into a ghost of a smile. "Hey."

I kissed the corner of his mouth and whispered, "Where've you been?"

His rich chocolate-brown eyes darkened and the smile vanished. "Demon fights and a disagreement with Maximus.

A lot of bullshit." Reaching up, he ran his fingers through my hair, studying me. "I'm sorry I was gone so long."

I shook my head. "You had a job to do."

"Yeah." The word was clipped, and resentment filled him. Because we were so connected, we both tensed. It was almost impossible for me to block out his emotions. He must've felt me stiffen, because he took a deliberate breath and let it out slowly. "Sorry," he said again. "There are things you need to know, but right now all I want is you."

The tenderness in his voice had me melting all over again. And the way his fingers were digging into my waist as if he never wanted to let go told me he really needed me at that moment. Not just physically but emotionally.

"It's okay. I have things to tell you, too."

He nodded once and then trailed his fingers down my neck, sending goose bumps rippling over my skin. "You're so beautiful."

I chuckled. "At five a.m. after I've been lying awake all night? Not likely."

When I'd gotten home after the calling at the lake and saw Kane still hadn't been home and that he hadn't called, I'd lain in bed staring at the ceiling, imagining the worst. At one point, sleep had been so elusive, I'd gotten up and made a cup of hot cocoa just for something to do. The full cup was still sitting on the nightstand.

"You're always beautiful, but right now, with your mussed hair and bright eyes, you're the most gorgeous thing I've ever seen." He ran his other hand up my bare arm to my shoulder and traced two fingers over my collarbone.

His light touch sent a delicious shiver over my skin, and I stretched my head to the side, giving him full access, ready to purr like a kitten. "That feels amazing."

"Yeah? How about this?" He leaned in and sucked my lower lip between his teeth, nibbling gently.

"Mmm," I moaned, heat shooting to my center. Pressing into him, I smiled when I felt him harden beneath me. We hadn't even been apart more than twenty-four hours, but so much had happened, it felt like days.

"I need you, Jade," Kane said, his voice a hoarse whisper. One hand moved to my upper thigh, his fingers digging into my flesh. He pulled back, staring at me with a pained expression. "I'm not going to be able to control myself."

That delicious heat spread everywhere, lighting my entire body on fire. God, I wanted him. Wild and on the edge of sanity, lost in the magic that bound us together. But reality crashed around me. The curse. My mind warred with my body's desire to ignore everything around us. To give him everything I knew he needed. I took a deep breath, clearing the lust haze. "Right now, that's the last thing I want you to do—"

He stood abruptly, almost knocking me on my ass, but caught me just in time and held me at arm's length. "Don't say that to me right now."

I swallowed the sexual frustration threatening to consume me, and in a soft voice said, "If you'd have let me finish, I was going to say that there are other things we can do. Things that won't result in pregnancy."

"You're sure?" His gaze searched mine. We both knew the suggestion wasn't ideal. Magic passed between us more easily and with more control when we were fully joined in the act of love, but this was hardly a sacrifice. I wanted him in any way I could have him.

"I'm sure," I said, my voice full of desire. "I want you, your hands, your lips, your mouth everywhere."

The tight expression on his face vanished, replaced by sultry determination shining back at me through his slightly narrowed eyes. He dropped his hold on me. "Show me, Jade. Where do you want my tongue first?"

His words touched that primal spot deep inside me, making everything tingle. My brain disconnected, and all I saw was my beautiful Kane standing before me, impatient with need.

My mouth went dry, and my nipples tightened.

He took a step forward and brushed his thumb over my cheek, and whispered, "I'm waiting."

I smiled, my heart squeezing from the love shining back at me. And then I reached down and pulled the cotton sleep shirt off, leaving me completely bare. Taking a step back, I trailed my fingers over my hip and up until I was cupping my breast. If he wanted to know what I needed, he was getting a full demonstration.

Using my thumb and forefinger, I gently squeezed my already taut nipple. Delicious pain rippled through me straight to my core, and I let out a tiny gasp of pleasure.

Intense need shot from Kane and straight into me, lighting a fire inside me so fierce I felt as if I were burning alive. Every nerve was so sensitive that I feared one touch would set me off.

"Tell me, Jade," Kane coaxed again. "What do you want me to do to you?"

Still pinching my nipple, I glanced down. "I want you to scrape your teeth over me right here until I gasp and shudder."

His eyes focused on my breast as he watched me tease myself.

"And then I want you to bite me."

"Oh, son of a…" Kane raised his heated gaze and took a half step toward me but then stopped himself. Balling his hand into a fist, he said, "And after that?"

Damn, he had control. Deserved a medal. I flattened my other hand across my belly and slowly inched my way down.

His breath quickened.

Bypassing my center, my fingers teased my inner thigh. "I want to be kissed here."

"Just there?"

I shook my head and moved my hand up until one finger found my slick heat. My muscles quivered from my touch, and as I imagined him taking over, a moan escaped my parted lips.

"Say it, Jade," Kane whispered.

"I want your tongue here."

He moved in close, his hot body brushing up against mine. The hard lines of his muscles sent ripples of unending yearning through my entire body, and I fought to not arch into him. "And once I'm done making you come with my mouth? Then what, love?"

I reached down and slid my hand into his pants, palming his thick length. I wrapped my fingers around him, caressing his velvety flesh. "Then…" I kissed my way up his neck, pausing to dart my tongue over his rapidly beating pulse. "Then, Kane, it's your turn. I'm going to take you deep into my mouth, torture you with my tongue, and make you forget your own name."

His shaft quivered under my touch, his breathing ragged and hot against my skin.

"That is, if you can last that long," I teased.

A low growl emanated from him as he grabbed me and flipped me onto my back on the bed. He hovered over me, his knee between my thighs, me completely naked while he was still fully clothed.

I felt wicked in the best possible way, ready for him to devour me, to possess me. To make me feel intensely, to know deep in my soul that I belonged to him and only him.

He lowered his mouth, stopping inches from mine, and whispered, "I'm going to show you exactly how thoroughly a man can love you."

Shivers took over my body, and I trembled beneath him.

He nibbled on my lower lip and pulled away. "Cold?"

I smiled and shook my head.

"That's what I thought." Then he lowered his head to my neck and kissed his way down to the swell of my breast.

I sucked in a sharp breath, anticipating his next move.

He chuckled against my skin and cupped my breasts, feeling the weight of them in his hands before moving down my body, alternately flicking his tongue and nipping my sensitive flesh. "You're burning up," he said hungrily and before I could answer, he clasped his teeth around one nipple, while using his fingers to pinch the other. Pleasure and sweet pain intertwined, and I arched, pushing myself against his mouth, demanding he give me more.

He answered by biting harder.

And in that moment, my magic flared to life and formed a connection with Kane. Everywhere he touched me, magic sparked between us, sending tiny shocks over my skin. It was a sensation unlike anything I'd ever felt. Delicate and yet a whisper of power. A force that could consume us both if I let it.

"There it is," Kane said huskily as he ran his hand down the center of my chest, sending those sparks over both of us. His lust-filled eyes met mine, and I swear I saw the magic dancing there in his heated gaze.

"Kiss me," I said.

He didn't hesitate. His lips claimed mine, and we ravaged each other, hands everywhere. And before I knew it, he was working his way down my body and had his mouth on my center. His first taste made me jerk my hips, begging for more.

He lifted his head, staring me in the eye. "While I'm torturing you, I want you to imagine me burying myself inside you, claiming you with each and every torturous thrust."

"Oh, God," I said, closing my eyes against the storm rolling through my center.

"Imagine me taking you hard and fast and deep."

"Kane," I begged, my body nearly convulsing just from his words. "Please."

"You're mine, Jade." He dipped his head, licking, sucking, and tasting. Everything pulsed. I was drowning in sensation, losing myself as I came totally undone, my magic sparking out of control around us in the form of tiny bolts of light. And then he shifted, and his fingers thrust up into me, making good on his promise to take me hard and deep.

My body tensed, and I cried out, waves of ecstasy crashing through me, leaving me boneless and completely satisfied.

I lay there, soft and pliable, as he repositioned himself and rested his head on my stomach. "You're gorgeous when you come."

I couldn't help my pleased smile and felt the flush claiming my cheeks. "You're gorgeous when making me come."

His hand tightened around my thigh, and it was then I snapped out of my postorgasm haze and felt the intoxicating sexual tension still streaming from him. He was barely holding on, nearly going crazy from lack of release.

"Kane?" I said.

"Yes, love?" he mumbled against my hip between heated kisses.

"It's your turn."

He stilled and glanced up at me, hunger consuming his expression.

I sat up, crooking my finger in a silent demand.

Kane's eyes gleamed as he pushed himself up and kneeled before me on the bed. He ran one hand down my bare arm, the heat of his touch igniting something primal within me.

I grabbed at his T-shirt and roughly pulled it off, breaking our eye contact for just a moment. There was so much emotion there, showing so much more than just his physical desire. Love, trust, vulnerability. My heart swelled.

But when his hands reached for me and connected with my skin again, his desire slammed into me once more, and I gave myself over to it. I reached for his pants, sliding them over his hips.

He quickly discarded them and then rolled onto his back on the bed, taking me with him. I lay on top of him, kissing him with all the welled-up passion pulsing between us.

"Jade," Kane said in a strangled voice. "I need you to touch me."

A devilish smiled claimed my lips as I trailed my hand down his side and moved to wrap my fingers around his pulsing shaft. "Like this?"

"God, yes." He closed his eyes and pressed his head back into the pillow, thrusting his hips up against my touch. The muscles in his neck strained with his will to control himself. How he'd lasted this long was a mystery to me.

"Just relax." I pressed quick, hot kisses against his chest, moving lower and lower, until I felt the angry red scars marring his abdomen. I stopped abruptly and jerked my head up. "Kane?"

"It's all right, love. I'll explain later."

"But—"

He reached out and caressed my cheek. "Honestly. I'm all right. All I need right now is you."

He pulled me up so I was straddling him and kissed me. Hard. His hands were everywhere, my breasts, my thighs, my ass. "You just feel so damned good. Perfect in every way."

The roughness in his voice, the way his body pulsed with physical need, and the way he felt wrapped in my arms was enough to push the worry from my mind. He was very much alive and all mine.

My power blossomed again and engulfed both of us as I kissed him, my tongue darting over his. I tightened my arms around him, needing to feel his hard body pressed to mine. It was then he started to tremble, almost unable to contain himself any longer.

I broke our kiss, pushed him down on his back, and, with my eyes locked on his, I slowly inched my way down the bed. Wrapping my hand around his shaft once more, I said, "Tell me what you need."

"You," he growled. "Your mouth. Work me until I come so hard, I can barely remember my own name."

Damn, that was hot. His words fueled the fire already burning within me, and I lowered my head, at first just tasting his swollen tip.

"Yes." He buried one hand in my hair and gently fisted it while the other clutched at the bed sheet.

Pleased with his response, I moved my hand to the base of his cock and took him deeper, feeling him grow even harder. Magic pulsed around us, his arousal pulling it from me. I gave it up willingly and moved my mouth over him, slowly first, then faster and faster, until his breathing was ragged and my magic pulsed with an almost painful intensity.

I took him even deeper, stroking him at the same time. His body tensed just before his hips unwillingly thrust up, and he spilled into me with a loud groan. I'd barely released him and swallowed when magic tore from my chest, streaming into him with such force we were both immobilized with the intensity of it.

It was terrifying and wondrous at the same time. The power heady, yet dangerous. And neither of us could control it.

Chapter 19

Kane

It was still early, just past seven, but I was wide awake watching my naked wife sleep soundly beside me. I should've kept my hands to myself, but I couldn't resist the urge to caress her porcelain skin. Propped up on my elbow, I lazily trailed my fingers over the soft curve of her hip.

"That's nice," she murmured in a sleepy voice.

I pressed a light kiss to her shoulder. A spark of magic tingled where my lips met her flesh, and she laughed.

"Seems you're recharged," she said without opening her eyes.

"Thanks to you."

She sighed and turned her head into the pillow, sleep already pulling her under.

There was little hope of me catching more Zs. Between the magic-induced sleep from the healer and the raw power Jade had transferred to me, I had more energy than I knew what to do with.

I waited until I saw Jade's chest rise and fall in a steady, rhythmic pattern and then rose and headed for the shower. I spent a long time standing under the spray of water trying to figure out my next move. Head back to the Brotherhood to find my dagger? Contact one of my brothers to look for it or help me secure a new one? If I went myself, I could look up the contract Ezra had shown me. See if the Brotherhood had any details on record of Chessa's transaction.

That's what I'd do. If she had dirty dealings with demons, the magical community needed to know about it. Not to mention I wouldn't hesitate to use anything I found to get Jade and myself out from under the high angel's thumb. Working for her had become too dangerous. Locking us away in the angel realm had crossed the line.

I was acutely aware there were no guarantees I'd find anything, but I had to check. At the very least there would likely be some background on Wes Lancaster. Maybe some clue as to why Chessandra was associating with him.

When I finally emerged from the bathroom with just a towel wrapped around my hips, the early-morning sun was streaming in the window. The sun splashed over Jade and her perfect naked breasts. Desire flooded back from just the sight of her and, unable to help myself, I crawled onto the bed, leaned over her, and brushed a kiss over her pouty lips.

I felt her smile, and then she kissed me back, her hands pressed against my chest.

"Good morning," I whispered, ignoring the slight twinge of guilt for waking her up again.

"Hmm." She slid one hand up over the back of my neck and pulled me down, tasting me as if she hadn't sampled me in days. My muscles tightened beneath her touch, and I felt myself stiffen and ache for her.

God, I wanted her. But even if we could make love, it was the last thing we should be doing after the power transfer we'd exchanged earlier. Judging by how much magic I had at the moment, I was willing to bet she'd completely depleted her reserves. She'd passed out almost immediately afterward, so it was likely she hadn't realized the full extent of what we'd done. Allowing this to go further before she knew her limits was reckless.

With a groan, I rolled to the side, flopping on the bed beside her.

"Hey, where'd you go?" she asked, curling into me.

"Nowhere. I'm right here." I gently kissed her temple and ran my fingers through her hair.

"But I thought…" She trailed her fingertips over my pecs.

"I know. But it's not a good idea. Not right now."

She opened her eyes and propped herself up on one elbow. "You're turning down sex?"

I laughed at the incredulity in her tone. "Not because I want to, believe me." I closed my hand over hers. "If you don't stop touching me like that, my control is going to be nonexistent."

Her brow furrowed. "Is it the curse?" She sent me a sexy little smile. "I thought we'd already proved there's more than one way to get the job done."

"It's not the curse." I brought her fingers up to my lips and kissed them. "It's this." I traced her wrist and forearm, leaving a shimmering trail of magic everywhere I touched her.

Her breath caught, and her expression turned serious as she focused on an unlit candle sitting on the dresser across the room. After a moment, she let out the air and groaned. "Oh, damn."

"Magic not working?"

"Yeah. I can feel it fluttering beneath my breastbone, but I can't call it."

Dammit. That was what I was afraid of. "I'm sorry, love. I didn't mean to take that much."

She shook her head. "You didn't. I mean, it was both of us. We were both out of control, and besides, I'd have given it to you willingly, anyway. It felt like you needed it."

"You weren't wrong." Still holding her hand, I moved it to my abdomen and guided her fingers over the raised scars, courtesy of Malstord.

She sat up, her eyes narrowed in concentration.

I held perfectly still, waiting for her to process what she was seeing.

She turned to me, surprise lighting her eyes. "They healed."

I nodded. Her explosion of magic had been powerful enough that the swelling had gone down, and the scars were now a fleshy pink instead of angry red. "They don't hurt anymore, either."

Her eyes narrowed. "You were in pain last night?"

"A bit." I shrugged and grinned at her. "I had other things on my mind."

"Clearly." She shook her head, amusement dancing in her eyes. But then she sobered. "What happened?"

"Demon attack."

"You don't say?" she said dryly.

I cracked an ironic smile. "I might have issued him a sanctioned challenge."

Her eyebrows rose and disappeared under her bangs. "You did what?"

I slid off the bed and walked to the dresser, feeling entirely too exposed in only the towel. *Damn. That's messed up.* This was Jade I was talking to. I glanced back at her, only to find she'd covered her naked body with a sheet.

Guess I wasn't the only one feeling uncomfortable.

After pulling on jeans and a T-shirt, I grabbed her robe and brought it to her. "Want to talk about this over coffee?"

She bit her lip and nodded.

I brushed her hair out of her eyes and gave her another quick kiss. "I'll get it started."

She clutched her robe. "I'll be right there."

Leaving her in the bedroom, I headed out to the kitchen and got to work on coffee. Once I had the pot filled, I moved on to breakfast. Omelets, because I didn't think this was a conversation we should have on empty stomachs. Plus Jade needed the nourishment.

The thought of her not being able to call her magic had me scowling. I'd definitely taken too much of her power. Had left her vulnerable at a time when she was a target. That was on me no matter what she said. I had the ability to control what I took, and instead of worrying about her, I'd taken everything she'd offered. Like a selfish bastard.

And the more I thought about it, the more frustrated I became. My hand closed over the egg I was holding, and before I knew it, the thing cracked, and egg slime slipped through my fingers.

"Son of a bitch!" I flung the mess into the sink and yanked the faucet on hard enough that the handle flew right off. "Goddammit!"

Water sprayed into the kitchen and all over me as I fumbled around trying to stop the water with my bare hands.

Jade appeared and watched me for a second, her head tilted to the side. Then she calmly walked over, opened the bottom cabinet, reached in, and turned the water off. She smiled at me as she poured herself some coffee.

I, on the other hand, stood there, soaking wet, like a damned fool. "Shit," I muttered and disappeared into the laundry room to grab a couple clean towels. After I wiped the kitchen down, I went back to work on the omelets, my irritation with myself growing by the minute.

When the omelets were done, I grabbed my own cup of coffee and the two plates and sat across from Jade.

She nodded her thanks and took a bite.

I didn't. My appetite had vanished.

She ate a third of her breakfast, then suddenly dropped her fork and pierced me with her stare, her smile long gone. "You want to tell me what's going on?"

I took a sip of my coffee, deliberately delaying my answer. I knew what she was asking. She wanted to know why I'd clammed up, why I'd suddenly turned into a raving asshole in the kitchen. But I wasn't ready to voice what was eating me up inside. "I have to go to the Brotherhood to do a records search."

Her eyes narrowed and her brow pinched in confusion. "You're leaving? Now?"

"Yes. I have something to do, but I'll be back soon. We can talk then."

Anger flashed in her brilliant green eyes. "You're joking, right? I can't believe you're talking about going to the Brotherhood without explaining what happened with that demon yesterday. Or filling me in on why you were tearing apart our kitchen. Whatever happened to 'let's discuss this over coffee?'"

She was fierce, her hands balled into fists as she pressed them into the table. Even without her magic, she looked like she could take on just about anyone and cut them down to size.

I leaned back in the chair, forcing out a breath. My chest was tight, and I felt like a twenty-pound boulder was weighing me down.

"Kane?" The anger had fled, and all that was left was worry. "Please tell me what's going on."

"Shit." I stood, running a hand through my hair. Forcing down all the self-doubt and shame trying to choke me, I rounded the table and pulled her into my arms. She stiffened, and I pulled back, meeting her troubled gaze. "I'm sorry."

"Kane you don't need to—"

I held my hand up and leaned against the island that separated our kitchen from our dining room. "I *am* sorry, Jade. What's happened to you? To us? It's thrown me for a loop. The fact that someone has cursed you and our future child is messing with my head. And after I realized I'd taken so much of your power that I'd left you vulnerable, I got really angry with myself. I know you're strong, that you're more than capable of taking care of yourself, but that doesn't mean I don't have a deep-seated need to protect you. To keep you far away from anyone who might hurt you." I averted my eyes. "Even me."

"Kane, look at me."

I reluctantly did as she asked.

Her expression softened, understanding dawning in her eyes. She took two steps and slipped her hands into mine. "*You* could never hurt me. Not like that."

"But I—"

"No," she said without any heat in her tone. "I heard what you said. Now it's my turn to talk. I know how you feel. Don't you think I go through the same thing every time someone I love is caught in the crosshairs of some magical disaster?"

I released her hand and ran my thumb over her jawline. "No one was caught in the middle of anything, love. This was me taking something from you. Something you need." I swallowed and rested my chin on the top of her head. In a whisper I added, "Do you have any idea what that does to a man? To know not only that I'm failing at protecting you but that I'm weakening you in the process?"

"Is that really what you think?"

I jerked and met her determined stare. "Well, yes."

"That you're failing me? That you somehow stole my magic?"

"Yes."

"Goddess above, Kane. Don't be an idiot." She shook her head. "I gave it to you. You couldn't have stopped me if you tried." Her lips curved into a small smile. "And if you think I wouldn't lay my life on the line for you, then you haven't been paying attention. Just like I know you'd do the same for me. The day we married, we became partners. Equal partners. In my heart, I know you agree with me. But maybe you need to be reminded."

Silence hung between us as I let her words sink in. She was right, of course. It didn't change the fact that I hated I was the reason her power was depleted, but it did help me accept it. I leaned in and kissed her gently on her forehead. "Thanks, love."

She reached up and brushed a fallen lock of hair out of my eyes. "You're welcome. Now, do you want to tell me what I missed?"

I nodded and leaned against the counter again. "Yesterday the Brotherhood was summoned to a demon invasion. Nothing too unusual at first, but then as the fight started, I noticed an angel. A young man. And he was moments from being killed."

"Oh, no." Her hand went to her throat, horror now claiming her beautiful face. "Please tell me he didn't die."

"No, he didn't, because I managed to distract the demon by extending the sanctioned challenge. And I justified the challenge by telling myself that if I saved the angel, it would reduce the tension that's been escalating between the Brotherhood and the Angel Council."

"But that's not why you really did it?" she asked with remarkable calm, no doubt feeling my conflicted emotions spewing from me.

I shook my head. "No. It's because he knew about the curse on you and our child…" My voice broke on the word *child*.

Jade's eyes misted with tears.

"And I lost it," I forced out, realizing for the first time exactly how much I wanted to start a family with Jade. Pain pierced my heart, knowing there was nothing we could do about it until we broke the curse.

Closing my eyes, I took a deep breath and tried to let go of the anger creeping its way back into my gut. "He knew, Jade. I can't even begin to tell you how that affected me. It scared me deep in my soul. I know the curse was done by an angel, but if the demons know, too, there's no doubt our child is destined to be in the middle of an angel–demon war. And I won't have it. Won't have anyone thinking they can touch you or our child. They'll have to go through me first. So I put myself in grave danger to prove a point. Can you forgive me for that?"

"Oh, Kane," she breathed, wrapping her arms around me and pressing her head to my chest. "There's nothing to forgive. You did what you had to do. No matter the reason, the fact is you did save an angel from death. That's noble. Something to be celebrated. And maybe you were protecting me in the process. There's no denying that demon won't be coming for me or our child now. Not as long as he's locked in Hell."

Our child. The image of Jade, her belly swollen with my child, flashed in my mind. It was enough to gut me. And I knew without a doubt I'd made the right choice challenging the demon. I'd do it again in a heartbeat. Anything to protect what was mine.

"You're probably right," I said, giving her a ghost of a smile. "Hopefully you'll remember this conversation the next time I lose my shit when someone's trying to hurt you."

"Just take it out on them and don't go caveman on our kitchen, all right?"

"Deal." I cupped her cheeks with my palms, gazing into her too-bright eyes. Raw emotions shone back at me, making my breath catch. God, she did things to me. The way she embodied such pure innocence at times but also had the ability to destroy the worst kind of evil was intoxicating. Good. Intense. Powerful. She was everything I ever wanted.

She reached up, trailing her fingers over my brow. Then she licked her lips and said, "Kiss me."

Powerless to her command, I lowered my head and pressed my lips to hers as I explored the curves of her hips. "What was that you said about not going caveman?"

She laughed softly. "I said don't go caveman in the kitchen. I didn't say anything about the bedroom."

Smiling, I lifted her into my arms and carried her back to bed, where I worshipped her until her soft cries filled the room.

Chapter 20

Jade

The chill in the late-morning air made me shiver as I walked the uneven streets of the French Quarter.

I pressed my hand to my abdomen, thinking about Kane's scars and remembering the pain I'd suffered the day before. I hadn't said anything to him, not after he'd been so upset about weakening me, but it seemed to me that my incident had happened right about the same time he'd been battling the demon. Had I experienced his pain? It was possible, I guessed. Because of my empath ability, I often felt his emotions as mine, but never his physical sensations.

Then again, he'd never almost died before either.

I shuddered as a chill ran over me.

He was fine. I was fine. I couldn't think about that now. I had work to do.

The day was overcast and slightly drizzly, which was a bummer, considering I was bound and determined to summon Avery from Hell later that night. The cloud cover and rain posed a bit of a challenge. Clear conditions were always better for summonings, but waiting wasn't an option.

At least I didn't need to worry too much about my magic anymore. After the morning's bedroom activities with Kane, my body hummed with enough energy to do what I needed to do. Kane had taken the lead and pleasured me until I'd gasped his name. And then he'd refused to let me do the same for him, saying I'd already given him what he needed earlier. As much as I wanted a two-way street when we were in the bedroom, I couldn't complain. His purpose was to give me back some of my power, and he'd succeeded.

Now I was on my way to Bea's shop, while Kane was headed to the Brotherhood to retrieve his dagger and to check out the records department.

The streets were mostly empty. It was mid-January, that time between New Year's and Mardi Gras that usually suffered a lull in tourists. This year was no exception, much to my relief. Dealing with demons and missing angels was quite enough without having to worry about navigating through hordes of partiers.

I strode through the door of the Herbal Connection and smiled as the familiar scents soothed me. Flickering candles lined the walls, creating a cozy atmosphere on the cool day.

"Bea?" I called, heading for the back room.

"Jade?" She popped out from behind a shelf, her hair mussed and her lipstick smudged.

"Uh, hi." What the heck was she doing back there? And with whom? "Sorry. I didn't mean to interrupt—"

"No, dear. You're not interrupting." She patted her hair and then straightened her red silk blouse. "I was just helping Maximus find a charm he was looking for."

"Oh?"

The demon hunter in question appeared, her red lipstick staining his cheek. He held up a truth charm. "Got it."

"Hello, Maximus," I said coolly. Right before I'd left the house, Kane had filled me in on their confrontation.

"Ms. Calhoun, it's nice to see you."

"Is it?" I asked, wondering exactly where Kane and I stood with the Brotherhood leader.

"Jade." Bea put her hand on my arm. "Maximus is here to talk about the curse. He wants to help if possible."

"Really?" I raised my eyebrows and fixed him with a stare.

"Yes, really," he said. "I was taken off guard by the revelation that your future child had been threatened. Had I known, I'm quite certain my conversation with your husband would've gone differently, and I regret the heated exchange we shared. Harming an innocent is beyond unacceptable."

"I see." My shoulders relaxed slightly, but I didn't completely let my guard down. Trust was getting harder to come by. "Thank you for that. We can use all the help we can get."

"You're welcome. I'm not sure what the correct course of action is at this time, but I assure you, the Brotherhood is on your side." He gave me a reassuring smile and then strolled to the checkout counter, oozing with dignity despite his slightly disheveled appearance.

I leaned into Bea. "You might want to refresh your lipstick."

Her hand flew to her mouth as she flushed pink.

"Busted." I grinned at her. "I'll be in the back while you, uh…take care of your customer."

"Oh, stop." She laughed and nudged me toward the lab. "Go see Lailah and Zoe. I'll be there in a minute."

"Just keep it clean out here." I winked and stepped through the door marked *Employees Only*.

Lailah and Zoe were seated at Lailah's stainless steel station, Lailah watching as Zoe chanted an incantation over a potion. I hung back, not wanting to interrupt.

Zoe had her eyes closed and her hands flat over a glass bowl of pale-pink liquid. "From the depths of the collective soul, may the love of two beings bring forth a new beginning. May their joining result in the conception of a new life."

Magic sprinkled down from Zoe's fingertips like little sparkling droplets of power. When the magic hit the potion, sparks skittered across the liquid and then turned to fire. Almost as soon as it ignited, the flame went out, leaving the potion bright red.

"Fertility potion," I said softly to myself.

"Jade?" Lailah spun. "When did you get here?"

"Just a second ago." I stared at Zoe. She'd cut her blond hair short, and her golden-brown eyes pierced me with intensity. I cleared my throat. "Zoe? Something wrong?"

She jerked back and shook her head as if waking from a trance. "Umm, no. Nothing."

Lailah and I glanced at each other. The angel shrugged one shoulder.

"Okay, then. Fertility potion? Looks like you're mastering it pretty well."

She shrugged, barely acknowledging I'd spoken. Without saying a word, she picked up the potion and began to transfer it into the tiny bottles already lined up on the workstation.

Well, that was weird. I signaled to Lailah to join me across the room at Bea's workstation.

She glanced at Zoe, nodded as if approving of the work the witch was doing, and then joined me. "What's up?"

"I want to summon Avery tonight. Now that we know for sure she's been taken into Hell, I don't want to wait any longer."

Lailah frowned. "Agreed. It sure explains why we weren't able to locate her with a finding spell. We knew this was a possibility. Now that we know for sure…dammit. We should've summoned her sooner."

I winced, a ball of guilt making me nauseated. This wasn't the time to berate ourselves, though, and I tried my best to be the voice of reason. "We can't know everything. Neither of us had any idea Avery was actually dealing with demons. For all we knew, she was lost in the shadows or had run away on her own. Or was even taken by a spirit or a goddess or witch for that matter. Summonings from Hell are a last resort. You know that better than anyone."

She pressed a hand to her forehead and closed her eyes. "You're right, but the thought of her living in Hell this whole time…"

"It's awful, I know. But tonight we'll do everything we can to bring her back."

Lailah took a deep breath. "Okay. We'll need the entire coven and Bea—"

"We'll need Maximus and some of his hunters," Bea interrupted as she strode into the lab.

"And they're willing to do that?" I asked. The Brotherhood wasn't usually keen on helping us, especially when it came to summonings. Their motto was as long as the demons stayed in Hell, they didn't care what happened.

Bea gave us a self-satisfied smile. "I think I might have some cachet when it comes to the leader of the Brotherhood."

I laughed, but Lailah's frown deepened.

"What is it, dear?" Bea asked, concern radiating off her in a thick fog.

Lailah stood, her fists clenched. "There's nothing funny about any of this. Avery was my responsibility, and I was more worried about trying to figure out what Chessandra was up to than about how to find her. Now we learn she's in Hell and could actually be a demon. And you two—" she waved an impatient hand "—are busy giggling about Bea's affair with Maximus. I can't deal with this." Lailah ripped her apron off and stalked out of the lab.

I didn't say anything at first, more than a little shocked at Lailah's outburst. Usually she was the calm, cool, collected one. Then I turned to Bea. "Affair? Really? It's not just a little kissing in the aisles?"

My mentor rolled her eyes and shook her head good naturedly. "I might be a little bit older than you, but I'm not in the grave yet."

"Of course you aren't." I slipped my arm through hers. "Perhaps we should go calm Lailah down?"

Bea nodded. "She's had a rough day."

I couldn't blame her and understood her outburst. The absolute worst thing to happen to an angel was to be taken to Hell. Their chances of survival were very slim. And she was right. We were being insensitive. Our ill-timed humor was our way of dealing with it.

Bea and I left Zoe in the lab and found Lailah in the shop, putting together a new-release display of a book titled *Loving*

Your Inner Wicked Witch. It was the newest self-help title for the modern witch.

"Lailah," Bea said, taking her hand. "Those can wait."

"No. Let me just get this done." She sniffled and wiped a single tear from her cheek.

Bea looked at her helplessly and, not knowing what else to do, I grabbed a pile of books and gave her a hand.

"You don't have to do this," Lailah said, her voice thick.

"I know. But I want to."

She shrugged and proceeded to ignore me as we stacked books.

When we were almost done, I said, "I know how you feel."

"I don't think that's possible."

"Maybe not. But remember my own mother disappeared for years. And instead of looking for her, I basically blocked it all out and pretended I wasn't a witch. Cut out everyone who was from her world. Fifteen years I lost because…well, the reasons don't matter now. But I do understand the guilt. If I'd embraced my magic, I probably would've realized a lot sooner what had happened to her, and it's possible I would've been able to do something about it."

"Okay. So we're both idiots, then. How does this help?"

I chuckled. "It doesn't. Not really. I'm just saying you're not alone. And you're not a terrible person because you didn't insist we summon her. There were almost no clues, no real reason to believe she was in Hell before now."

She slammed one of the books down and whirled on me. "No? Where else did I expect her to be? Doesn't it seem stupid to you that I never really seriously considered this was an option?"

I met her gaze with a steady one of my own. "No. Why would you think she'd be taken by a demon? She was Chessa's assistant who'd been sent to the shadows. Lost souls usually fill the shadows, not demons. And if demons are there, the Brotherhood finds them. It's not rational to think Avery would've been meeting a demon on behalf of the high angel. You know that. Now you have to stop sulking so we can get on with planning this summoning. Because I need you. You and Bea and the rest of the coven. This isn't something I can do on my own."

She lowered her gaze to stare at her feet. "Yes, you could."

"Maybe, but I sure as heck don't want to find out." I pulled the last book from her hands and placed it on the pile. "Let's form a plan, all right?"

"Fine. But no more joking around. I'm not in the mood." Before I could say anything else, she stalked over to the counter, pulled out a notepad, and started scribbling.

Bea took her place beside her and flipped open one of her ancient spell books, while I watched them both with a little bit of awe. I might've had a lot of raw power, but those two women had something else. Knowledge. Backbone. Heart.

"Well?" Lailah said when I didn't move.

"I'm right here," I said, hurrying to the counter. "Just trying to figure out where I fit in."

Lailah stopped scribbling. "You're the muscle—the one who's going to make this happen." She handed me the list she'd just made. "Now grab these things from the shelves. We have potions and charms to prepare."

"Yes, ma'am." I gave her a mock salute and went to work.

Chapter 21

Kane

A line stretched out the door of Pyper's café, the Grind. Instead of waiting for my turn, I walked straight into the back, grabbed the only apron I could find, and joined her at the espresso machine to help move the customers through the line.

"Hey, you," she said, grinning at me. "You look really good in pink."

I grimaced. "What happened to the black aprons?"

She shrugged. "I wanted a little color in my life."

"Right. Because you don't have enough of that." Considering she was an artist and spent quite a lot of time body painting, color wasn't really an issue for her.

"Okay, you got me. They were on sale. And totally worth it now that you're wearing one." She winked and handed an order to a waiting customer. Then she turned back to me. "What brings you here?"

"Coffee." I poured milk into one of the metal containers and handed it to her to steam. "But this line was so long, I figured it would be faster if I helped."

"Aww, you're too sweet."

Not really. Pyper had spent a few years helping me manage the club next door, so when it looked like she needed an extra pair of hands, I was happy to pitch in. It was what best friends did. I spent the next half hour immersed in making lattes and cappuccinos, perfectly content to have something other than angels and demons to occupy my mind.

When the line died down, I was just walking into the back to grab a fresh tray of pastries when I heard, "Rouquette, since when did you become a barista?"

I stopped mid-step and turned to find Ezra leaning against the counter, a smug smile on his narrow face. Wiping my hands on the apron, I raised one eyebrow. "How did you know where to find me?"

He shrugged. "I didn't. Actually, I was going to look for you next door but came in here for a coffee first. Now I'm killing two birds with one stone."

Pyper glanced between the two of us, and then her gaze landed on me. "What's going on?"

I shook my head. "Nothing. At least not yet." I untied the apron and handed it to her. "Here. I've got to talk to him. Can you get us two coffees?"

She nodded and waved me off when I tried to pay for them.

"Over here." I gestured to a table in the corner.

Ezra sat across from me and stretched his feet out in front of him, crossing them at the ankles.

Pyper sauntered over and placed our coffees in front of us. She patted my shoulder and said, "Thanks for the help."

"Thank you for the view." Ezra scanned her body, his gaze lingering on her denim-clad ass.

Her smile vanished.

"Jesus. You tappin' that, Rouquette?"

"Watch it, kid," I said, a growl in my voice.

"Dude, don't worry. I'm not trying to horn in on your action, but damn. She's fine."

Pyper cleared her throat. "Excuse me."

He gave her a slow, lazy grin. "Yeah? You want my number? I'm not free tonight, but I could use someone to warm my bed tomorrow, say around eleven?"

"Jesus," she muttered. "Not even if your dick came with batteries and was twelve inches long. Now get your eyeballs off my ass before I burn your retinas with that coffee I just gave you. Got it?"

His grin widened. "You can't fault a guy for askin'."

"Yeah. I can." She turned to me. "Get this jerk out of my café."

Grabbing my coffee, I stood. "Sorry, Pypes."

She waved a hand, indicating not to worry about it as she headed back to the counter.

"Come on, kid. Let's go." I strode out, irritation making my skin itch. Pyper was more than able to take care of herself, but his sleaze still pissed me off. Once we were outside, I said, "Talk to her that way again, and you'll answer to my fist."

He gave me a what-the-fuck look, but when I didn't back down, he shrugged. "Whatever, man. I was just messing around."

"Well, mess around somewhere else." I took off down the street, heading back toward my house where my car was parked. He fell into step beside me, and I glanced over at him. "What is it you wanted to talk to me about?"

He shook his head. "Not here."

His cocky, over-the-top attitude had vanished, and he'd morphed back into the introverted, almost wounded young man I'd met the day before.

"All right. I'm headed to the Brotherhood now. Want to ride along? We can talk in the car."

He nodded and shoved his hands into his pants pockets, hunching his shoulders as if he wanted to fold into himself.

As irritated as I had been at him back at Pyper's café, now all I could muster was pity. He'd had a shit life, and no amount of money Chessandra threw at him was going to fix that. What he needed was a good therapist. And a strong support network. I was willing to bet he had neither.

Once we reached my Lexus, I hit the remote and nodded toward the passenger side. "This is it."

He eyed it and said, "Sweet ride." But there wasn't any emotion behind the words. He was just going through the motions.

Both of us were silent as I navigated out of the French Quarter. After a while I couldn't take it anymore and glanced over at him. "All right. What's up?"

He stared straight ahead, and for a moment, I thought he was going to ignore me. But then he turned, his face contorted into something that resembled rage. "My mother's the one who orchestrated that curse."

Ice climbed up my spine at his words. I jerked my attention back to the road and gripped the steering wheel until my hands ached. "You're saying Chessandra cursed my wife?"

"No."

"Oh." The feeling started to come back into my hands as I relaxed my grip.

But then he said, "I'm saying she's the one who ordered it."

I swerved toward the curb and slammed the car into park. My entire body stiffened with tension, and static filled my ears as raw, unadulterated rage filled me. Chessandra, the high angel, overseer of souls, had had Jade cursed. She'd tried to take Jade's soul at one point, and now she was trying to take our child. Unable to sit any longer, I jumped out of the car and paced. What could we do? Go back to the angel realm and demand she do something about it?

The last time we'd gone there, we'd ended up in lockdown. And it wasn't like we could fight her in the angel realm. She had all the power. No. We were going to have to get help from the leaders of the rest of the magical community. That meant Maximus and probably the head of the Witch's Council—who I didn't know, but I was sure Maximus or Bea did.

Frustration coiled in my gut. My last meeting with Maximus had been strained at best. Well, too damned bad. He'd just have to see reason. But he wasn't going to do anything without proof. I took a deep breath and climbed back into the car.

"You all right?" Ezra pierced me with his dark gaze.

"It's not me anyone needs to worry about." I fired up the car and pulled back out onto the street, not wanting to waste even another minute. I came to a stop at a streetlight and faced him. "How do you know Chessandra is responsible for the curse?"

He shook his head. "I can't tell you that."

I narrowed my eyes and inched in closer. "You're going to tell me. In order to bring her down, we're going to need proof."

A gleam lit his gaze, and his lips formed a twisted smile for just a moment before vanishing. "I'll do what I can, but my source has to remain anonymous."

"Fuck." I pounded my fist on the wheel and then ran a hand through my hair. "I need more than speculation."

"I have more."

"Well? What is it?"

Ezra pointed out the window. "Make a right."

"Why?"

"There's something you need to see. Proof of Chessandra's crimes."

"What proof?"

"You said you needed it. I'm giving it to you to see for yourself." He pointed again. "Turn here."

I didn't hesitate. If he had something tangible on the high angel I could take to the leaders, everything would change. The tires squealed as I rounded the corner and headed toward Central City. "Where are we going?"

"We'll be there in a few blocks." Ezra peered straight ahead. A minute later, he gestured to the right and again said, "Turn here."

I steered the car onto a rundown street full of houses still in serious need of renovation after Hurricane Katrina. A few had bars on the windows. Only one appeared to be lived in, with a red car out front and Christmas lights hanging from the roof.

"Here." Ezra indicated a beat-up white Creole cottage with ivy growing out of the plank siding.

I stopped in front of the house, leaving the car idling.

"Let's go. What you have to see is inside." Ezra slid out of the car and didn't look back as he climbed the questionable wooden steps. The entire porch seemed to sway under his weight.

"Jeez," I muttered and flipped the ignition off, praying the Lexus would still be there when we got back.

"Move it, Rouquette," Ezra said from the open doorway.

The place looked deserted, but after my time spent with the Brotherhood, that only heightened my unease. Walking into such a place without my dagger was asking for trouble. But Ezra had already disappeared into the house, and leaving him there wasn't an option, either.

I moved up the porch, thankful my foot didn't crash through any of the rotted boards, and stood in the doorway, waiting for my eyesight to adjust. Old, ratty furniture filled the front room, and the musty air all but choked me. The only sign of life was the footprints Ezra had left in the dust covering the scuffed wooden floors.

I sucked in a breath of clean air and made my way through the dark house, hearing nothing but the scuff of my boots on the floor. I found Ezra standing in the threshold of the back door.

"This way," he said.

Gritting my teeth, I followed him into the overgrown back yard. He stopped under an old oak tree and turned to stare at me.

I stilled and waited under a thick limb of the tree. "Well? Where's this proof of yours?"

Ezra backed up and sat on a wooden bench that was being claimed by the vegetation. "This morning I learned that Chessandra had compelled a newbie witch to cast the black magic spell on your wife. The one who just got a new soul. Do you know who she is?"

Zoe? Was that even possible? Hadn't Jade told me it was angel magic? And why had he brought me here to tell me this? Nothing was making any sense. "I'm not sure—"

"My contact overheard her talking about it. Good ol' Mom has bewitched...what's her name? Zoe?"

I nodded. "Yes. She's the one who got a new soul."

"Yeah. Her. Anyway, Mom has her doing her dirty deeds for her. If your wife is as powerful as everyone says she is, it won't take much for her to see the enchantment on the new witch once she's looking for it."

Anger surged through my veins. I practically vibrated with it. What Ezra had said sounded exactly like something Chessandra would do. She was forever getting everyone else to do her dirty work. First her sister, Mati, to try to close a demon portal, then me and Jade to deal with the shadows, and even when she wanted to keep Pyper in the angel realm to clean up their open case files. If she thought she needed power over Jade's child, would she do this too?

She might. It wasn't something I could rule out. She was ruthless when it came to her agenda. I had to let Jade know Zoe was compromised. I reach for my phone, but came up empty. Dammit. I'd forgotten it'd gone missing after I'd battled Malstord.

"Kane Rouquette," a smooth voice called from behind me.

That all-too-familiar prickle of unease settled in my bones and I froze.

Demon.

I turned on my heel, automatically reaching for my dagger, and came up empty.

Shit.

The demon, an inch or so taller than me, stood a few feet away. He appeared almost human except for his electric-green eyes and the two small horns poking out of his shaved head. Everything else about him said older gentleman, from his pin-striped suit right down to his wingtipped shoes.

"What do you want?" I asked, acutely aware that he'd called me by name.

He smiled, showing his ultra-white, perfectly straight teeth. "You, of course."

"And what exactly do you want from me?" I glanced back, checking on Ezra, only to find he'd completely disappeared. Betrayal made me see red. That bastard. He'd set me up.

"Your little friend is long gone." The demon raised one hand, signaling to someone over my shoulder. I started to turn, but stinging pressure slammed into me from the back, indicating not one but at least three demons. I was surrounded with no dagger. No backup. Nothing but Jade's magic running through my veins.

I leaped up, grabbing the lowest branch of the oak tree, and scrambled to climb. But the moment my foot touched the trunk, two hands clasped over my calf.

Heat seared up from the ground, and without even looking, I knew they'd opened a portal to Hell. A brand new one. Because it hadn't been there a moment ago. I'd have felt it. Which meant these four were extremely powerful. Not just any demon could create a portal. Only the really old ones.

Christ, what did they want from me? My only hope was to hold them off long enough until my demon hunter brothers came running. Portals did not go unnoticed.

I kicked out hard, catching one of them in the face, and managed to free my leg. With a shot of adrenaline, my feet found purchase, and I climbed, barely staying out of the grasp of the demons below.

My heart raced and sweat ran into my eyes, but I kept going until I was well above the portal and the angry demons below. And just when I was pulling myself up one more limb to settle and wait for backup, I heard a cry from above, followed by the flash of black as Ezra jumped down and landed with both feet on my fingers.

My grip slipped, and the last thing I saw as I fell through the portal was Ezra's evil, triumphant smile staring down at me.

Chapter 22

Jade

Bea, Lailah, and I sat in Bea's Prius in the parking lot near the coven circle, waiting for the downpour to stop. It was nearing midnight, and the heavens had opened up a few hours ago to dump buckets of water on the greater New Orleans area.

"Conditions could not be worse for a summoning," Lailah said, staring out the window.

The rain was so heavy we couldn't even see the other coven members' cars parked just a few spaces away.

"If this doesn't end soon—"

"Don't even say it," Lailah said. "Everyone's here. All we need is a break in the weather."

"Everyone except Maximus and the demon hunters." I turned to Bea. "You did say they're coming for backup, right?"

"Yes." Bea closed the spell book she'd been consulting. "Max said he'd send a crew. They're probably waiting for a break in the rain as well."

"I hope so." Antsy, I checked my phone for the hundredth time that day. No calls. No texts. Nothing from Kane. Surely he was still busy researching, right? Or maybe he was preparing for the summoning. If he knew Maximus was sending a team, he'd be here. No doubt about it.

I swallowed the unease trying to rise in my throat. He was fine. He'd been going to the Brotherhood, after all. It was just about the safest place in the entire city besides Bea's house.

"Hey." Lailah tapped me on the shoulder. "The rain has slowed to a drizzle. This is probably our window."

"Yeah. Okay. Bea?"

She glanced out the window and nodded. "It's now or never if we're going to do this tonight."

I jumped out of the car and tightened my raincoat against the wind. The chill in the air had me shivering almost instantly. Perfect. Gritting my teeth against the cold, I sidestepped a large puddle and knocked on Lucien's Jeep window.

The glass lowered, and I was blasted with a wave of warm air from the heater. I had to stop myself from leaning into the open window. "We're doing this now."

"Okay." He tapped his horn, indicating to the rest of the coven it was time.

I scanned the parking lot, searching for anyone who might look like they were from the Brotherhood. Nothing.

"Let's go," Lailah said and tugged me off into the soggy grass toward the trees. The smell of damp moss permeated the air, making my nose twitch.

Within seconds, my feet were soaked through. By the time we emerged from the trees into the clearing, mud caked my shoes, and just keeping my balance became a major chore.

The coven members silently went about preparing the circle with a salt ring and pillar candles for each member, while Lailah and I separated the potions we'd brought. I held four tiny bottles of healing potion in my hands, praying we didn't need them. The potion was only good for demon attacks, able to cure just about any wound left by a demon. It also could be used as a weapon against any demon who got close enough, as whatever it was that helped humans heal actually seared the leathery skin of demons.

I glanced around, once again looking for someone from the Brotherhood, and frowned, disappointed.

"They'll be here." Bea handed me a small bag of healing herbs.

I shoved them along with the potions into my front pocket and nodded my thanks. Eyeing the dark skies, I said, "We can't wait for them."

"I know. They'll probably feel the pull of the circle. Try not to worry about it."

How could I not? Demons meant black magic and spending eternity in Hell. Images of souls trapped in distorted statues flashed through my mind, and I shuddered. That was what happened to the unfortunate souls who were claimed by demons. Only a very few lucky ones ever escaped. I shook myself, putting it out of my mind, and then took my place on the northernmost point of the circle.

Bea met my gaze and nodded that she was ready.

I held my candle out in front of me, a pure black one intended to tap into the darkest forces, and whispered, "*Elevate*."

The candle trembled on my palm, the magic seeming to stutter as it tried to take hold.

"*Elevate*," I said more forcefully.

Power zipped from my palm and wrapped around the candle, lifting it into the air and holding it perfectly steady a few feet in front of me.

"*Ignite*."

The flame flickered to life, and all around me the coven closed in, not yet taking their places on the circle. Bea was walking the perimeter, chanting protection spells, strengthening the magic. Once she was done, it would be almost impossible to cross the circle barrier after we erected it. I wasn't taking any chances.

The mood had already been somber, but ever since I'd lit the black candle, the electric current in the air had turned ominous. The circle seemed to know something dark was coming.

I swallowed, sweat breaking out on the back of my neck despite the chilly temperature.

"It'll be all right." Lucien came to a stop beside me. "With all of us here, we're strong enough to deal with just about anything."

I nodded, certain he was right. We could deal with it. But that didn't mean no one would get hurt in the process. As strong as the circle was, if an ancient demon appeared, there was no stopping him. And Lucien knew that. "Where's Kat tonight?"

"At home. She made me promise to call her the minute we complete the summoning."

I smiled at that. There was no way Kat was sitting on her hands at home. "You don't think she'll be waiting in the car down the street?"

He chuckled. "Now that you mention it, you're probably right."

"We'd better get this show on the road, then." I turned and called, "We're ready."

"Wait." Lailah held a hand up, then walked to the middle of the circle and placed a small music box on the ground. "Jasper gave it to me. It's Avery's. It will help us form a connection to her."

"Thanks, Lailah," I said, relieved she'd secured something personal of Avery's. Without it, the chances of locating her were greatly reduced.

My coven members, along with Lailah and Zoe, filled in around the circle. After seeing how powerful Zoe was in Bea's shop, I'd requested she come along even though technically she wasn't part of the coven yet. She was strong, and we needed all the help we could get.

Bea took the southern spot on the circle, while Lucien and Lailah claimed the east and west. Seven of our coven members, plus Zoe, filled in the spaces between us.

"Thank you all for coming. We all know how dangerous this is. Anything can happen during a summoning." I glanced around at their somber expressions. "So this is it. If you have doubts, now's your chance to back out. No one will judge you."

It was late in the game for anyone to leave, but having them make a final decision while they were standing on the circle solidified their commitment to the summoning. So when no one said anything, I let out a sigh of relief.

"Good. I'm glad we're all on the same page." I held my arms out to my sides. "Everyone join hands."

Magic pulsed from my ribcage to the tips of my fingers, and the second Rosalee's and Zoe's hands slipped into mine, power zinged up my spine, completely filling me. My black candle rose a foot in front of me, and the flame flared brighter.

The circle's power had intensified. Our coven was growing stronger.

"Goddess of the night, keeper of the worlds, hear my call. Our coven joins the darkness under the cloaked moon to seek what's been taken from us."

A bolt of magic shot from my hands and reverberated through each of the members until it got to Bea. The magic seized her, and she stood straighter, her shoulders back with her head tilted skyward. Her power was clearly buzzing just beneath the surface. Good. She was as ready as I was.

"Goddess of the night, we are here seeking one who was taken against her will. Help us to summon her soul, bring her back to where she belongs. Wrap her in your compassion and carry her home."

I let go of Zoe's and Rosalee's hands and raised mine high in the air. All the rest of the black candles elevated with my movement.

"Bring forth the light!" I commanded.

With strong, sure voices, the coven members called, "*Ignite!*"

The candles came to life, illuminating the circle with light and electric magic.

"That's it!" I raised my arms higher, reaching for all the power I could muster. "Avery Freeman, angel of the realm, open yourself to my call. We the New Orleans coven call you, bring you forth, bind ourselves to your spirit and request—"

A loud boom thundered overhead, and for a second, I thought the storm was starting to brew again, but it was followed by a bright white light that shone down from the heavens.

A collective gasp came from the circle, followed by a high-pitched, "Stop!"

I lowered my hands and let the magic dial back to a simmer as I tried to process the interruption. Squinting, I peered into the circle and then scowled.

"Chessandra. What are you doing here?" Anger rose from deep in my gut and threatened to strangle me. Hadn't she caused enough trouble?

"Stopping you from making a big mistake." Her high angel robes were gone, and she stood in our circle wearing jeans and a bulky long-sleeved sweater. Her chestnut hair was piled high on her head without care, and from what I could tell, she had little to no makeup on.

"And what mistake would that be?" I asked. "Finally getting to the bottom of your double-dealing secrets?"

"You shouldn't talk about things you know nothing about." She stalked toward me, her eyes narrowed. Unease and trepidation mixed equally with her frustrated anger.

Interesting. She was mostly scared of what we were trying to do. Why? Was it because she didn't want us to know her secrets, or was it something else?

"I think you should go," I said, my voice steady and full of conviction. "We don't need—"

"Oh gods!" Lailah exclaimed and pointed at the high angel, her finger shaking as she glanced between Chessandra and Zoe. "You spelled her."

Chessandra spun and glared at Lailah. "Stay out of this. It's none of your concern."

"Yes, it is!" Lailah yelled. "Everyone here—" she waved a hand around "—I'm responsible for them, for their souls, and you—" She shook her head violently and turned to stare at Zoe.

Zoe's eyes were wide with fear as she stared back at Lailah. "I didn't want to. I tried to break the hold, but her power… it's too strong." She held up her hands.

It was then I noticed the pure white aura that coated Zoe's lavender one, and there were at least a half dozen threads that were connected to Chessandra.

Fury rippled through me, and I turned on Chessandra. "Lailah's right. *You* spelled her."

"Bewitched," Bea said, still holding her spot on the southern point of the circle. "It means Chessandra can take over and control her if she wants, only she couldn't this time because the coven power was too much for her. Isn't that right, Chessa?"

"You stay out of this, Beatrice. It's none of your concern." Chessandra leveled me with her authoritative gaze. "You have to let this go. It's too dangerous."

I shook my head, my tone hard, completely void of compassion. "It's been far too long since Avery went missing. If you'd told us right away what had happened, you might have gotten a say in how things were handled. But you didn't. Your opinions are no longer welcome here. And now I find out you've bewitched Zoe, too? I guess I'm supposed to believe it wasn't you who had me cursed?"

"Cursed? What?"

Her act only pissed me off more. Of course it was her who cursed me. Why else would Zoe be so afraid of her and confessing her sins in front of everyone? "Don't play innocent, Chessandra. We all know what you've done. Release the bewitchment on Zoe and then reverse the black magic spell on me. Maybe then, if we find Avery, your own kind will take pity on you and not lock you away for years in the room where time stands still."

"But I didn't—"

At that moment, the flame on the black candle that had been hovering in front of me suddenly went out, and the smoke shot around us, extinguishing all the other candles. The entire circle lit up with an eerie red glow.

"The summoning. It worked," Bea called.

"Chessandra, get out of the circle!" Lailah demanded.

The high angel spun around and stared at the shimmering ground.

"Chessa!" Lailah said again.

She stood still as if she was in a trance. But then she shook her head hard and ran toward Lailah. When she got to the edge of the circle, she came up short and glanced around in panic. "Release the barrier. I can't get out."

Lailah met my gaze, asking a silent question.

I shook my head. It was too late.

The eerie red fog solidified and morphed into a woman's form.

No, not a woman.

A female demon.

Oh, crap.

"Chessandra," the demon hissed.

"Avery?" Chessandra said, horror in her tone.

The demon appeared almost human, save her red glowing eyes and her clawed hands. She stepped forward, her deformed hand extended toward the high angel. "This is your fault. And now you're going to pay."

Chapter 23

Kane

The smell of meat barbequing on the grill wafted through the open window. My stomach turned as I imagined what exactly the demons were cooking for dinner. My captor, a demon who called himself Aiken, was seated behind an ornate banker's desk in the adjoining room, his pen flying across a piece of paper.

The contract.

That was what he'd said he was working on. The one he was expecting me to sign after the feast tonight.

I paced my wrought iron cell, cursing my stupidity for trusting Ezra. Now that I had nothing to do but think, it seemed obvious he'd been a setup from the start. Why else had he been in that warehouse with those demons who hadn't seemed all that intent on actually hurting anyone except Ezra? It also explained why Malstord had baited me. They'd been there to capture me and likely would have if I hadn't issued that challenge. Why else had there been such super-powerful demons on the prowl without any other explanation?

Aiken rose from his desk, his black duster jacket sweeping behind him as he strode over to me. "The festivities are just about to begin."

I stood with my arms crossed over my chest, glaring at him through the bars.

"And you're the guest of honor." He'd likely been a handsome angel at one time. Tall, broad shouldered, athletic build. Only now, his hands were gnarled, complete with misshapen talons. Scars and pockmarks marred his face. And the crown of horns sticking up through his dark hair didn't help matters. But he did have the type of confidence that came with power. Likely he didn't have trouble with the female demon population.

I gritted my teeth and said nothing.

"After the sacrifice, you'll sign the contract in front of the Inner Circle." He thrust a folded-up piece of paper between the bars. "Of course I'll give you plenty of time to process it. It is a contract, after all."

The paper balanced between the bars, teetering in my direction. I plucked it out and tore it in half without even looking at it.

Aiken sighed. "You disappoint me, Kane." He glanced at the two halves now scattered on the floor of my cell. "I suggest you piece it together. You'll be signing the original one way or another."

"And if I don't?"

A chilling smile spread across his ugly face. "Your wife will be the next target. And any child she conceives will be mine." Aiken turned on his booted heel and somehow managed to glide across the cement floor without making a sound.

My breath had left me at his words. They'd go after Jade. She was powerful enough and had enough help that it was likely she could avoid capture. But she'd come after me. Chances were high they'd contain her then. And her future child.

Pain pierced my heart. If I became an agent of Hell, there wasn't any chance for a child between the two of us. But assuming she didn't end up right here next to me, she'd move on eventually. Start a family the way she should. Her life would continue, while mine would be here, serving Aiken.

No.

I couldn't let them target her. I'd do anything to avoid that.

I crouched down in my empty cell, grabbed the two pieces of paper, and started to read.

Contract #9889876543.0006669

I, the incubus, demon hunter Kane Rouquette, hereby forfeit my life from this date forward till the end of eternity to Aiken the Second, son of Vilkor, in exchange for the freedom of my wife, Jade Calhoun, and any children she bears. Neither she nor her children will be targeted by any demon of Hell unless the demon's actions are in self-defense. I shall serve in the capacity of an agent of Hell and will carry out any and all such duties as Aiken the Second orders, including but not limited to obtaining souls for the Collection.

Besides a place and date for both parties to sign, that was it. Short and to the point. I would be a slave to the demon, and my wife would be free from the agents of Hell forever. Only I highly doubted the contract would hold up when she came barreling into the place with her magic so charged she could light up a square mile.

Because if there was one thing I knew about my wife, it was that she would not sit by and let any of this happen.

Signing the contract wasn't an option. It wouldn't save her. Her actions would see to that. And I'd forfeit my life for nothing.

I'd just have to think of something else. Find some way to get out of this place. Be ready when her coven came looking for me.

My instinct was to burn the contract. To completely destroy it. I could do it. I had just enough power running through my veins to ignite a small flame. But as I called up my magic, usually reserved for my missing dagger, I hesitated. A nagging doubt at the back of my mind had me folding the bits of paper into a neat square. I tucked it into my back pocket and sat in the middle of my cell, waiting.

More smoke wafted in from the patio. The roasting meat made my stomach turn. It didn't smell right. Almost rancid, as if they were barbequing roadkill. Disgusting.

A moment later, deep laughter filtered through the window, followed by the murmur of voices.

I strained to make out what they were saying, but only heard something about Aiken turning someone to gain power.

Turn who into what? An angel to demon? That didn't make sense. Angels fell; they weren't turned.

"Rouquette. On your feet." One tall, thin demon with a shock of electric-green hair appeared from somewhere deep within Aiken's residence. "Time to get this party started."

I didn't move from my spot on the cement floor.

"Yo, incubus." Green Hair peered in at me, his expression disgusted. "Satan's arse. You're worse than useless. Tell you what. Get up on your own two feet, or I'm going to send a curse right up your backside that will sear your intestines from the inside out."

Well, didn't that sound pleasant.

"I'm not fucking with you." Black magic danced at his fingertips.

Reluctantly, I rose, keeping my gaze straight ahead.

"Good, pet," he cooed through the bars. "Now put your arms straight out and hold your hands together."

I did as I was told, reserving any resistance for a time when I might actually have a chance of escaping this literal hell hole.

A tendril of his magic snaked from his fingers and wrapped around my wrists, creating shackles and a thick chain that wove from his fingers to the base of my restraints. Grinning, he snapped his fingers, and the smoke chain turned to steel. Green Hair nodded to himself, clearly satisfied, and gripped the chain, yanking me forward.

We stood face to face, peering at each other through the bars.

"You'll do as I say, or else this chain will turn back into that black magic I forged it from and we'll be talking about searing your intestines again. Got it?"

I nodded. What else was there to do? Besides fantasize about crushing his larynx so I wouldn't have to hear any more about intestines.

With a touch of his hand on the security pad, the door on the iron cage opened. Green hair nodded to the patio. "Let's go."

I started to follow, but he jerked so hard on the chain, I lost my balance and went to one knee.

A satisfied gleam hit his eyes. "That's it, incubus. Get use to kneeling for your kings."

I silently vowed he'd be the first one I'd destroy once I got out of this mess.

Without acknowledging him, I pushed myself to my feet and followed like the obedient slave they wanted me to be.

The outside, or what passed for outside in Hell, was more of a carved-out cave with stadium-type seating of five rows on one side. Off to the right was the barbeque pit, where something unidentifiable with four legs was turning on a spit. At least it wasn't human, thank the gods.

"This way." Green Hair jerked me forward again, but this time I was ready for him and kept my footing.

A group of demons who'd mostly adopted human characteristics were sitting at a large wooden table, liberally drinking wine so dark it appeared the color of blood.

Green Hair pulled me up onto an ornate platform that was decorated with what appeared to be real gold-accent inlays and pointed to the larger of the two matching thrones. "Sit."

I raised my eyebrows. The setup made it appear as if I'd be presiding over this function.

"Do it," Green Hair barked.

Shrugging, I took my place on the throne and scowled as the hot sear of magic coated my limbs, weighing them down. The spell was in effect keeping me strapped to the chair without the actual restraints.

Green Hair snapped his fingers once more, and the black magic shackles released from my wrists and vanished. "Now we can get started."

"Take your seat, Bevel," Aiken said from the head of the table below. "Your service is complete."

Bevel nodded, his green hair flopping over the side of his face. He glared at me with his one exposed eye. "Your servant will be along shortly. Take care to treat her well, or you'll answer to me."

The saliva gathered at the back of my throat, and I had an almost uncontrollable urge to spit in his face. I probably would have, too, if Aiken hadn't barked, "That's enough, *boy*. I said take your seat."

Boy. Interesting. Bevel was low demon on the totem pole. I filed that away for later, just in case I needed leverage.

The demons at the table ignored me for the most part, and after a while I started to wonder what exactly I was doing there. The entire scene reminded me of an afternoon frat get-together. Just a bunch of guys—or demons—hanging out drinking, with me as the pledge forced to sit patiently until they were ready for me.

I had started to doze off in the chair, ignoring the ache from sitting in the same position for so long, when a wooden door across the cave slammed open. I startled and blinked, trying to make sense of the scene in front of me.

The demons stood and nodded their greetings to three human women who'd walked in. They were all wearing small scraps of fabric that covered only their breasts, and long flowing skirts. Each was adorned with a diamond pendant and had multiple gemstone rings. The three of them were flawless in their perfection.

A group of well-dressed demons, both male and female, followed them and took their seats in the stadium.

The three women circled the table, slightly bowing to the standing demons, and then stood at the back of the room, lined up against a wall.

Aiken waved for the rest of his pack of demons to be seated. Keeping his gaze trained on the women, he walked slowly over to them, stopping in front of each one for just a moment. All three of them curtsied at his signal, making my stomach turn.

What were they doing here? Human slaves? Only they appeared to be well cared for. None of them seemed harmed. Or particularly unhappy. Maybe resigned.

Aiken finally stopped in front of the last woman. She bowed her head, but he jerked her chin up and claimed her in a kiss so fierce, the other women gasped.

I felt my eyes widen, surprised the human seemed to accept him so easily. Were they here voluntarily? I shook my head, trying to make sense of everything.

Aiken lifted the woman off her feet, pulling her closer, and as he did, a shimmer of power burst from her, engulfing them.

Holy fuck. She wasn't a human woman. She was a sex witch.

The nausea returned full force. Less than six months ago, I'd learned incubi were the product of demons and sex witches. That demons had enslaved sex witches for hundreds of years until their offspring, the incubi, freed them. Now there were three sex witches here, in Aiken's service.

The rage I'd been carefully holding back sprang to the surface, and if it hadn't been for the magic restraining me in the chair, there was no doubt in my mind I'd be on my feet and gunning for Aiken. Instead, I was forced to fume on the throne and imagine eighteen different ways to tear his head off.

Aiken released the witch and stepped back as he gestured toward me. "Bianca, please take the chair beside our honored guest."

With a sharp nod, the witch strode toward me, her shoulders back and her head held high. It wasn't until she was a mere few feet away from me that I noticed a flash of anger in her eyes. But then she blinked, all traces of emotion gone.

I nodded a greeting.

She returned the gesture and sat perched forward on the edge of the throne as if she was trying to limit the contact between her body and the wooden structure.

Aiken moved gracefully into the middle of the cave, his arms spread wide. "Welcome, honored guests. As you're well aware, tonight is a special night. The night I officially announce my intention to run for the Minister of the Damned. And now that I have Malstord's defeater as my devoted servant, support for our cause will reach critical mass."

A cheer rose from the crowd, but the two witches standing near the wall stayed still and silent.

I seethed. It appeared not only was Aiken trying to force me to forfeit my life to him, he also planned to use me in some political power struggle. How Malstord fit into that, I wasn't sure. But the fact that I'd beaten him in the challenge obviously had something to do with it.

Aiken moved back to the table and poured a large glass of the dark wine. The cheering from the crowd grew louder. His self-satisfied smile grated on my nerves.

Holding the wine high in the air, Aiken strode over to the spit and tore off one of the short legs with his bare hand.

Grease slipped through his talon fingers, and with a roar of triumph, he bit into the flesh, tearing a large hunk of meat from the bone. Juices dribbled down his chin as he chewed and jabbed the leg in the air in some sort of sign of victory.

A frenzy rippled through the crowd, and my unease intensified. A room full of rowdy demons was the last thing I needed.

Aiken turned toward us. He barely glanced at me before his lust-filled gaze swept over Bianca, lingering on her ample cleavage.

She sat stock still, staring straight ahead the way assault victims did in order to survive the ordeal.

My blood ran hot, and my arms involuntarily strained against the magic. There was nothing I could do but sit there and watch Aiken violate her with his mind. Disgust ate away at my soul. And I vowed right then and there that before this was over, I'd do everything I could to end him. One way or another, the cocky demon was living on borrowed time.

Aiken finally lifted his gaze to meet Bianca's and said, "Release the incubus."

"What?" I said, eyeing the witch. Of course I knew she had power, but it hadn't occurred to me the demons let her use it. If I could make an ally of her then—

Her hand closed over mine, and a sharp stab of pain went straight through my palm as if she'd nailed my hand to the wooden throne.

"Ouch!" I yelped, trying to pull my arm back, but it was no use. I was still magically bound to the chair.

"Relax," she said in a smooth, silky voice.

I stared into her cornflower-blue eyes and got lost in the undisguised despair she couldn't seem to keep hidden.

"This is going to hurt," she whispered and then shut her eyes tight.

Her magic radiated from the center of my palm and seared its way through my veins, effectively burning away the demon magic holding me to the throne.

The air rushed out of me, and I grunted, unable to do anything but take the assault. And just as suddenly as it had started, the pain vanished, leaving me slumped over, weak, and at the mercy of every demon in the room.

Humiliation mixed with outrage as I willed myself to stand on my own two feet.

The demons all watched me with rapt attention, and when I took a very unsteady step toward Aiken, a ripple of laughter reverberated through the crowd, followed by a cheer of approval.

"He's perfect, Aiken. Well done!" one of the demons at the table called.

Another stood and clapped him on the back. "Damn, man. Brilliant. There's no doubt you've got this in the bag."

I narrowed my eyes and glared at them all.

But the demons were too busy congratulating themselves to pay any more attention to me. I glanced over at Bianca. "Do you know what this is all about?"

She nodded. "They've chosen a warrior."

"What?"

"You. You're a warrior. Anyone who can fight through the magic I just subjected you to is very special indeed. Aiken needs someone like you if he's going to rule. They're pleased with this development."

"I see." Standing before them, I arranged my face into a neutral expression. They didn't need to see the stone-cold determination that had taken over every fiber of my being.

If they wanted me, they were damn sure going to pay for it.

"Rouquette, my warrior," Aiken said, striding toward me. The meat and the wine were gone, replaced by a towel he used to clean his hands. "The only thing left to do is for you to sign the contract."

He swept a hand out, and a short demon dressed in a business suit shot out of his chair. With quick movements, he jumped up on the platform and presented me with a gold pen and the official-looking document on a marble clipboard.

"Thank you, Gerald," Aiken said.

Gerald looked up at me expectantly, his eyes shifting from yellow to green and back again. What was it with the color of the demons' eyes? Did they shift with power or emotions? Or maybe intent?

"Take it," Gerald said, his voice kind.

I held my hand out and welcomed the coolness of the marble as I gripped the gold pen with the other.

Gerald bowed in Aiken's direction and then jogged back to his seat.

"Now then, Rouquette. Because I'm a fair leader and understand you're making a great sacrifice, I'm willing to make one as well." The humor left his expression and he turned serious. "As a signing bonus, you'll receive in your possession the lovely Bianca to use as you please."

Bianca shifted beside me, covering her mouth as she muffled a gasp. Loud whispers circulated through the crowd as they all stared at me, waiting for my reply.

I ignored them all, tamped down the icy fury building in my chest, and said to Aiken, "I have some conditions first."

Aiken jerked his head back and blinked. "Excuse me? The sex witch isn't enough?"

I shook my head. "No. I want the angel Ezra as well."

A dark shadow fell over Aiken's face. "The angel has nothing to do with us."

"I think he does," I said, my tone matter of fact.

The demon leader walked slowly back over to the table and held his hand out for another glass of wine. After he took a long drink, he rolled his shoulders, visibly forcing himself to relax. "The angel Ezra is no longer in our company. The request is denied."

"Then no deal." I placed the marble slab on the chair behind me and crossed my arms over my chest.

A loud protest went up around the room.

Aiken waved his arms for them to quiet down. "You do realize this means we'll wage an all-out attack on your wife. That she'll never be safe from our kind."

I shrugged, pretending disinterest. "My wife can take care of herself."

Aiken peered at me and then let out a bark of laughter. "You're right, she can. But I wonder what a dozen of my best demons could do to her before the Brotherhood even so much as scented a whiff of their presence."

My jaw ached from keeping my mouth clamped shut, and I resorted to trying to solve complicated math problems in my head in order to block out the disturbing images running through my mind. When I got a grip on myself, I said, "If you want me to sign this, you'll bring me Ezra. Otherwise we're at an impasse."

I had no idea what I planned to accomplish once Ezra arrived, but at that moment, I needed to stall. And I couldn't think of a better candidate for Hell than the double-dealing angel.

Aiken's pockmarked face turned red and his demon fangs grew, indicating I'd thoroughly pissed him off. Good. What was he going to do? Kill me in front of his guests after they'd all cheered for their new "warrior?" He slammed the wine glass down on the table and said, "Fine. Sign the contract, and I'll bring you the angel."

I shook my head. "The angel first. Then I'll sign."

He let out a loud roar, and I thought he might lose control and rip my head off right there in the cave. But he quieted and stared at his feet. And then he suddenly turned to Bianca. "Restrain him."

Bianca gave me a pained look and touched my arm.

A thousand white-hot knives prickled my skin, the magic spreading over me as if it was a poison. All the energy drained from my body. Fog clouded my thoughts, and I watched Bianca reach out in slow motion to retrieve the contract from my chair. Sighing, she pressed her other hand against my chest, applying just enough pressure that she pushed me back into the chair.

I fell hard, unable to control my reactions. And the minute I connected with the throne, the restraining magic was back, once again invisibly tying me to the chair.

Aiken turned to his companions at the table. "Find Ezra and bring him to me immediately."

Chapter 24

Jade

Avery opened her mouth, and black magic spewed toward Chessandra. The high angel froze, her eyes wide with shock.

"Move," I cried, harnessing the coven's collective magic to mix with my own. The power burst from me, barely colliding with Avery's right before it engulfed Chessandra. What the hell was wrong with her? She had magic of her own. Wasn't she even going to try to save herself?

I sucked in a steadying breath as the dark magic inched its way forward, eating away at the coven's lighter magic. She was strong for a new demon. Or just really pissed off.

Avery snarled in Chessandra's direction, barely paying any attention to me at all. Yes, she was pissed. And if she did decide to put her full attention into warding me off, I was going to be in trouble. My power was probably at half speed since my activities with Kane, and right then, I was giving it all I had and losing.

"Bea!" I called, noting my mentor wasn't feeding the coven's collective. She was focused on Chessandra, who'd finally taken action and was casting a protection spell. Flashes of light sparked over the high angel's skin, cocooning her in a shimmering layer of magic. It wouldn't keep the demon from overpowering her, but it would give her enough time to either flee or fight back. "A little help, please?"

Bea's gaze landed on the spot where the coven's magic met Avery's, and she cursed. A second later, her magic joined seamlessly with ours, and with her in the mix, we easily gained control of the situation.

Avery growled and turned her attention to me. "This is between me and Chessandra. She owes me a life and I'm going to collect."

"I can't let that happen," I said, not backing down for a second. No matter what Chessa had done, I wasn't going to let a demon snatch her into Hell. Even if I did think that was a just punishment, she'd only turn demon, and that would be one more enemy we'd have to fight.

"She's been making deals with demons for over twenty years," a male voice said from behind me.

I glanced over my shoulder and spotted a tall young man with spiky blond hair. "Who are you?"

"Her son." He walked the perimeter of the circle until he was only a few feet from Chessandra.

She turned to him, relief shining through her guarded expression. "Ezra. You're okay. Where have you been?"

"Hell. Where do you think I've been?" he spat and produced a piece of paper, waving it in front of her. "Gathering proof of your double dealings."

It was the contract to pardon the demon Kane had told me about. And he was confronting her right here in front of everyone.

Avery redoubled her efforts, her black magic stream eating away at our combined attack, and moved slowly in the direction of Chessandra.

I stayed focused on Avery, and dug deep into my own reserves until we were locked in a standoff.

"Ezra—" Chessandra started.

But he cut her off. "It says here, the high angel granted a pardon to a demon by the name of Wes Lancaster in return for his silence. Good old Wes killed someone and blackmailed Chessandra here into letting him live."

"Wes Lancaster!" Avery cried. Her magic vanished, and she ducked below the coven's stream of power, surging forward, her arms outstretched as if she was going to strangle Chessandra. "It's your fault I'm like this, you selfish bitch. I'll kill you."

Before I could process what had happened, Avery tackled Chessandra, and the pair went down in a heap of arms and legs. Avery got the better of her almost instantly and climbed on top of her, straddling the high angel with her hands wrapped around her throat. "You're coming with me."

Avery's black magic spiraled out into ropes, wrapping itself around the angel.

A collective gasp rose from my coven members, while I stood frozen, watching the angel–demon fight in stunned fascination.

"Jade!" Bea called from across the circle.

I shook myself and gathered up the magic still pulsing from the coven. I met Bea's gaze and said, "Now!"

Our magic blasted full force into Avery, lifting her right off Chessandra and slamming her into the spelled earth in the very center of the coven circle. A sad wail of music shot from the music box, and then winked out as the box was crushed. Tendrils of white magic grew out of the ground and shackled all four limbs of the demon, anchoring her to the earth.

"Whoa," Zoe said, her face pale.

Without hesitation, I stepped into the circle, gesturing for Zoe to join me.

The young witch shook her head and tried to step off the circle, but Lucien reached over and grabbed her arm. "No. If you disengage, you'll weaken our power, and the magic holding the demon might fail."

She took a deep breath and nodded. "Okay, but I don't want to go inside, either."

"You have to, dear," Bea said. "You were the vehicle that cursed Jade, weren't you? We need to use you to break it."

I smiled at Bea, pleased we were both on the same page. Now that the demon was temporarily restrained and we had Chessandra trapped in the circle, I wasn't letting this moment go by without reversing the black magic clinging to me.

Tears filled Zoe's eyes. "I didn't mean to. I had no choice."

I held my hand out to her. "I know. But now's your chance to help correct this injustice."

The tears spilled down her cheeks, and my heart ached for her. Not long ago she'd been trapped in the Shadows and had most of her spirit as well as her soul stolen by a lesser goddess. Luckily she'd gotten a soul back, but her spirit was still rebuilding. Now she'd been a pawn of the high angel. Trust couldn't be high on her to-do list.

"We'll also break the connection Chessandra has to you," I said. "This is as much for you as it is for me."

She hesitated, and then with a decisive nod, she took a step into the circle.

"Lucien?"

"Yeah?" he said.

"Can you keep the demon restrained if Bea withdraws her magic for a few minutes?" I'd already broken off from the coven when I walked into the circle. And while I was determined to reverse the curse on me, I wouldn't do it at the risk of the coven.

"As long as Lailah stays connected," he said with an air of confidence.

"I'm not going anywhere," Lailah said.

Thanks, I mouthed to her.

She nodded and her stream of power brightened with intensity as she refocused on the restrained demon.

I felt a burst of power surge from Bea into the coven's collective, and then she too walked into the circle.

"Didn't anyone hear me?" Ezra bellowed from behind me. "She deserves a trip to Hell."

"We heard you, son," Bea said evenly. "But no one except that demon is going to Hell today. The Angel Council will deal with your mother for any perceived crimes."

"You're making a big mistake."

"No, we're not," I said quietly, staring down at the high angel, who was kneeling in the grass.

She looked up at me with tears in her eyes. "I failed with him."

"You failed to give me the life I deserved," Ezra said, hatred in his tone. "Now you'll pay for it." He raised his arms, magic crackling all around him.

I let out a sigh, already tired of his hysterics. He couldn't get past the coven circle, but any magic he threw at us would weaken the circle wall. I had to shut him down. Fast. "Ezra?"

"What?"

"I'd cool it if I were you."

"Don't tell me what to do, witch. She's my mother. The one who abandoned me to strangers. Let me—oomph." A bolt of magic came from behind him, knocking him to his knees.

"It's about time you guys showed up," I said to Vaughn, one of the demon hunters.

"Our apologies." The handsome twenty-something incubus smiled at me. "We got caught up."

I glanced past him at two other demon hunters I didn't know. "Where's Kane?"

Vaughn frowned. "I'm not sure. We'll have to ask Maximus."

Too bad he was conveniently missing as well. I returned my attention to Chessandra, now standing behind me. Her eyes were fixed on her unconscious son, worry streaming off her in waves. Whatever had passed between the two of them, she clearly cared about him.

"Let's get on with it," I said to Bea.

She stood beside me. "You know what to do."

I'd done a curse transfer before, but I'd taken it from Lucien, filtered it through myself, and forced it back into the witch who'd cursed him. I glanced at Zoe and shook my head. "No.

I don't. If she's responsible for cursing me, I can't transfer it to her."

Bea studied Zoe for a second then asked her, "How did you do it?"

Zoe sucked in a shaky breath. "I spiked Jade's chai concentrate with the fertility potion Chessandra cursed. I did it on New Year's Eve when we were all at Jade's house."

Son of a… No wonder I'd gotten sick the next day after drinking my morning tea. How simple and utterly stupid that I hadn't realized anything was off.

"I see." Bea's tone was full of anger as she glared at Chessandra. "Then Zoe can be left out of the equation, and we can just give it back to the person it belongs to."

Chessandra stared at the ground, appearing completely resigned. Most likely, since it was her black spell, she could neutralize it, but it would cost her. She'd be weakened afterward. I just didn't care. The fact that she'd wanted to control my child was quite possibly the worst thing she could've come up with to do to me. I had half a mind to take Ezra's side and send her off to Hell. But the room where time stood still would be better. She'd be out of commission, and we wouldn't have to worry about her coming back as a demon.

"You're a real piece of work, you know that?" I said to her as I grabbed her wrist and squeezed until she winced. "Abandoning your own child and then trying to take mine from me. You deserve everything that happens to you after this night."

Then before she could say a word, I focused on the dark pit of magic curling in my gut, gritted my teeth against the burning pain, and called it forth. Everything left my mind as the black curse took over, spiraling me into a world of confusion and static. My head spun. My stomach turned. I couldn't see anything. All I knew was the ugly pain of black magic consuming me. It filled me up and took over, leaving me completely lost.

"Jade! Transfer it," Bea's faint voice broke through the walls of confusion. "Do it now!"

It was the sound of her voice more than the actual words that reached me, and in that moment, I fought for her. For Kane. For my future child.

"Release!" I cried.

The magic burst from my hands, and I watched as the dark curse wound its way around Chessandra's arms and climbed up her neck. She didn't fight it, just stood there letting it happen.

But before the black magic fully engulfed her, it stopped, balled up, and shot across through the air, straight through the wall of the circle, and slammed into Ezra.

He let out a loud moan and bent at the waist, clutching his chest.

"Oh my God," I heard Zoe say.

My focus narrowed to Ezra as he straightened and stared straight at me, hatred in his eyes. "What did you do to me?" he asked.

I shook my head, not at all sure myself. I turned to Chessandra.

Tears streamed down her face. "The curse controls the first-born child."

Holy gods. I'd been forcing her curse back into her, but because she'd already given birth, the curse attached itself to her child. Now he was controlled by…who? Chessandra? Or me? I'd been the one to transfer the curse. I had no idea. But the thought that I might have control over him sickened me. It wasn't something I wanted.

"Jade!" I turned just in time to see Avery break free of her bonds. When the black magic had penetrated the circle wall, it had weakened the coven's magic.

She stood tall, with her arms stretched out, blocking all attempted magical attacks. Her eyes blazed red as she pointed to the ground and unleashed a torrent of her own magic. A hole opened up, and she stood at the edge, glaring at Chessandra. "I'll be back for her."

"She won't be here," I said.

The demon turned her wrath on me. "She'd better be, or you'll never see your husband again."

"What?" My heart thundered against my chest.

"You didn't know?" Her lips turned up into an evil grin. "He's been taken to Hell. Claimed by one of the most powerful players of our realm. But I'll make you a deal. You give me Chessandra, and I'll help you get him out."

"It's not true," I said, praying with every fiber of my being that she was lying. But the fact that Kane wasn't here... I glanced over at Vaughn. His pitying look told me everything I needed to know. Kane had been taken, and Maximus was either trying to find a way to save him or was too cowardly to face me.

When I met Avery's wild gaze, she said, "I'm your only chance." Then she jumped, and the hole slowly started to close.

"No!" I ran forward, stopping at the edge of the portal, teetering on the edge.

"She's lying," I heard Ezra call. "No one can help him now."

I spun. "You knew?"

He glared at me. "Of course I knew. When one spends nine months in Hell, he learns a few things. Rouquette is never coming back. They have plans for him."

Two thoughts hit me simultaneously. The first was that the longer Kane was in Hell, the harder it would be to get him out. The second was that Ezra had information about the players I didn't. And while I didn't trust him, I absolutely believed he'd do whatever he could to survive.

Without weighing exactly what I was doing, I said, "Come here."

Ezra struggled against Vaughn's grasp, unable to break free.

"Let him go," I ordered. The coven's protective wall had shattered when the black magic had shot through it. Ezra would have no trouble joining me in the circle.

Vaughn did as I said and stepped back.

Ezra scowled but moved forward, his limbs jerky and uncoordinated. "How are you doing this? What's happening to me?"

"You're obeying my command." It was the curse. I had complete control over him. My stomach turned at the thought, but I squared my shoulders and swallowed the unease. Now wasn't the time to worry about it.

When he got to my side, I wrapped my hand around his and said, "Jump."

His eyes widened with horror as we both disappeared into Hell.

Chapter 25

Jade

My knees ached from where I'd slammed into the stone floor, and sweat coated my skin. Nerves coiled through my belly, and for a minute I thought I was going to vomit right there on the demon hovering over me.

"Have you lost your goddamned mind?" Ezra hissed. He was sprawled on the stone floor of Avery's quarters.

I ignored him and spied the demon in question standing over us, a snarl on her blood-red lips. Her wild dark locks frizzed in the humidity of Hell, and she looked every bit the evil demon she was. Black sparks of magic hit the stone floor right in front of me, and I jerked back, barely avoiding being taken out with whatever nastiness she'd thrown at me.

"Not now," I said to Ezra and scrambled to my feet, throwing up a wall of magic to block another attack from Avery.

"Fuck," he muttered, joining me. To Avery he said, "Stand down, demon. Or you'll have to answer to Aiken."

Her sharp gaze landed on him, but she didn't drop her magic. "What do you mean, I'll answer to Aiken?"

A smug look filtered over his face. "He owes me. Now back off."

"Fuck you," she spat and threw another bolt of power at our magic wall. The pressure in the air between us and the barrier intensified, and I fought to keep from taking a step back.

"You dumb demon," Ezra said, narrowing his eyes. "I know you're Wes's property. What do you think Aiken will do to him if he finds out you failed to inform anyone of my presence—someone who makes deals with demons and is also the son of the high angel?"

"I don't care what happens to Wes." Her movements were stiff now, full of agitation.

Ezra sighed and took a step forward, almost pressing himself against the magical barrier. "If anything happens to Wes, you'll only be sold to the highest bidder. Do you want that? To be a demon slave to those who will do with you as they please?"

I sucked in a sharp breath. Avery was a demon and beyond help, but still, it was hard to see her like this. To not only be damned but to be a demon of the lowest order. My hatred for Chessandra grew. This was her fault. She'd sent Avery to deal with Wes.

"I won't be…sold," she said, but nothing about her declaration was convincing. She was worried.

"Just take us straight to Aiken, love," Ezra said. "You might even gain favor. Maybe find a way to be out from under any other demon's thumb. Do you have any idea how powerful he is?"

She stepped back, dropping her magical attack. Her nostrils flared with frustration, but then she turned to me. "You sure you want to do this? If I were you, I'd take my happy butt right back up to the surface."

I nodded. "I'm sure. I'm not leaving here without Kane."

"Fine. But if you even think of trying anything—"

"I'm not interested in causing you any trouble. If you keep your magic to yourself, I'll do the same."

With a sharp nod, Avery pulled back a ratty curtain, revealing a small area where she kept her personal effects. She took out a brush and quickly tried to tame her hair. But it was useless. She'd only succeeded in creating a larger mass of frizz.

"I'm sorry," I said to her and waved a hand around the dank quarters. The room was small, like a college dormitory with a single bed and no décor except one sad, faded cityscape of New Orleans that hung on the gray-tinged wall. "I wish we could've saved you from this."

She gritted her teeth. "There's no saving anyone. We're all doomed."

Her response saddened me, but I couldn't say as I could blame her. A life relegated to Hell would quickly become one without hope. I clamped my mouth shut and followed her and Ezra out of the small room.

Avery held her head high and acted as if having an angel and a witch trailing after her was completely normal.

Ezra had an odd mix of confidence and trepidation streaming from him. It wasn't a comfort. I patted my front pocket, searching for the herbs and potions I'd tucked there before the summoning and scowled. They hadn't survived the trip into Hell. Damn. That wasn't a complete surprise. Most objects didn't, but the potions would've been useful against the demons.

I'd been in Hell once before, but I didn't recognize the area we were in now. In fact, I had no idea where we were or where we were going. The last time, I'd memorized a map and Kane had been with me. Now I had a double-dealing angel who I didn't trust at all and one pissed-off demon. If I found Kane and we actually made it back home, it would be a dammed miracle.

The pit in my stomach grew, and nerves made my hands start to shake. What in the world had I gotten myself into? And tossing an angel into Hell against his will, no matter what sins he'd committed, was beyond wrong. Shame filled my heart. White witch my ass. My actions were no better than a demon's.

Stop it, Jade.

I shook my head violently. Second-guessing my choices wasn't going to change anything. Right then, I had two tasks and two tasks only: find Kane and get us out of there.

We moved along a dirt-walled corridor. Gas lights hung from the rock ceiling. The entryways into new rooms were just carved-out holes, most covered with a fabric partition. It was like the slums of Hell.

I wrapped my arms around myself, stifling a chill despite the heat. Avery was clearly on the bottom rung when it came to the demon social class. I could only hope that Wes treated her with a modicum of decency. She was easily the most reasonable demon I'd ever met. But then, she hadn't had much choice, had she?

My heart started to ache for her, but as I caught myself clutching my chest, I forced my hands to my sides.

Demon, I told myself one more time.

That meant her humanity was either stripped away or there was so little left that it wasn't worth looking for. And if I allowed myself to feel sorry for her, it was as good as surrendering myself to her. Avery wouldn't take pity on me. If she had her way, I'd already be a pile of goo on the floor of her room.

Sliding a shield around my heart, I straightened my shoulders and buried all the fears trying to bubble to the surface.

"Hold up," Avery said, coming to a stop at the end of the corridor. She pressed her hand to the closed old-fashioned wooden door and scowled.

"What is it?" I asked.

She turned around, her eyes narrowed and glowing red. "There's a group of demons on the other side of this door. They're surly and like to drink, which means getting around them is going to be a bitch. We can either wait here until they move on, or you can take your chances."

I couldn't wait. Who knew what Kane was going through? The longer this took, the greater the likelihood I'd never see him again. We had to risk it. "We're not waiting."

Her nostrils flared again, but she didn't argue. "Don't say I didn't warn you."

I glanced at Ezra. "Say whatever you have to, but don't mention we're here for Kane."

He gave me a disgusted look. "Do you think I'm an idiot?"

I shrugged. He was the one who'd made deals with demons, wasn't he?

"When this is over, Calhoun, you'd better watch your back. No one crosses me and gets away with it."

Anger surged from the depths of my core and got caught at the back of my throat, but I swallowed it, not allowing him to bait me. Now wasn't the time to battle with the prodigal son of the high angel. "Let's go," I said to Avery.

She shook her head but reached for the door handle anyway. Ezra beat her to it in some rare show of male chivalry.

Avery glared at him as she moved past him.

My internal B.S. meter went off, and I stopped in front of Ezra. With the will of my magic behind my words, I said, "Don't even think about betraying me. You'll do whatever it takes to ensure I make it safely to Kane's side." The impromptu spell I'd cast on him tickled my lips. Good. It was working. "Or I'll make sure you stay here for good."

His expression turned to one of detached obedience, and I prayed I hadn't spelled whatever charm and cunning he had right out of him. He was going to need it.

"Well, what do we have here?" a deep voice boomed from the small crowd of demons gathered at a community table.

"Looks like Wes's bitch needs some taming," another one said with a snicker.

"Shut up." Wes stood and knocked the drink out of the offending demon's hand. "Don't ever talk about my property that way."

Property? Every fiber of my being longed to curse Wes as my guilt intensified for not being able to help Avery. Her existence encompassed my worst nightmare.

"Avery." Wes circled the table and moved to stand right in front of her. He'd morphed into human form. Nothing about him said demon except his color-changing eyes. He was tall, had dark hair, and if it hadn't been for the air of aggression coming off him, he'd almost be handsome. "Did you bring me a present?" Wes eyed me from head to toe. An eager grin spread over his face. He turned his attention back to Avery. "Looks like you might have just gained a little favor, sweet cakes."

Oh, for the love of… "I'm not your present. We're here on business."

"Business?" Wes let out a loud laugh. "The only business you're going to be engaged in is cleaning my suite."

He reached out to grab my arm, but I jerked back, simultaneously calling up a magic shield that coated my skin. It wouldn't keep anyone from grabbing me, but if they did, they'd get quite the zap.

Ezra stepped around me. "We're on our way to see Aiken. I suggest you take us to him if you don't want him to find out how you got Avery as your bedmate."

Whoa. I glanced between them and then at Avery. Her face flushed a deep shade of maroon as she glared at both of them. Bile stung the back of my throat, and I wanted to scream for the angel she had been.

"Ezra?" Wes's eyes went wide and then narrowed. "I heard you traded your life for an incubus. What are you doing back here?"

And there it was again. Another demon who clearly thought Ezra had sold Kane out. I had to clench my fists to keep from striking out at the angel.

Ezra sent him a blank look. "That's none of your concern."

"Actually, I think it is." Wes took a step forward, standing nearly chest to chest with Ezra. "Since I'm the one who brought you to Aiken in the first place, what you do reflects on me. You're not here to cause trouble, are you?"

A muscle pulsed in Ezra's jaw, and his whole body tensed. For a second, I thought he was going to snap. Then Ezra said, "I'm bringing him another gift." He waved to me. "If you want to gain favor with your master, you might want to stop this interrogation and help us get there."

"What?" I whispered harshly. "A gift?"

Hatred mixed with self-satisfaction gleamed in Ezra's eyes. "You demanded I get you safely to Rouquette's side. You didn't say anything about what happened to you after that."

"You little—"

He waved a hand, and suddenly my words were gone. My mouth worked, but nothing came out. That bastard! "That's to make sure you're done with your commands."

I raised my hand to strike out, but he blocked my blow easily. "Behave, or I'll have Avery restrain you."

Avery smiled, clearly enjoying our battle, and although every instinct was calling for me to silently curse Ezra, I tapped into a self-control I didn't know I possessed. Instead, I concentrated on trying to break his spell. I couldn't go into a room with a bunch of demons and not have my voice.

Calling up my magic, I imagined the white light collecting at the back of my throat, and then in my head I chanted, *return*. A sharp pain shot down my throat as my mouth burned, and I had to fight to keep from crying out. I instinctively knew my magic had worked, but the last thing I wanted to do was let Ezra know that. When we walked into Aiken's chambers, I was going to be ready.

Ezra turned to Wes. "Take us to Aiken."

The other demon laughed. "You do have a way about you, Ezra. If you weren't such a conniving weasel, I'd join forces with you. But I'm not interested in finding a knife in my back."

"You'd know all about that, wouldn't you?" Ezra asked.

Wes shrugged. "I only did what I had to in order to survive."

Ezra glanced at Avery. "Since when does survival mean forcing a demon to warm your bed?"

"Since I haven't had a woman after your mother left me twenty years ago. I'm done waiting." Wes's eyes landed on Avery, and a spark of lust claimed him.

Oh, holy shit. My eyes widened, and I had to stifle a gasp to keep from giving myself away. Chessandra had been with a demon? Or had he been an angel then?

Wes tore his eyes from Avery. "Let's go. The little demon and I have plans later."

My stomach rolled at his words as I followed Wes and Ezra out of the room and into another crude corridor.

Chapter 26

Kane

A small party of three demons headed toward the heavy wooden door on the other side of the cave, but before one could open it, the door swung open and smashed against the rocky wall.

A tall demon wearing a suit strode in, a smug smile on his face. He had companions, but I couldn't make them out through the demons now standing and jeering at them.

"Well, well, well. What do we have here?" Aiken's smooth voice boomed over the growing chatter. "Looks like you boys don't need to make a trip to the surface after all."

I struggled against the chair, frustrated I couldn't see what was going on. Leaning over to Bianca, I said, "Who's here?"

She stared straight ahead, her expression blank. "Your charge."

"What?" Craning my neck, I tried to peer around Aiken, but I only caught a flash of pale skin and long strawberry-blond hair that looked very familiar. Fear rippled through me, and my mind whirled. *Jade?*

"Kane!" Jade broke through the crowd and leaped onto the raised platform. She fell to her knees in front of me, relief and horror swimming in her eyes. "What have they done to you?"

"Nothing…yet." I glanced around the room, spotting Aiken. Glee lit up his expression. I swallowed the epithets on my tongue and refocused on Jade, ignoring the mixture of panic and relief I felt at seeing her. "You shouldn't be here."

Her eyes narrowed, but she was unable to hide the love and worry shining back at me. "Neither should you."

"I didn't have a choice."

"Neither did I." She placed her hands over mine and instantly drew them back. "They've bound you to this chair?"

"Yes," Bianca answered for me.

Jade cut her gaze to the sex witch, appearing to notice her for the first time. "Who's she?"

"I'm his reward for signing the contract."

"His…what?" Her bright-green eyes met mine again. "Contract?"

I shook my head, meaning to say I never had any intention of signing the thing, but Aiken was striding toward us with the tall demon beside him and…was that Ezra just behind him glaring at Jade? "You double-crossing piece of shit," I spat at the angel.

He folded his arms over his chest and gave me a flat stare. "I didn't have a choice."

Aiken flicked a glance at Ezra. "Shut up." Then he ordered the rest of the crowd to take a seat. When the commotion died down, he eyed the demon in the suit. "You've brought me two great gifts today. Your obedience will be rewarded. Jasmine—" he waved toward one of the sex witches still leaning against the wall.

The curvy raven-haired witch moved around the large table in the middle of the room and stood meekly next to Aiken.

"Join hands," Aiken said to the demon and the witch.

The suit held his hand out, and Jasmine, still staring at the floor, raised hers. The demon clutched it possessively. Jasmine winced, even though I was certain the demon hadn't hurt her physically.

"Very good," Aiken said. "I hereby bequeath the sex witch Jasmine into Wes Lancaster's service for the next fifty years."

I sucked in a sharp breath. Wes Lancaster was the demon

Chessandra had pardoned from some unknown sin. Was he in on Ezra's deception? All I knew was I trusted no one but Jade.

"You two may leave," Aiken said, waving Jasmine and Wes toward the open door.

Ezra moved with them, but Aiken grabbed his wrist, stopping him. "You're staying."

He jerked his arm out of Aiken's grasp. "Why?"

"Your presence was requested." Aiken pointed to a chair at the table, snarling at him. "Sit down."

Ezra shot Jade and me a look of pure hatred as he dragged his feet across the stone floor.

"Very good." Aiken clapped his hands together, a pleased smile claiming his ugly face. "We can get started."

"What's going on?" Jade whispered, still kneeling near me.

"He wants me to sign a contract binding me to him as some sort of warrior." Her expression was fierce, full of determination. I prayed she had a plan, because I had no idea how we were going to get out of this mess. "He said if I don't, he's going to go after you and your first-born child."

Jade's expression shifted into one of hardened steel. "Did he now?" She stood, her back straight, magic barely sparking at her fingertips.

I was caught somewhere between gut-wrenching fear for what she had in mind and utter pride. My wife wasn't letting anyone take her down. Or me, apparently.

"Now that the offering has arrived, we can commence with the signing." Aiken nodded to Bianca. "Hand him the contract."

The witch did as she was told, but Jade grabbed it out of her hands. After quickly scanning it, she let out a humorless laugh. "Kane will never sign this."

Aiken glided toward us, an amused expression on his face. He stopped right in front of Jade. A full foot taller, he stared down at her, making her appear small and weak by his sheer bulk. But I could feel the magic building in her and knew better.

"He will, white witch," Aiken said. "Otherwise we'll take you instead."

"I doubt it," she said without even a hint of fear coloring her tone.

Pride welled in my chest. I had to hand it to her. She had brass balls and wasn't afraid to show it.

"You're way out of your league, little witch," Aiken sneered. "Now sit down, or I'll have you chained to the wall." He jerked his head, indicating a section to the right that had shackles bolted to the stones.

"Why do you want Kane?" she asked, ignoring his command.

Her question seemed to surprise him, and he stepped back, shaking his head.

"Political reasons," I said. "Something about needing a warrior so he can take over as leader or something."

Aiken looked at me. "You don't know? Neither of you do." The realization made him belt out a laugh. "This is too much."

Jade and I glanced at each other, both of us remaining confused.

"Mr. Rouquette, you're my direct ancestor. When the two of us join forces, my power will be unparalleled. No one will dare to challenge me. Not even my father Malefant, the oldest demon of the realm, our oldest living relative. Life in Hell will change. We'll no longer be required to collect souls for the oldest among us to further their power. The souls we harvest will feed our own magic. We shall rise up, be free to roam the surface, and take what we want for ourselves, not for those who only wish to exploit us."

The demons in the cave roared their approval and cheered by pounding their fists on the wooden table.

"Gods." Jade whispered and reached for my hand but pulled away before she touched the magic coating my skin. "We have to do something."

I nodded. If I signed my soul to Aiken, one evil would be traded for another. Conditions would be worse, in fact. As it stood now, these demons were tasked with harvesting a certain number of souls for the elders. If things changed and it became every demon for himself, the soul harvesting would be a thousand times worse. Demons would be taking over our world and wreaking more havoc than ever. It was a rebellion of devastating consequences.

"As per our agreement," Aiken continued, "the angel Ezra and the sex witch Bianca will be awarded to Mr. Rouquette once the contract is signed. His wife—"

"You can't do that!" Ezra shot up from the table, his face stark white with fear. "We had a deal. I brought you the incubus in exchange for my freedom. You agreed."

"Do you have a contract?" Aiken asked calmly.

"I have your word and witnesses!"

Aiken scoffed. "I'm a demon. My word means nothing."

"Then I want a revised contract," I interjected. "If your word can't be trusted, then I require written confirmation that Ezra and Bianca will indeed be under my charge."

"Kane?" Jade's voice was barely audible.

I gave her a tiny shake of my head and met Aiken's stare once more. "And I want a couple of hours alone with my wife before I do anything."

"Not acceptable," Aiken said.

"You're expecting him to give up his life, but you can't even spare a few hours for us to say our goodbyes?" Jade asked.

"Sit down, witch, or I'll have you removed." Aiken ordered.

I ground my teeth. "You have two choices. Let us have a little bit of time. Or you can just forget having me as part of your operation. I'm not doing anything until I say goodbye and know Jade is safely back at home."

Aiken's chest puffed up, and a muscle in his already strained neck twitched. He was seconds from losing control. "You're done calling the shots, Rouquette."

"All I asked—"

He turned toward Jade and unleashed a stream of dark-gray magic that hit her in the chest. Her eyes went wide with shock and then narrowed in pain. Her mouth dropped open, but no sound came out as Aiken's magic lifted her into the air, her feet dangling a few inches from the platform floor.

"Stop!" I demanded, straining against the magic binding me to the chair. My muscles bunched and protested. Sweat poured down my back. Welts cut into my wrists from the invisible restraints. And through it all, the only thing I felt was a sharp pain centered deep in my chest. "Put her down. She's not a part of this."

Aiken growled and lifted her higher in the air. "She is as long as you're more concerned with her than with the contract. Consent to sign, and I'll let go."

White bursts of magic shot sporadically from Jade's fingertips, blasting small craters into the stone floor.

Goddammit. I couldn't sit there and watch him torture her. The fact that she was barely fighting back spoke volumes. She was in serious pain.

"Well?" He curled his fingers, and Jade started coughing as if he was choking her. The crowd urged him on, cheering their approval.

"Put her down. I'll sign it. Just leave her alone and let her go home."

Aiken dropped the magic, and Jade crumpled to the ground, holding her throat as she sucked in large gasps of breath.

"You son of a bitch," I said, my voice low and full of hatred. I'd sign his fucking contract, but the first chance I got, I was going to kill him. My hand started to tingle with magic the way it did when I was ready to battle and my power connected with the magic of my dagger. But that wasn't right. My dagger wasn't here, and it was highly unlikely any of the demons had one. It was possible, but a demon hunter's dagger was a power drain for demons. One would have to be out of his mind to carry one.

Jade moaned beside me, and the desire to murder Aiken intensified along with the tingling in my hand. I felt the pulse of magic streaming through my body, but I didn't have a way to release it. I glanced at Jade and made an instant decision.

"I'm ready," I said to Aiken. "Release me, and I'll sign the contract."

"No." Jade forced herself to stand, even as she swayed on her feet from the effects of Aiken's attack.

I stared at her, willing her to see my intention. *Please let her be strong enough for this.* If she wasn't—I forced the thought from my head. There was no need to doubt her strength. My wife was a powerful white witch.

"I can't let you do this," she whispered.

"I'm not. *We* are."

Something about my tone must've clued her in, because a small light of understanding lit her eyes. It vanished almost instantly, and she turned to stare straight ahead, stone-like as if she was shutting down, but I knew she was bracing herself.

"Let him up," Aiken said to Bianca.

The witch to my right touched my arm once more, searing my skin with her neutralizing magic. The invisible restraints burned away, this time leaving tiny but deep gashes over my exposed skin. I hissed and then scowled, knowing it was likely those scars were going to be permanent. I didn't care. If we survived this, then I'd wear them with pride. No demon was going to enslave me or separate me from the love of my life. Not without a fight.

Aiken walked over, grabbed the marble clipboard from Bianca, and thrust it at me. "Sign it. Now."

I took a moment to read the contract one more time. It hadn't changed. It was still a simple agreement, nothing much to think over.

"Do it!" Aiken snarled.

I glared at him and grabbed the pen hard enough that a piece of the metal cap broke off. It scattered to the floor, making a *tink, tink, tink* sound. We all watched it in silence as it rolled off the platform.

And then I moved. Dropping the clipboard, I grabbed Jade's hand with my left, and with my right I lunged, stabbing Aiken in the shoulder with the gold pen.

The demon jerked back and roared, making the whole room vibrate. He ripped the pen out of his chest. Green-tinged goo dripped from the wound. "You stupid incubus. How dare you lay a hand on me?"

"Now, Jade." I pushed a small bit of my itching magic into her palm, counting on her ability to manipulate my energy.

She responded instantly, pulling everything I had to offer into her control. And just as Aiken unleashed a torrent of his dark power at me, she cut off his stream with one of her own, no doubt saving me from being obliterated right there in the cave in front of everyone.

I held on to her hand, feeding the demon hunter magic into her, while she stepped forward, pushing Aiken back.

"No one is signing your contract." Her raspy voice was strained. "I'd tell you to go to Hell, but that's too good for you." Jade's body lit up as her lavender-tinted white aura materialized. Her hair streamed out behind her as she vibrated with strength. "I think we'll make sure you never see the light of day again."

She ripped her hand from mine, but the lavender-white aura continued to cling to my wrist. Even though we were no longer physically touching, we were still connected by her magic. Taking a step forward, she said, "Let us leave this place now, or—"

"What, witch?" Aiken spat and increased his efforts, pushing her back a half step. "You'll kill me?" His humorless laughter filled the room.

"No." She jabbed her head toward the top of the wooden door. "I'll trap you in the stone snake carved up there."

Chapter 27

Jade

Kane's demon hunter energy coursed through me, filling me with bravado. I'd battled demons before, but fear had always been present. Now I was confident, sure I could take the demon down. He couldn't get past me *and* Kane. Even now he thought he was beating me back with his magic. He wasn't. I was only letting him think he was gaining ground.

The power consuming me could've likely melted him into a puddle of green demon slime if I'd wanted it to. But I had other plans. He could suffer the existence that so many of the demons' victims did—trapped in a stone statue where other demons fed off their power. It was so far beyond the pale that it seemed the perfect end for him.

Aiken and I stood about ten feet apart. He increased the pressure on his attack, while I reined mine in just a tad, creating the illusion that he was winning. But when I saw a flicker of triumph in his expression, I pushed my hands out and curled my fingers, visualizing that I was grabbing hold of his magic.

He gasped, and when I tightened my hands into fists, his magic pooled around him in a cloud of black smoke.

"How is she doing that?" I heard the sex witch ask Kane.

The jeers of the other demons now closing in around Aiken drowned out his reply.

"No!" I jumped off the platform and cursed when they created a demon barrier as they each met my stream of magic with a combined attack. Using Kane's incubus magic, combined with my own, I swept my arm to the side. Our powerful force slammed into them, instantly bringing them to their knees. Triumph spurred me on.

"Get out of my way," I ordered, leaping over the two demons now writhing on the ground.

Just behind them was Aiken, propping himself up with the edge of the long table. Our gazes met for half a second, and I let go of one more powerful blast, hitting him right in the chest. Aiken's mouth popped open in a silent scream. I smiled in triumph as he fell backward, his eyes rolling up into the back of his head.

Take that you son of a bitch.

I kept moving, intending to make good on my promise to trap Aiken in the stone snake, but was cut off by a green-haired demon. He held up a large ruby-red amulet. I blasted him, expecting him to go down as easily as the others. Except the moment my magic got near him, a force overcame me, and my power was sucked right into the eye of the amulet.

I tried to shut the magic down, but it was no use. My feet were glued to the floor, and I was completely unable to move while the demon drained my only weapon.

"Jade!" I heard Kane call over the buzzing in my ears.

The demons moved together in a crowd toward the door. Directly behind Green Hair, I saw two of them hauling Aiken away. He was still unconscious, burn marks from his own magic marring him.

Good. Even though I hadn't had the opportunity to trap him in the stone sculpture, at least I'd done some damage. My arms started to shake, and I was certain if I didn't break the hold Green Hair had on me, I was going to be just as unconscious as Aiken. Closing my eyes, I focused all my energy on the tips of my fingers. My magic sputtered and sparked, but Green Hair increased his effort, smiling with evil satisfaction.

"Let go, demon," I said, putting my will behind the words.

He hesitated, and the grip he had on me wavered.

I stepped back and then plowed head on into another demon, forcing him forward right into Green Hair. They both sprawled to the ground. The ruby amulet flew out of Green Hair's hand. I dove for it, my hand wrapping around the silver setting at the same time as Green Hair's did.

"You dumb bitch," the demon said, his spittle spraying me in the face.

"Ugh, gross." I brought my knee up but missed his groin as he rolled, taking me and the amulet with him until he was straddling me, both of us still clutching the magical artifact.

"Get off my wife." Kane grabbed one of the demons attacking him, threw him against the wall, and kicked Green Hair in the shoulder, knocking him off me. The demon's hold on the amulet was so strong that he ripped it right out of my hand.

"No!" I pointed, meaning to tell Kane to get the weapon, but he was already on it. In one swift movement, he reached down and palmed the amulet. It turned bright red at his touch, and Green Hair screamed as magic shot from the ruby straight into his eyes.

He let go and rolled away, cowering under the table.

"It recognizes you," I said to Kane amid the chaos.

"No, it recognizes my magic. It looks like someone fashioned this from a demon hunter dagger a long time ago."

"Watch out!" Bianca yelled from behind us.

I spun, finding her battling two demons as two more came straight for us.

"We have to get out of here. Now," I said to Kane.

He nodded.

"You're not leaving without me," Bianca announced.

Kane reached out to grab her hand, but Ezra came up behind her and snatched her around the waist.

"You're not taking her anywhere," Ezra yelled, threw her over his shoulder, and ran toward the door. Despite her cries of protest, no one stopped him. And Kane and I had our hands full.

"That little shit," I said to Kane as he pointed the ruby at a demon and blasted him across the cave into the far wall.

His free hand wrapped around mine, and he tugged. Together we shot demon after demon, forcing our way through the room until we made it through the cave opening.

"Run," Kane said.

But his order was unnecessary. I was already sprinting back toward Avery's room. If we could get there, we could slip back through the portal that led to the coven circle. Hopefully. If the coven hadn't sealed it.

"This way," I said, ducking into the unfinished passageway, my limbs heavy and my chest aching from the massive amount of energy we'd used back in the cave. But adrenaline and sheer willpower kept me moving. Resting wasn't an option.

"Wait!" a female voice yelled from behind us.

I paused. It was Bianca, with Ezra right on her heels.

Kane turned and squared his shoulders. "Leave her be, Ezra."

He ignored both of us and reached for her.

Kane pointed the amulet at Ezra. "Touch her again, and I'll knock you unconscious."

Ezra snarled and wrapped his arm around Bianca's neck. "She's my ticket out of here."

"Jeez." I shook my head. "Let her go and just come with us."

He shook his head. "You two can't be trusted."

"*We can't?* You've got to be kidding me." He was out of his mind.

"Do you think I'm an idiot? What would you do once we made it back to the surface? Let me go on my merry way?"

Kane put his hand up, stopping me from saying anything more. "Let Bianca go, and you're free to do whatever you please."

He shook his head violently. "How do you think I'm getting out of here?"

I met Bianca's gaze, and the resignation I saw there fueled my determination to save her. She didn't think she'd ever leave. I clutched Kane's hand. "Wherever they're going, we're going with them."

"No. You're not." Ezra pulled a dagger out of his back pocket and waved it at us.

I didn't pay much attention to it, as I was watching the fear roll over Bianca. But Kane stiffened beside me, and something close to hate sprang to his surface. I looked up at him. "What is it?"

"He stole my dagger."

I cut my eyes to Ezra and focused on the weapon he held. Sucking in a hard breath, I straightened my spine, ready to battle once again. "You had it this whole time?"

He shrugged.

"You're an incredible bastard," I said quietly and moved forward. But before I could curse him or just plain slap him, the door behind us burst open, and demons sprinted down the hall toward us. "Go!" I yelled, and the four of us took off down the unfamiliar hallway.

A few yards down, we took a sharp left, and before I knew it, we were passing the meeting room where we'd first found Kane. Only a few demons were still sitting at the table, drinking wine from ceramic chalices. They didn't even glance up at the pounding of our footsteps. Apparently they were more worried about food and drink than intruders in Hell.

Ezra skid to a stop, grabbed Bianca once again, and burst through a door adjacent to the cave room.

"What the hell are you doing?" Kane asked, glaring at him.

Ezra tried to shut the door on him, but Kane thrust out his hand, keeping the door from slamming shut. Ezra once again brandished the dagger and held it out at Kane. "Don't test me, incubus."

"Go ahead and try it," Kane challenged.

An uncertain expression claimed Ezra's face just mere seconds before he called, "Freeze!"

Magic shot from the ruby stone on the dagger's hilt in the form of frost, covering Kane and me from head to toe. I shivered uncontrollably. Kane swore and lunged forward, reaching for the dagger.

But the door had already slammed shut, cutting us off from both Ezra and Bianca.

I concentrated on that pulse in my chest and focused my magic, sending it through my body. The frost melted, leaving my clothes wet and my skin damp. "He's going to wish he'd never been born."

"I think he already does," Kane said and took my hand once more. Frost still clung to his clothes but had already melted from his skin. He blasted the door open and led us across an ornately decorated room with rich, warm wooden floors.

"It feels like you know where you're going," I said.

"This is Aiken's quarters and where I was held before the gathering. There's only one more room. Unless Ezra has already figured out how to leave Hell, that's where we'll find them."

Aiken's place? Dammit. He could be in that other room, already recovered from my last blow. I'd only knocked him out. Chances were he'd have woken up by now. I sucked in a steadying breath, braced myself, and followed Kane through the doorway.

Sure enough, Aiken and Green Hair were standing in the middle of the room. Green Hair had Ezra in a chokehold, while Bianca was on her knees in front of Aiken, her head bowed.

"Release them," Kane ordered.

Green Hair laughed. Aiken didn't even acknowledge our presence.

"You've been disobedient," he said to Bianca.

She nodded but didn't look up at him.

"You cursed more than half a dozen of my followers." His words were a statement rather than a question.

Bianca took a shuddering breath but didn't respond.

"You disrespected me."

I was half a second from cursing the demon myself, but Kane's light squeeze and small shake of his head kept me from making a move just yet. What was he up to? I sent him a questioning glance, but he was focused on Ezra and Green Hair.

Green Hair had Kane's dagger in his left hand and was holding it close to Ezra's face. The fact that the demon could touch it told me Kane was low on energy and couldn't activate its magic. Of course he was. I'd just used a torrent of his power back in the cave. If Kane's magic had been strong, he would've been able to connect to the dagger and force the demon to drop it. Or at the very least cause a nasty burn on the demon's hand.

"I just want to go home," Bianca said to the floor.

"You are home!" Aiken pulled his arm back in a wind-up to strike a blow.

I didn't even think before I reacted. A thick stream of magic burst from my palm and slashed Aiken's raised arm.

Thick black blood gushed from his wrist while Bianca rolled away, her hands raised to protect herself against any incoming attacks.

But the demon had turned his attention to me, a murderous expression in his crimson eyes. "You will die for that, witch."

"You first," I said and sent another burst of hate-filled magic at him. The blast was so strong, so powerful, and fueled by so much bitterness that I was terrified I'd tapped that dark place inside me that could call up black magic. Only, as I watched my magic pour into the demon, it was nothing but brilliant white light.

Aiken stood with his mouth open in a shock of horror at my attack.

I heard a commotion behind me, and from the corner of my eye, I saw Kane and Bianca rushing Green Hair. But I didn't have the luxury of paying attention to that fight. All my attention had to be focused on the old demon in front of me. If I could keep the magic going, I was certain I could obliterate him. Just a few more minutes and—

"Jade!" a familiar female voice said into my ear.

Without breaking my assault, I glanced over my shoulder. Limbs jabbed and kicked as Green Hair and Kane battled fist to fist, no dagger in sight. Ezra had dropped to his knees and was cowering behind an armchair. Bianca was on her feet chanting a binding spell, one meant to keep Green Hair anchored where he stood.

"Jade!" the familiar voice said again.

I squinted and finally spotted an outline of Lailah. Her transparent body floated near me. "Lailah? What's going on?"

"Sorry it took us so long. The portal sealed, and we had a devil of a time making a connection to either you or Kane until we remembered the binding spell Jasper cast. He's how we found you. We're here to bring you home." She pointed over my shoulder, indicating another transparent angel. Jonathon Goodwin, her mate.

My heart thundered against my chest. "Kane! Time to go."

He issued a bone-crushing blow to Green Hair, spun, and produced the dagger, shooting a weak stream of magic past me. Aiken let out a cry of frustration, his magic zapped momentarily.

Son of a…crap on toast. While I'd been watching the fight behind me, Aiken had pushed back my magic so far that he'd been seconds from burning me with his black magic. Thank the gods for Kane and the small bit of magic he'd juiced from the dagger.

Bianca turned her attention to Aiken, and ropes of magic rose up from the stone floor around the old demon in an impressive display of power. Her pupils were dilated into huge black saucers, a frightening snarl claiming her twisted lips.

"Aiken!" Green Hair jumped up, rushing to help his would-be leader.

"Oh, hell no," I spat and imitated Bianca's chant, my own ropes of power coiling around Green Hair.

"Hurry," Kane said. "We have to get out of here. I can feel more demons coming."

Bianca narrowed her eyes and swung her hand in a circle, whipping her powerful rope around Aiken's neck. "That's for every demeaning word, every time you dared touch me, and for every single time you thought I belonged to you, you sick bastard."

Aiken's eyes bulged, and his face turned a sick color of grayish-green as he tried and failed to suck in a last gasp of air.

"Never again," Bianca whispered, one lone tear trailing down her face.

Green Hair was on his knees, trapped in my magic. I didn't have enough strength left to end him, but he was bound enough that we could make a break for it.

Kane held his hand out to me. I grabbed it and yelled, "Bianca, time to go." The witch paused, hatred streaming from her as she stared at Aiken, trussed up and suffocating on her magic. "If we meet again, demon, it'll be the end of you." With her head held high, she turned her back on him and held her hand out to Kane.

With the three of us joined in a circle, I glanced at Lailah. "Take us home."

Jonathon and Lailah each held a hand out. And then Lailah chanted something in Latin. Magic crackled around us. When it faded, they were each left with what appeared to be a pile of ash in their palms. Both of them raised their hands to their mouths and blew. The ash floated through the air and coated the three of us.

Warmth spread through my limbs as we were lifted off our feet. We hovered there in the room for a moment, and then we began to fade into the otherworld. Only while the other two disappeared, I stayed in limbo by myself, seeming to be stuck in transit.

Panic filled me. Darkness closed in, and nausea took over. "Lailah!" I cried.

Nothing.

"Kane!" My voice echoed into the emptiness. I took a deep breath and focused on Kane, our home, the connection we shared when he was dream walking, and I felt myself start the fade into the otherworld again, but I was somehow pulled back to Hell once more. What was happening?

Why couldn't I transfer?

Clearing my mind, I forced every thought out except the coven circle, of the magic that must be there right then. It was the only way Lailah and Jonathon could've transcended into Hell the way they had. But no matter how hard I tried, I couldn't move. "You can't leave me here!" Ezra's voice rose up from the middle of the room. "We're bound."

"Ezra?" Righteous indignation made me scoff. He'd sold both Kane and me out and now he expected my help?

"We're connected. You can't leave without me," the angel cried.

How was that possible? I had no idea. Maybe it was the curse that transferred from me to him. I peered down at him, panic seizing me. The magic Bianca and I had used to bind the demons had already faded into the ether, and Green Hair was on his feet, stumbling toward Ezra, while Aiken pulled himself up off the floor.

Gods, if I left Ezra there, he'd turn demon. It didn't matter how I felt about him personally; I had to take him with me.

"Lailah!" I cried out, still floating high in the air. "Help!"

Green Hair jerked his head up. "You bitch. You're going to pay for this."

"Jade?" Lailah's outline materialized beside me, both of us floating high in the air. "What happened?"

I pointed to Ezra. "We're connected. I can't leave without him."

Understanding dawned in her expression. "Of course. Distract that pissed-off demon for a second."

Lailah darted down toward Ezra, and I followed, hovering just over Green Hair. "Hey, asshole."

He glanced once at Ezra, then leaped. Fire shot from his hand and singed the back of my arm as I rolled away, barely missing being crispy fried.

"Hurry," I said to Lailah, who was blowing more ash on Ezra.

"Now!" she cried and disappeared. Static filled my ears, and I knew this time it was working. Ezra was across the room, his body fading into the ether just as I knew mine was. The outlines of my coven circle appeared in my field of vision.

Jasper stood in the middle, holding hands with Lailah and Jonathon. To their left were Kane and Bianca, winded from our battle.

All the minor details started to come into focus: a silver dragonfly comb in Lailah's hair, the glint of Jonathon's wrist watch, the hilt of Kane's dagger.

"Jade!" Lailah cried.

I jerked my head up and met her frantic gaze.

"Her physical form won't transfer," I heard Bea call, only I couldn't see her or any of the other coven members.

"What's happening?" I asked, trying not to panic. I was here with Kane in the circle. Everything would be okay. It had to be,

Kane moved toward me, but when he reached out, his hand slid through me just as it had back in the room where time stood still.

"What the—"

"She's still tied to Hell," Jonathon said, cutting me off.

"Jasper!" Lailah gestured to him. "You're her only shot. Do something."

The young angel released Lailah's hand, raised his arm and sent a thick stream of magic straight at my chest.

An electric shock reverberated through my system, holding me frozen in place. I felt nothing else as a sharp pain gutted me and darkness took over.

I floated in a haze of nothingness for what seemed like ages, only to open my eyes to a shrill cry of panic.

"She's bleeding. Bea. Help her."

A warm hand clutched mine, and I blinked. Dark, worried eyes met mine.

Kane.

"Don't worry, love. You're going to be just fine."

"What…" I licked my lips. "What happened?"

He shook his head. "I'm not entirely sure. For some reason you were having trouble crossing."

Images started flashing in my mind and everything clicked. "Ezra. I was still bound to him. I couldn't leave while he was there."

Kane frowned and looked around. "Where is he, then?"

"He didn't make it back," Lailah said sharply.

"What do you mean?" I asked, glancing around in confusion. "I saw him fading with us."

"Jade?" Bea's soothing voice reached me.

I turned my head to the side and noticed her kneeling beside me, her hands hovering over my abdomen. "I've already administered a numbing spell, but the spell I need to close this wound is going to hurt. So brace yourself."

"What wound?" I tried to glance down at myself but was so weak I couldn't even move.

"You came back with a tear in your abdomen, Jade. But Bea's here. Don't worry," Kane said, squeezing my hand. "You're going to be fine."

I would've believed him if he hadn't been touching me. My empath ability was still running strong, and although he was putting on an excellent front, worry was eating him alive. It was bad.

"Did a demon do this to you?" Kane asked, casting a quick glance down my body.

"No. It must've happened when I crossed over. But I don't know why."

Kane jerked his head up, staring hard at someone off to the left. "Was it that spell Jasper used to complete her crossing?"

"No," Lailah said, tears in her voice. "Not exactly. Jasper's spell was able to anchor her here because of the binding he cast on both of you. But in the process, her connection to Ezra was severed. That's what caused the wound."

Kane squeezed my hand and narrowed his eyes as he glanced around. "What happened to him? Ezra I mean."

Lailah's face went white. "It was the ash spell. It didn't work on him. It only works on souls who are pure. Those souls who don't deserve to be in Hell."

She cut her gaze to me and stared me in the eye. "I can only guess that Ezra made too many deals with the demons, so once you both crossed the barrier back to the surface, the circle was trying to cast him back into Hell. And because you're bound by the coven and the magic of seven other witches, the pair of you were trapped in limbo until Jasper's spell broke whatever bond you shared with Ezra, leaving you here, gutted, and Ezra back in Hell."

"That's…awful," I said weakly, still numb, still waiting for Bea.

Lailah frowned, and her usually white aura turned gray with distress. "That's all you have to say?"

I nodded, too tired to care. Closing my eyes, I shut out everything until Bea's magic reached in, scrambled my insides, and stabbed me with a thousand razor-sharp knives.

Chapter 28

Jade

I can't remember much of what happened after Bea healed my wound other than Kane shadow walking me home. That was a week ago, and since then I'd spent much of my time in bed being waited on hand and foot by Kane, Pyper, and Lailah. They kept a steady rotation, making sure I didn't go much farther than the connected bathroom.

But today I was up, showered, dressed, and ready to go, if not exactly moving fast. I hobbled into the kitchen, holding my abdomen. I wasn't sure how extensive my wounds had been before Bea had magically mended me back together and, honestly, I didn't want to know. A doctor had checked me out and said I'd suffered some major bruising, but after a couple of weeks' rest, I'd be as good as new. Right now everything was just sore.

"I guess this means you're determined to go to the hearing?" Lailah said from the kitchen bar.

"Yes." I poured chai concentrate into my cup and sniffed it. Only spice and honey filled my senses. My taste for chai tea hadn't diminished one bit, but I did think about the curse every time I fixed myself a cup.

"No one but me, Pyper, and Kane have been anywhere near your kitchen in days," Lailah said. "Not even Kat."

My best friend had been by a few times, and thankfully had brought greasy takeout food, the way a good friend was supposed to. "I was just checking." Smiling, I shoved the cup into the microwave and hit the on button. "How is Zoe, anyway?"

Lailah shrugged. "She's all right, I guess. She told me she started going to therapy. Apparently there's a witch psychologist in Metairie. Bianca is seeing her as well."

"Seriously?"

"Twice a week."

That was interesting. I'd heard Bea had taken Bianca over to Coven Pointe and asked Mati, another sex witch, to take Bianca under her wing. Her entire family was filled with sex witches, so that seemed like a good choice to me. "I hope it helps. They've both been through so much."

Lailah nodded. "Zoe's been mentally violated by the one who was supposed to protect her. It's going to take her a while to recover. And Bianca, she's been physically violated, and although she appears to be acclimating well, her emotional scars run deep."

There was no denying either of her assessments. Both women had lived through nightmares.

Footsteps echoed from the other room, followed by Kane striding in. He smiled at me. "Hey, pretty witch. It's good to see you up."

"She thinks she's going to the hearing," Lailah said.

"Of course she is." Kane winked at me.

I smiled. There was no way I was missing this. Not after everything that had happened over the last months.

"Okay, then. Time to go." Lailah stood up and held her arm out to me.

I glanced at Kane. "Coming?"

"Wouldn't miss it."

The three of us walked to the living room. Kane and I glanced at Lailah.

"Hold on." She sent a text. Her phone buzzed immediately, and a silly grin spread over her face.

Both Kane and I stared at her, our eyebrows raised.

"Jonathon. He's meeting me there," she explained.

I pursed my lips. "Where's he been all week?" Lailah had barely stepped foot out of our house, only leaving to go home to shower and find clean clothes. She hadn't even slept there. She'd been occupying our guest room instead.

"In the realm, helping put the case together."

"Ah. I thought maybe he was staying away because of me."

Lailah's smile vanished. "He does feel badly about the history you two share. I think he wants to make amends, and that might be why he's working so hard on this. To bring justice to everyone who was hurt."

"Well...that's good of him." I felt sort of neutral about Jonathon these days. At one time, he'd treated me horribly. I'd been making an effort to put the past behind us, but sometimes I found it difficult to let go of my resentment. Though his help getting us out of Hell certainly had gone a long way toward mending fences.

"He's trying." She glanced up at the ceiling. The bright-white light shone down on us, and a second later, the three of us were standing in the angel realm's version of the Saint Louis Cathedral.

Every seat was filled with an angel in formal dress robes. Chessandra sat at a table in front of all of them, facing the Angel Council members.

"Whoa," I said.

"This way." Lailah led us down the center aisle and turned right in front of Chessandra.

When I met the high angel's gaze, I didn't see anything except regret in her dark eyes, and remorse streamed off her in waves.

Even though she'd been the reason Avery had been turned demon, I couldn't help but feel sorry for her. She'd lost her son to Hell. Whatever decisions she'd made about his upbringing, she had to be grieving that loss.

Kane put his hand on the small of my back. "You okay?"

I nodded and gingerly followed him into the witness box. We hadn't been summoned to testify, but Lailah said she'd put us on the list of volunteer witnesses in case the council wanted to call us. Our attendance wasn't mandatory, however.

Lailah sat next to Jonathon, while Kane and I sat in front of them.

"I didn't know if you'd make it," the angel beside me said.

I glanced over and did a double take. "Jasper."

He gave me a sad smile.

"I'm so sorry about Avery."

He stared straight ahead. "Me, too." After a moment he said, "I'm sorry about the binding spell. I know it wasn't cool, but by then I was just so frustrated and scared for Avery. I was willing to do anything to find her."

"Don't be. I'm not." I reached out and placed my hand over his. "Because of you, Lailah and Jonathon were able to find us in Hell. And if it wasn't for that binding, I could quite possibly still be trapped there."

He closed his eyes and sucked in an audible breath. "It still doesn't make it right."

"Jasper?"

"Yeah?"

"Don't be so hard on yourself. We all push boundaries when it comes to protecting those we love."

"Some of us more than others."

"You can say that again." There wasn't much I wouldn't do to save Kane when he was in trouble. A binding spell was minor compared to what I'd done to Ezra…no matter his crimes.

The familiar guilt settled around me, and I wondered if I'd ever come to terms with my actions. Jasper had a point. Just because something could be justified, that didn't make it right.

I leaned forward and glanced around the room, scanning for Drake. He wasn't up on the dais, though I hadn't expected him to be. He wasn't in the witness box, either, which surprised me. Because he was Chessandra's mate, his testimony would be considered partial, but I'd thought they'd force him to testify anyway.

Maybe he was skipping the proceedings altogether. It would be hard to watch your partner be accused of demon dealing, bewitching a witch and fellow angels, and abusing power.

Up on the dais, an older angel I recognized as Endora stepped up to the podium and banged a gavel. She licked her lips and in the process smudged lipstick all over her teeth.

I cringed and stifled a laugh at the same time. Her demeanor was so regal despite her blue eye shadow and frizzy bright red hair.

"The proceedings in the case against High Angel Chessandra Ballintine are now called to order." Endora banged a gavel, and the light chatter that had been rumbling through the sanctuary vanished. The only sound that could be heard was the soft click of footsteps on the white-and-gold tile floor.

I peered down the aisle, spotting Drake, my father. He didn't speak or look at anyone as he strode to Chessandra's side and sat in the chair reserved for her representation. She glanced up at him with tears in her eyes. If I hadn't been privy to everything she'd done, it would've been heartbreaking as my father gently took her hand in his.

Endora cleared her throat. "If everyone is settled, then?"

"We are, your honor," Drake said, now holding Chessandra's hand with both of his.

"Very well." She put the gavel down. "Chessandra Ballintine, you've been charged with willfully endangering the lives of those who serve you, engaging with demons, and casting illegal spells." Endora paused, sucked in a breath, and then continued. "How do you plead?"

Chessandra rose from her seat and held her head high. "I plead guilty to all charges."

A collective gasp filled the room. No one had been prepared for her statement.

Kane's hand tightened over mine. I held my breath, certain the other shoe was going to drop.

"Guilty?" Endora asked, surprise coloring her tone. "You're sure?"

Chessandra nodded.

Endora made a note on her paperwork, and when she looked back up, she stared pointedly at the high angel. "The council will need to deliberate your sentence. Would you like to explain your actions?"

Chessandra shook her head, tears now streaming down her cheeks.

"Ms. Ballintine," Endora said forcefully, "I hope you understand your sentence is likely to be severe. If there are any extenuating circumstances at all, I urge you to disclose them now."

Chessandra shook her head again and sat down.

Drake leaned over, urgently whispering in her ear. She just sat there, her head bowed.

"Chessa!" he said sharply. "Tell them."

She jerked her head to the side and glared at him. After a moment, she closed her eyes, took a deep breath, and stood once more.

"Do you have something to say?" Endora asked.

"I…" She waved a hand. "I don't deserve any sort of leniency, but I do think some people here today deserve an explanation."

Endora leaned forward, placing her elbows on the podium. "The floor is yours."

She turned toward the witness stand, her body rigid, but her gaze didn't land on anyone in particular. She just stared past us all at something only she could see.

We all waited in silence for her to collect her thoughts.

And when she started talking, her voice was monotone, void of all emotions. "When I was eighteen, I had a romance with an angel I met at college. It was intense and serious and, at that time, I thought forever. I thought I'd found my future mate. Only it turned out the angel I fell in love with wasn't in love with me, and we parted ways after about six months."

She paused and glanced once at Drake before continuing. "A month later, I found out I was pregnant."

When she didn't continue, Endora gently asked, "Did you have the child?"

Chessandra nodded and turned toward the angel. "Yes, I did. By myself. No one else knew except my doctor."

Endora raised her eyebrows. "No one?"

"That's right. When I went to tell the father, I found out he'd been taken into Hell. It was highly suspected that he'd fallen demon. But I had to know. So I went after him. That was when I found out I had extraordinary powers. I was able to enter and leave Hell at will. It was as easy as stepping into the shadows."

The breath left me in a whoosh. Was she joking? I didn't think so. Her posture was tense. The last thing she wanted to do was tell this story.

"So I went after my former lover, Wes Lancaster. But when I got there, he'd already turned, as so many do. Terrified I'd be next, I ran and slipped back to the surface with no difficulty. But what I'd seen in Hell gutted me. I was only eighteen, pregnant, alone, and the implications of my power hit me hard. Even though I didn't fully understand what my role would be in the angel realm, I knew because of my power, my life was about to change. And I also knew any child of mine would be a huge target. So I made the decision to give him up for adoption."

Endora nodded, and I felt a wave of pity pierce through the animosity that was coming from the audience.

"I kept tabs on him, always tracking what happened to him. He had good parents for his early years, but their lives ended in tragedy. After that, he was in foster home after foster home. I did my best to be sure he was kept out of the worst ones, always interfering when his environment was unacceptable. It meant he moved a lot. But by then, I was already the high angel, and I couldn't bring him home to me. I was too dangerous to be around. My enemies were growing by the day."

Endora scribbled more notes.

I stared open mouthed at Chessandra. As much as I wanted to hate her for her choice, I couldn't fault her. I knew better than anyone that power attracted trouble. And as the high angel, she was a giant target. She wasn't wrong that her child would be in danger.

"Five years ago, Ezra's father surfaced from Hell and found him. He filled Ezra's head with lies about who he really was, pretended to be a witch, gained my son's trust, and then black-mailed me to get himself out of a jam. I hated to do it, but I had no choice. Wes was threatening to take Ezra into Hell with him. And it would be way too easy. Ezra already trusted him."

The contract Ezra had shown us. That was what her testi-mony was about.

"But the blackmail didn't stop there. He kept asking for more and more from me. And that's how Avery got involved. I would send her with harmless information to keep Wes at bay, but he got tired of my games and took her." A single tear spilled down her cheek.

She sniffed. "At that time, I hired the witch Jade Calhoun and her incubus husband to find Avery in the hopes that they'd bring her home, but I never told them what I knew. That in all likelihood she was already in Hell. I was afraid. And ashamed. I thought if Wes had Avery, he'd leave Ezra alone. Only he didn't. By then I was in too deep and did everything I could to keep everyone in the dark."

Her gaze swept over me then. "After it was clear Avery had been taken, I couldn't stand the idea of anyone else being hurt because of my actions. So in desperation, I bewitched Zoe so I could have her sabotage the search for Avery. Everything I had her do was an attempt to keep Jade Calhoun and her coven safe. Some things were minor, like deleting phone messages. Others, like the curse…well, I was desperate to keep as many souls as safe as possible. And I didn't want the white witch battling demons when it was all but certain we'd already lost Avery. I failed, obviously."

Was she really sitting up there claiming she was only trying to protect her people? Was that the real reason she'd put a curse on me and my future child? To keep him or her safe? It was likely I'd never know the truth.

"And none of that was about protecting your secrets?" Endora asked.

Chessandra shrugged. "It might have been, but honestly, that wasn't my main motivation."

"I see. Do you have anything else to add?"

"Yes. Only that I don't want nor do I deserve any sort of leniency. I endangered those working for me. In the end, I lost my son anyway. I deserve everything I have coming to me."

Opinions, combined with jeers, erupted throughout the conflicted room. There was a mix of understanding and forgiveness as well as hostility and distrust. The crowd was divided. Chessandra sat back down and stared straight ahead.

I was certain she'd committed more crimes than she'd copped to, but her confession was more than enough.

"Ezra was her son?" Jasper asked me.

"Yes."

"My God."

"You knew him?" I asked.

"Yes. The apartment I took you to, that was his."

"You're kidding. So all that evidence. He put it together?"

Kane leaned forward. "Ezra was very bitter. In fact, I think it's fair to say he wanted to take her down more than anyone."

Jasper's eyes widened. "Were any of his accusations true?"

"Sure. But it's all probably a lot more nuanced than we know." For a long while, I'd thought Chessandra was just selfish and maybe morally corrupt. Those things were still true, but at least I understood why she'd done the things she did.

I put my hand over Jasper's and squeezed lightly, offering him a modicum of support. The poor kid's world had been turned upside down. He'd learned his fiancée was a demon, had lost someone he called a friend, and now it looked like he'd need a new job as well. His days as Chessa's assistant were over.

The council deliberated for more than two hours. By the time they finally reemerged, my entire body protested from sitting in the hard chair.

Endora strode to the podium, and after taking a few minutes to settle the spectators, she cleared her throat and said, "Chessandra Ballintine, please rise."

Chessandra stood as if in a trance.

"Chessandra Ballintine, you are hereby stripped of your title of high angel. Your salary, all privileges, and active contracts are now void. You've been sentenced to thirty years confinement with two years psychological therapy. Your time will start immediately."

Drake got to his feet and wrapped an arm around her, but she stood stiffly beside him, her expression blank.

And when the guards came for her, she didn't resist.

An inkling of relief blossomed in my chest, followed by a hollowness in my gut. I should've been elated. Vindicated. Triumphant. But I felt none of that. Mostly, I was empty and worn out. All I wanted to do was curl back up in bed with Kane and my ghost dog Duke.

We sat in the witness area until most of the angels had cleared out.

"I can't believe it's over," Lailah said from behind me.

Too drained to talk, I nodded my agreement.

"Ready to go home?" Kane asked me.

"More than ready." We stood, but before I even took my first step, Jasper grabbed my hand. I glanced down at him.

He looked up at me with wild eyes. "I have to know. Is she really…?"

My chest constricted with pain. He couldn't finish his sentence because he was talking about Avery. "Oh, Jasper. I'm so sorry. She'd already fallen—"

"Demon," he finished for me.

"There's nothing we could've done."

"I guess not." He lumbered to his feet and, without another word, hunched his shoulders and shuffled out of the sanctuary.

Epilogue

Kane

Three months later

The stove door creaked as I pulled it open. Inside was a perfectly golden cheesecake, baked for Jade and our celebration dinner. What we were celebrating, I really had no idea. It wasn't our anniversary, her birthday, or any major holiday. Trust me. I'd checked just as soon as she'd left this morning to spend the day at the café with Pyper.

All I knew was this morning she'd told me we had plans, and we were celebrating. Our last three months had been relatively quiet. For once. Now that Chessandra was incarcerated, our shadow walking contract had been voided, and we'd declined to sign a new one. Since we'd been coerced into the first one, no one was surprised.

I was still demon hunting, but even the demon attacks had decreased. Maximus suspected my time in Hell had diminished Aiken's following, and tensions had cooled a bit. I didn't know, and frankly I didn't care. I was just enjoying being with my wife.

Jade had been spending most of her free time studying up on healing magic with Bea and working with Pyper at the café.

She'd said she was ready for a quieter life. Well, she'd gotten it for the most part. There hadn't been a major crisis since we'd come back from Hell. Thank the gods.

I placed the cheesecake on a cooling rack and headed for the shower. When Jade got home, I'd be ready for her.

Within moments, the steam filled the bathroom, and I stood under the water, letting the heat sluice over me, relaxing my shoulders.

"Need some help?" Jade's voice carried over the rush of the water.

Grinning, I pulled the shower door open. "If you're offering."

She stood barefoot on the tile floor, already naked. Just the sight of her swollen breasts and her slightly pronounced curves sent my blood rushing to my groin, and I felt myself harden beneath her intense gaze. After three months of the easy life, Jade had gained a few extra pounds that I found sexy as hell. She'd been beautiful before, but now she was just plain luscious.

I crooked a finger. "Get in here, pretty witch."

Her gaze traveled the length of my body, lingering on my groin area. "It looks like you're more than ready for a *little* help."

I grabbed her hand and pulled her into the shower. "Honey, there's nothing little about it."

She giggled and pressed her palms to my chest, her head tilted up, joy radiating from her sparkling green eyes.

God I loved that sound. I could spend forever listening to the tinkle of her laugh. "Come here." I wrapped my arms around her, warmth filling my heart. "How was your day?"

"Hmmm, just about perfect." She gazed up at me, her face radiant.

"Really? Did something special happen at the café?" There was something decidedly different about her today. She practically glowed from the inside out.

She shook her head. "Nope. Just a regular day filled with chocolate cupcakes, chai tea, and Pyper badgering me about what we were celebrating."

I laughed. "I see it didn't work. She was under strict orders to call me the minute she figured it out."

"So she didn't, then." Her smile turned self-satisfied.

"Obviously not. I haven't heard from her."

"Good." She pushed up on her tiptoes and nibbled on my lower lip, feeding that need to have her that was never quenched.

I let out a tiny moan and pulled her closer, loving the way her nipples hardened against my chest. "You are perfection."

"You think so?" She pulled away slightly and turned in my arms, pressing her back against me. Threading her fingers through mine, she wrapped my arms around her belly.

"Absolutely."

"I hope you still feel that way six months from now."

I frowned. "What's that mean?"

She glanced back at me, her smile lopsided.

I narrowed my eyes, suspicion taking up root in the back of my mind. Her swollen breasts, slightly rounder belly and hips, the expectant-mother glow. "Jade? Are you—?"

"Pregnant?" she asked.

I nodded.

She placed my hand over her belly and whispered, "Yes."

"A child," I whispered, disbelief warring with awe for my dominant reaction.

"Our child." Jade leaned against my chest, caressing my fingers that rested on her barely-there baby bump.

Powerful emotions rose up and stole my voice as I realized I finally had everything I'd ever wanted right there in my arms.

Jade. Our child. A family.

The backs of my eyes burned, and I tightened my hold on my wife, wishing I could keep her and our child wrapped tightly in my embrace forever.

Safe.

"Kane?" she asked softly.

"Yes, love?"

"You're happy, right?" There was more than a little trepidation in her tone.

I turned her around, lifted her up, and pressed her against the tiled wall of the shower. Staring into her glassy bright-green eyes, I gave her a slow smile. "Nothing on this planet could make me happier than knowing you're carrying my child."

Her lips curved up as two happy tears slowly slid down her cheeks. "You're not worried?"

My smile turned wistful. "I think I'll be worried every minute of the day for the rest of my life, but that doesn't have anything to do with the fact that you're the coven leader and I'm a demon hunter. That's just part of the territory."

Shaking her head, her voice hitched as she said, "I know all parents feel that way. But our lives…it's not the same."

I sobered and pushed a lock of her strawberry-blond hair from her cheek. I knew what she was saying, and although I'd made a joke of my answer, there was already an ache deep in my heart for everything our children would have to endure. Even though the curse had been broken, there was no guarantee our child wouldn't be targeted again. But I refused to live my life in fear. And I knew the same was true for her. Our children would know exactly what it felt like to be loved. And Goddess help anything or anyone who tried to harm them.

"You're right. It's not. But this child"—I glanced down at her belly—"is going to grow up surrounded by love and magic and wonder. And she'll have two badass parents to keep an eye on her. Poor thing. That's probably going to be harder on her than any demon who tries to get in her way."

Jade laughed. "She?"

"Yes. A little girl with blond curls and jade-green eyes just like her mother."

"Or a dark-haired little boy with rich dark-chocolate eyes and lashes so long they make all the girls jealous."

"How about both," I whispered and leaned in, covering her lips with mine.

She let out a quiet, satisfied moan and tightened her hold on me, pressing her body into mine. "I think that can be arranged, Mr. Rouquette."

"How about now?" I teased, dipping my head to kiss my way across the swell of her breast.

She giggled. "I'm not sure it works—oh!"

I'd scraped my teeth over her nipple and, unable to control myself, I sucked hard, my fingers digging into the soft flesh of her hips. She was so warm, so pliable, so perfect. A rush of blood pumped through my body, every nerve alive with desire.

She arched her back into me, her nails already scoring my back. "Take me to bed, Kane. Show me exactly how much you love me."

"Gladly." I flipped the water off, and with Jade still wrapped around me, I strode into our bedroom. And there, right in the middle of the bed, was the cheesecake.

Jade gave me that sexy little smile of hers and said, "I figured we could make do without the forks."

A seductive grin claimed my lips, my mind flashing to all the wicked places I was going to taste her. Her breath hitched as I lowered us onto the bed and ran my fingers over her heated flesh. "I hope you're ready, Mrs. Rouquette. This is going to be one hell of a celebration."

Jade's hand came up to cup my cheek. "It's going to be one hell of a life."

My heart stuttered from the intense love shining back at me through her gaze. And for the first time in my life, I finally understood what it meant to feel complete. I pressed my lips to hers and murmured, "It already is."

About the Author

Deanna is a native Californian, transplanted to the slower paced lifestyle of southeastern Louisiana. When she isn't writing, she is often goofing off with her husband in New Orleans, playing with her two shih tzu dogs, making glass beads, or out hocking her wares at various bead shows across the country. Want the next book in the series? Visit www.DeannaChase.com to sign up for the New Releases email list.

Made in the USA
Middletown, DE
19 June 2016